DECEIVED BY A KISS

"Did he ever kiss you?"

"No." The answer was more a breath than a word.

Her eyes grew large and lovely and her lips parted, just enough to emit a breath. Gently he cupped her cheek. He lowered his head and brought his mouth to hers. He found her as pliant yet firm as he'd suspected, and every bit as sweet. In her inexperienced way she kissed him back.

It wasn't much of a kiss, little more than a mingling of breath, and he wanted more. His fingers found the wild pulse at her temple, threaded into the hair she wore firmly coiled about her head. Closing his eyes, he let her scent and taste and the texture of her lips wash over him. She felt clean and pure. He wanted to pull her into his arms, to discover the body hidden by ill-fitting layers of wool, and most of all to kiss her properly, until she was gasping and crying out for more.

Her untouched enthusiasm touched him, and shamed him too. A man like Marcus Lithgow had no business with this artless girl.

Too bad. He needed her and he couldn't afford scruples.

Romances by Miranda Neville

MIRANDA NEVILLE

The Ruin of a Rogue

AVON

An Imprint of HarperCollinsPublishers

AVON BOOKS
An Imprint of HarperCollins*Publishers*
10 East 53rd Street
New York, New York 10022-5299

Copyright © 2013 by Miranda Neville
ISBN 978-0-06-219951-5
www.avonromance.com

First Avon Books mass market printing: September 2013

Avon Trademark Reg. U.S. Pat. Off. and in Other Countries, Marca Registrada, Hecho en U.S.A.
HarperCollins® is a registered trademark of HarperCollins Publishers.

Printed in the U.S.A.

10 9 8 7 6 5 4 3 2 1

The Ruin of a
Rogue

Chapter 1

The Countess of Ashfield to her sister
London, November 1800

This dull season has been rendered more than usually piquant by the presence of Anne Brotherton, granddaughter and heiress to the last Earl of Camber, at evening parties. Since Miss Brotherton lost the Duke of Castleton to her cousin Caro Townsend, unwedded men with any claim to eligibility have descended on town by the hundred. Little wonder since the Camber estates are enough to make a fortune hunter of the richest aspirant. I believe the hunting shires are empty of single gentlemen, while officers of the better regiments have all applied for furlough at once. Heaven help us if we should be invaded by the French. I believe she would be just the match for dear Algernon . . .

Eyes straight ahead, Anne Brotherton wove through the packed saloon, dodged a moustached guardsman, avoided the eye of a red-faced sportsman, and resolutely ignored the efforts of Lord Algernon Tiverton to offer her refreshment.

"Miss Brotherton! May I . . ."

No, thank you, she answered silently as she made her escape into a blessedly empty passage. *No, you may not ply me with ratafia and bore me with tales of your ancestors.*

Second door on the right, the footman had told her. It was cool in Mr. Weston's private sanctum. Neither a fire nor the press of bodies moderated the chill of a November evening. She made a quick survey: two doors, one leading to a completely dark room or closet. She should be safe from that direction. She turned the key in the other with a satisfying click and released her breath.

Oh the bliss of escaping her suitors! Half an hour, she guessed, until Lady Ashfield, her chaperone for the evening, sent someone to find her. Half an hour away from the inane compliments of insincere fools. Half an hour to feast her eyes and calm her spirit with the ineffable creations of the ancient past. Mr. Weston's celebrated collection of antiquities was the only reason she'd chosen to attend his wife's rout.

She peered through the glass cabinet door at the statue of a woman, her child at her feet. Though both were devoid of a scrap of clothing, they appeared quite comfortable. Greece was, presumably, warmer than her native Buckinghamshire. She longed to touch the marble skin. Without thought she removed her glove, then guiltily dropped her hands to her sides.

She almost missed the sound of the side door opening. Confound it! Was she never to be allowed any peace? She fixed her attention on the next object in the case.

Footsteps trod softly over the polished parquetry floor and she sensed a figure, taller than she, standing at her shoulder. Reflected in the glass she identified the intruder as a man by his dark coat and the white linen around the throat. She continued to stare, now at a small male figure who'd lost his head, one arm, and all of his private parts.

"Interesting piece." His voice, of a pleasant low timbre, proclaimed him a young man.

Another man attracted by her rolling acres, magnificent mansions, and thousands upon thousands of pounds in the funds. Annoyance blended with a twinge of embarrassment at being caught staring at a naked man, even one nine inches tall and lacking vital evidence of his sex. She kept her eyes on the antiquity and her elbow ready to repel any effort to hold her hand or steal a kiss. She had no intention of being compromised into marriage to someone unsuitable.

For one thing, she'd never hear the end of it from her guardian. At the moment she only had to put up with his letters. When he returned to England he'd harangue her with all the force of his dominating personality. The poor Irish! She felt sorry for them with Morrissey as their governor.

"A Greek original, I believe." The agreeable voice interrupted her thoughts and actually said something interesting. "From Attica, most likely Apollo."

She jerked her head around. "What makes you think that?"

"The laurel tree, sacred to the god and the games given in his honor."

This remarkably intelligent speaker merited her attention. She liked what she saw: a tall, well-proportioned figure, good-looking, distinctly elegant, with an open countenance. He seemed different from the other men she'd met in London, something about the impeccable neatness and fit of his clothing, perhaps.

"Have you spent much time in Greece?"

"I've been to Athens," he replied, "and to some of the isles."

"And Rome?"

"Indeed. I've had the good fortune to spend a good deal of time in Italy."

"I envy you. I always longed to go. Now, with the war, I doubt I'll have the chance."

"I returned myself earlier this year. Escaping from Naples once the French arrived was quite an adventure."

"Were you able to bring anything back?"

"I'm no collector. But I picked up some knowledge of antiquities staying at Sir William Hamilton's house."

Hamilton, she knew, was the British envoy to the court of Naples and Sicily, a noted collector, and author of a treatise on Greek vases. Anne thought of asking his name, this sensible and pleasant gentleman with the foreign air. But things usually became difficult when a man learned he was talking with the wealthiest woman in Great Britain. It was, of course, possible that this man knew who she was and was either an excellent actor or didn't care. For once she decided not to find out, and merely, for a few minutes, to enjoy a conversation with one who shared her pursuits.

"There are some lovely things on these shelves but I know little about them. That lady with the child, for example. Can you tell me if she's Roman or Greek?"

He tilted his head and concentrated. She'd seen a similar look on the faces of cognoscenti in the British Museum. This was a man who took his antiquities seriously. "A Roman copy of a Greek piece. I'm sure you recognize Aphrodite. That's her son Eros at her feet. Do you see he is riding a—"

"—a dolphin!" she broke in. "So he is. The head of the fish has broken off so I didn't notice at first. I was admiring the way the sculptor breathed life into stone." Again she raised her hand to the glass barrier.

"Wouldn't you like to touch it?"

His low voice, humorous with a touch of mischief, tempted her. "I couldn't do that. I don't have Mr. Weston's permission."

"Are you always so dutiful?"

Aside from the occasional peccadillo, the answer would have to be yes. Her bare fingertips pressed against her silken skirts as the glowing marble beckoned.

Mr. Handsome-Knowledgeable, whoever he was, had no such scruples. He opened the cabinet and gestured with one hand and a wicked little smile. Why not? No one would know and she wouldn't do any harm.

"So cold," she said, fingering the intricate braids of the goddess's hair. "I always think marble is pure white but it isn't really, is it? It has almost a golden hue."

He nodded. "There's nothing like seeing and touching the real thing, and it's even better under the sun. There's only so much you can learn from illustrations. Have you seen many of the English collections?"

"No. What I know is from books."

"If Admiral Nelson prevails, Europe will again be open to the English traveler and you'll be able to see the ancient sites for yourself."

"Sometimes I think the fashion for travel makes us overlook what we have under our feet. Most of England was a Roman colony. There must be buildings buried everywhere, and so little has been discovered, outside the larger towns. My greatest ambition is to unearth a villa." She looked at him anxiously. Even the most ardent suitor grew wary when exposed to her abiding enthusiasm. The Duke of Castleton's eyes had regularly turned to unpolished stone at the very mention of the word *dig*.

The Countess of Ashfield, a lady of impeccable *ton*, had told her a dozen times that gentlemen found ladies with knowledge tedious. Lady Ashfield also said it didn't matter a whit if Anne drove them into catalepsy. "Nothing can make a great heiress unappealing to a man." Anne didn't find the pronouncement comforting. While not expecting to be admired for her beauty—she had none—she wished gentlemen saw something to like about her besides her fortune. Her companion could be feigning politeness. They all did.

"I do tend to carry on once I mount my hobby-horse," she said. "I fear I will bore you."

"I'm not bored," he said with a sincerity she let herself believe in.

And then he touched her, a featherlight contact of fingers on her bare wrist. Unaccustomed to much physical contact in her restricted, well-ordered life, she especially rejected any attempt at a caress from her despised suitors. Yet there was something different about this casual touch that sent a quick shock through her.

She had felt at ease with this interesting stranger and conversed with him with an openness she usually managed only with those she knew well. She stepped away in alarm and pursed her lips.

Even before she stumbled back, Marcus knew that touching her had been a mistake. The graceful hand, pale and unflawed as the polished marble before them, had lured him to act on instinct, an unaffordable luxury in a life led with finely honed calculation. Used to the free ways of the louche European circles he frequented, Marcus had for an instant forgotten the circumscribed habits of English society, especially the kind of company frequented by a well-guarded heiress. He hastened to correct his error. Without offering an apology, which would give importance to the awkward moment, he smiled guilelessly.

"I always prefer conversation with substance. If they can dig up Pompeii, why not England? Have you seen the remains at Bath?"

"I'm sorry to say I have not. Have you?"

Marcus decided it was better not to mention his sole visit to that spa. He'd been ten years old at the time, accompanying his father, who was in pursuit of a rich widow, ripe for the fleecing. Antiquarian exploration had not been on the menu.

The irony that he was essentially on the same mission did not escape him. His presence in this room was no accident and every word between them had been carefully planned, except his reaction to Miss Brotherton. She wasn't what he'd expected. Caro claimed her cousin was delightful, but Caro was ever kind to those she loved. He'd preferred to believe Robert when he called the wonderfully rich Miss Brotherton dull, proud, and plain as any proper English virgin.

Marcus had entered the room to find a slender lady peering into the display case. He didn't make the mistake of assuming from her outmoded gown that he'd found the wrong woman. Any courtesan or social aspirant with a few guineas and a competent dressmaker could look fashionable. His practiced eye recognized the first-quality cloth, the quietly expensive trimmings, and the air of confidence that came from shopping without regard to cost or the necessity of impressing anyone. The double string of modest but exquisitely matched pearls, her only adornment, proved to the discerning observer that she came from the best circles.

The full-skirted gown made it impossible to assess her figure, but her face, not beautiful by any standard, was appealing, features regular, and her eyes a pretty hazel. Skilled as he was in reading expressions, he found her inscrutable, perhaps why he'd offered that potentially harmful caress on her wrist. The necessity of pursuing an heiress hadn't thrilled him, but she was more of a challenge than he'd anticipated. Neat as a pin in her attire, her hair and her manner were equally unruffled.

He'd quite enjoy ruffling her.

Gazing at her well-bred, English face, he thought of the green fields, neat hedgerows, and wholesome air of his distant childhood, before he became an adventurer. The foolish idea crossed his mind that she deserved better than him. Ridiculous because he had no conscience.

During a grueling game of *primiera* with some Italian Jesuits in Berlin, he heard his opponents claim that if they had a boy for his first seven years, they had him for life. Whatever the power of Catholic priests, Marcus was living proof it didn't work for English ladies. Any influence of his mother had been stamped out when she'd died, leaving the seven-year-old Marcus under the sole influence of Lewis Lithgow, one of the world's greatest rogues.

Miss Brotherton cocked her head at him. What was the question?

"No," he said. "I'm not familiar with Bath." It was too soon to express a wish to explore the Roman baths with her, a suggestion likely to send an English virgin into the vapors. Better leave her now, before he said something indiscreet. He'd made a good start and it was always preferable to leave a mark intrigued and eager for further play. More importantly, he'd rather keep her wondering, before she learned that he was the notorious Viscount Lithgow, prominent on any list of men that women of reputation avoided.

Luck had left them alone so far, but the way things were going for him, it wouldn't last. "I'm keeping you from your friends," he said. "But before I let you go, have you read Mr. Warner's *Illustration of the Roman Antiquities Discovered at Bath*?"

"I haven't come across that particular book." Marcus could almost see her memorize the name of the obscure volume.

"I recommend it," he said.

Taking his leave with a respectful but not deferential bow, he slipped out of the house, to which he had not been invited, by the same back way he'd entered.

Chapter 2

Marcus was half asleep, but the moment the door opened his mind was alert and his muscles tensed. Not even his late-night indulgence at a local tavern could erase the instincts developed over a lifetime.

"Good morning, my lord."

He relaxed and groaned. He was in London where no one wanted to kill him. Yet. After several months he should be used to being woken by that odiously cheerful voice, but he'd never had a personal servant before and wasn't entirely sure why he had one now.

"Lovely day, sir. Not raining at all."

"Your praise of the English weather is, as always, unfounded in fact. I wish I were back in Italy. Even in November it's warmer than this hellhole."

"Now, now, sir. You're only saying that because you haven't had your tea." Marcus heard the tray deposited on the table without so much as a clink of china. He blinked sullenly as Travis swished open the curtain to admit the leaden London light. "Sit up and I'll bring you a cup."

As he swallowed the hot drink, his head and his temper improved. Not having to make his own breakfast was the greatest advantage of having acquired such a superior attendant and pretty much the only one. Travis was a nuisance and one Marcus couldn't shake off. The man clung like a burr. Served him right for saving the valet's life. Next time he'd know better than to engage in unnecessary acts of altruism.

"And how was Mrs. Weston's rout?" Travis delivered his question with the disinterested expression of the well-trained servant, but Marcus knew how anxious he was to hear. He swallowed his tea, feeling the warm liquid enliven his chilled sinews, and let Travis wait.

"Another cup," he requested.

Travis poured the tea and waited some more, his long, lugubrious face not at all the kind of features Marcus preferred to wake up to.

"Did your former employers confide in you about their engagements?"

"Not the marchese, sir. But he was foreign." Just the first of the nobleman's heinous faults in the eyes of his valet. "My previous master, Lord Sutton, was sometimes good enough to remark on the events of an evening."

"That must have been fascinating."

"Lord Sutton is a gentleman of great propriety."

"That bad, eh?" Draining his second cup, Marcus put an end to the torture. For the moment.

"Your information was correct. Miss Brotherton was there and I made her acquaintance."

"Ah!"

"She seems an agreeable girl."

"So I've heard." Travis's head bobbled eagerly. "It will be a fortunate man who wins Miss Brotherton's hand."

"*Very* fortunate."

Now the conversation was going his way, Travis stopped looking like an anxious French basset hound and busied himself with the clothing Marcus had discarded the night before. He carefully folded the breeches, placing them in a press, while soiled linens and stockings were set aside for laundering. The evening coat in dark blue satin velvet—purchased in Naples after a run of luck—already hung on one of a row of pegs in the small chamber. Travis removed it, shook it out, and made a great play of rearranging it on the peg.

"If you allowed me to wait up for you, I could make sure your clothes were properly put away." This was an old argument and had resulted in a compromise by which Travis agreed to go to bed at eleven if Marcus hadn't returned. Knowing he was keeping the man up made Marcus uncomfortable and he preferred to come and go as he pleased, without reference to the convenience of another. Explaining that he was quite accustomed to taking care of his own wardrobe, that he'd acted as valet for his father from the age of seven, had failed to impress.

"It's bad enough seeing your sorry face in the morning. Spare me at night."

Travis accepted Marcus's needling with his customary serenity. "It's the duty of a valet to see to his gentleman at all times."

"But I'm no gentleman."

"Of course you are, sir," Travis said in his most annoyingly indulgent tones. "And one any young lady would be lucky to have as a husband."

"You do realize that it's in the highest degree unlikely that Miss Brotherton's guardians would approve such a match?"

"Then they will have to be persuaded otherwise, sir."

"I suppose you'd prefer to serve a man of fortune. One who actually paid wages."

"I'm quite content in my situation."

Marcus gave up. Travis was wrong. Morrissey would never be "persuaded" to allow the heiress's marriage to Marcus, unless the girl was compromised. Even then he might still dig in his heels and refuse his consent. This didn't bother Marcus. Either way was fine but he'd prefer the latter. Matrimony lasted for life and he'd always been leery of encumbrances. A wife would be even more tedious than a servant. If he played his cards correctly, the trustees would buy him off with a fat settlement. The fifteen-year-old daughter of a Genoese nobleman had been mad for his eighteen-year-old self. Her father, on discovering that Marcus hadn't actually ruined the girl, paid him a handsome sum to absent himself from the city, forever. Marcus, a man of honor when there was no reason not to be, had never set foot in Genoa since. With a richer pigeon in Miss Brotherton, he intended to pull off that trick again. Unless . . .

"Hand me my dressing gown and bring a pack of cards."

"Please, my lord, no." The valet put his hands behind his back.

"Yes, and stop the my-lording. *Sir* is good enough." He stepped down from the bed and found his own banyan. "Come on." Travis trailed him into the dismal sitting room, which, together with the bedchamber and the tiny servant's room, comprised the whole of their cheap lodging. "Sit down. We'll try Beggar-My-Neighbor."

He chose the children's game because there wasn't an ounce of skill in it. It was the perfect test of luck. Travis sat stiffly at the coarse gateleg table and accepted half the cards.

Marcus had once spent an idle evening trying to work out the mathematics of Beggar-My-Neighbor, to see if it was possible for the cards to fall so the game would never end. Certainly it always felt endless. Not today. He watched in detached amazement as Travis won pile after pile of cards, until Marcus was down to two. Travis turned up a king and Marcus produced a knave. He held his breath as his opponent revealed the next card in his hand. Another knave. Marcus's last card was a worthless five and the game was over. It had taken less than five minutes, surely a record.

"Damnation, Travis. I swear you bring me ill luck."

"Sir!" The man's indignation managed to be both comical and pathetic.

"Don't worry. I don't blame you. I've never held with the superstitions that rule many of my fraternity. It's all in the odds, and for some reason they've been against me for a while. I'll recover eventually."

Brave words! There seemed no end in sight to the longest losing streak in his long career as a gamester. There was no help for it: It would have to be the heiress.

"I need to know Miss Brotherton's plans. Will you see her maid today?"

Travis cracked a smile, always a distressing sight. "If I take Your Lordship's shirts to the laundress now, I believe I shall meet her going about her business."

"Exercise your charms then." The girl must be desperate to find Travis's mug appealing.

"Ahem. I regret to say that the establishment does not care to extend Your Lordship credit."

Marcus produced a coin from his dwindling purse. He'd left Italy in a sound financial state but he'd never dreamed of the ill luck that had haunted him since he crossed the Alps. He could only trust his strategy with Anne Brotherton would be more successful than his effort to cheat her cousin. No, not quite cheat, but close enough. And he regretted it. Caro's late husband, Robert Townsend, had been his best friend, and he and Caro had been close. The Townsends' house had been a welcoming haven during his visits to London. Now Robert was dead and Caro, the new Duchess of

Castleton, refused to speak to him. He missed them far more than he missed cards. Gaming was his profession, not his passion.

When Travis left, Marcus took up the volume on Roman antiquities of Bath. The author was no stylist, and he found the work hard going. He'd barely taken in enough to convince Miss Brotherton of his familiarity with its contents when he was gratefully interrupted by a knock at the door. Marcus opened it to find a man carrying a small trunk that he recognized at once.

"Mr. Lithgow?" Evidently the fellow was unaware of his acquisition of a peerage. "Had the devil's own time finding you. Delivery from foreign parts."

During his childhood, the box had been a familiar sight, accompanying him and his father between shabby lodgings and angry victims. It hadn't been among Lewis Lithgow's effects when Marcus arrived in Naples to find his father dead and buried. He had no key, but picking a simple lock was a skill he'd acquired along life's way. The lid opened with a creak. Laid on top of some folded cloth was a letter addressed to Mr. Marcus Lithgow, England, in a hand he guessed was German. No, Austrian. From Vienna.

Dear Mr. Lithgow. Perhaps you know my name, he translated. *Your father has perhaps mentioned the Countess von Hoffenburg. We became acquainted in 1784.* The year after his father left England for good, leaving the eleven-year-old Marcus to the care of his mother's uncle.

The countess explained that Lewis was forced

to leave Vienna in a hurry. Not the first time he'd found a city too hot for him. *I always looked for his return but it was not to be.* Some poor deluded female who didn't realize how lucky she was that her lover had abandoned her before he took her for all she was worth. *When he was cruelly torn from me, he left this trunk. He intended to return but made me promise that if I heard of his death I would send it to you in England. I lately heard the sad news of dear Lewis's demise. So I keep my promise and send this to London, hoping it will find you there. The son of so distinguished a man must be well-known in the English capital.*

Distinguished? Distinguished only as a scoundrel.

Marcus was sure the contents would be worthless. It wasn't like Lewis to leave behind anything of value. Still, he couldn't help hoping there would be something. Even a small coin or two. He pulled out a black silk domino. His father always enjoyed a masquerade.

As expected, his inheritance proved sadly meager.

A velvet mask. A pair of dice.

Marcus tossed them. Double sixes. And again. Loaded.

A pack of cards. These he knew well. A barely perceptible and intricate system of pinpricks identified each card in the deck. Lewis had made the young Marcus learn those marks by heart, over and over until he could recognize each card by a glance at its back. His father's idea of education. He drew one and examined the back. Queen of hearts. Correct. Ten of spades. Right again.

He'd always had an excellent memory. Much later he studied the odds and learned to win honestly—unlike his father. Under Lewis's approving gaze, he'd cut his winning teeth by cheating stable boys and bootblacks out of their wages.

He returned to the trunk. A single shoe buckle, a pair of white gloves, soiled, and another letter. This time he knew the writing.

Dear Marcus,
  If you are reading this it means I am dead. Thanks to a little trouble with some angry Russians I have to leave Vienna in a hurry. My intention is to return soon and complete my plans, but if I surrender to force majeure in the form of the prince's unreasonably brutal servants, I want you to know that I left handsome insurance when I departed England last year. Your uncle Hooke has it in his care, though he knows not what a treasure I left in his hands. I doubt he would approve. Find it, and you will be set up for life. Never say that I haven't been a good father to you. I close in haste.
                                Yrs affectionately,
                                L. Lithgow

A year or so earlier, Marcus had unwillingly traveled by ship from Lisbon to Naples at Lewis's urgent behest. He liked Lisbon, finding the Portuguese poor cardplayers and amiable losers. Why he allowed his sire to exercise any pull over him, he didn't know. Reluctant fascination at what the old man was up to, he supposed, along with a battered remnant of filial deference. He arrived to find Lewis had been dead a week, and buried too—they didn't keep bodies lying around in southern Italy—and that he, Marcus, by a twist of genealogy, had inherited an obscure viscountcy from his father's distant cousin. The letter informing his father reached Naples after his death. As usual, Lewis had the last laugh. Not only was there nothing of value among his possessions, but Marcus had to pay for his funeral.

Now, it seemed, he had a legacy beyond his thorough education in villainy. But what?

Sitting at the table, mindlessly throwing the loaded dice, he tried to guess what the *insurance* was. Hard to credit Lewis had left anything that was both valuable and easily carried behind him when he left England. And supposing he had, it was by no means certain he hadn't returned to retrieve it. As far as he knew, Lewis had never again set foot in his native land. Whatever brouhaha drove him abroad, it was bad enough to send him into permanent exile. But Marcus had too much respect for his father's cunning to eliminate the possibility he had crept back sometime in fifteen years.

Marcus considered, and rejected, posting down to Hinton. On such slender grounds, the price of a journey to Wiltshire looked a poor investment, not worth more than the price of a sheet of paper, for the delivery of which his mother's uncle, Josiah Hooke, would have to produce a sixpence or two.

Which left Lewis's other legacy, a concrete one.

Marcus took the marked pack and dealt a hand of piquet. Without looking at the telltale markings, he examined his cards. Not bad. In fact, quite good. Unless the other hand possessed a guarded queen of spades, he'd win. Nothing spectacular, but better than he'd enjoyed in months. Perhaps his luck was turning at last. With practiced ease he calculated the odds and found them in his favor. He eyed the extra cards available to the other hand and read the minute combination of pinpricks and ink, invisible to any eye that wasn't looking.

Queen of spades. Eight of spades. Seven of spades.

Unbelievable.

He, one of the best piquet players in Europe, couldn't even beat an insentient opponent with marked cards. It would definitely have to be the heiress.

Chapter 3

Travis had struck up an acquaintance with Miss Brotherton's maid at the laundress's establishment and advanced to friendship based on fervent and mutually held opinions regarding the correct application of starch. Well-informed of the heiress's habits and movements, two mornings after their meeting Marcus entered Dangerfield's, the Berkeley Square circulating library. Across the spacious reading room he spied Miss Brotherton perusing a section of shelves devoted to history. Rather impatiently, she stood on tiptoe to reach a volume on a shelf above her head, without calling an attendant for library steps.

"Allow me." He reached over her shoulder. "Was this the one you wanted?"

She jumped a little, but when she turned to face him she didn't seem displeased. "Thank you," she said with a faint blush.

He read the spine of the stout quarto as though he didn't know exactly what it was, from the previous afternoon's reconnaissance. *"The Medallic History of Imperial Rome*? Interesting."

"I think it must be. Do you know it?"

"Never heard of it. You must let me know."

"I came to find the book by Mr. Warner you told me about. Dangerfield's doesn't have it."

"What a shame." He reached for the first of a set of volumes. "Have you read Gibbon's *Decline and Fall of the Roman Empire*?"

She averted her eyes. "I would like to but my grandfather was particular about what I read. He told me it wasn't a proper book for a lady."

"Do you know Greek and Latin?"

"I'm afraid not."

"Then you should be quite safe. The questionable passages are in the footnotes, in the original languages. As schoolboys we found them quite an incentive to study."

Her eyes widened. "Are there many such passages?"

"Not nearly as many as schoolboys wish."

"I shall take the first volume, and this one. Then I think I'll walk to Piccadilly and see if Hatchard's has the Warner book."

"Are you alone? May I keep you company?"

"My maid is waiting for me, studying the latest edition of *La Belle Assemblée*." Then, after grave consideration, "I would be happy to accept your escort, but we haven't been introduced."

He made a play of looking about him. "I was hoping to find a mutual acquaintance to perform the office, but I don't see a soul I know. We shall have to remain in ignorance of each other's identities."

Since she smiled at his joke, he summoned his luck, as he did when about to cast the dice with a large sum at stake. "Viscount Lithgow at your service, ma'am."

"Oh." Oh, indeed. Then, happily, she smiled again. "Lord Lithgow! Caro's friend Marcus! I've heard about you for years."

"Nothing bad, I trust."

"Oh no!" The way she averted her eyes told him she wasn't being entirely truthful. How could she? No one ever heard of Marcus Lithgow without hearing something bad. He trusted she had heard only old stories of his wild youth, rather than any recent and specific sin. God bless Caro for her loyalty. She might be furious with him, but she wouldn't carelessly blacken his name to others. He had bet on Caro keeping the cause of their quarrel to herself—and won.

"Forgive me," he said; "but should I know you?"

"I am Caro Townsend's—the Duchess of Castleton's, I mean—cousin Anne Brotherton."

He seized her hand and shook it heartily. "How extraordinary! Caro's cousin Annabella. I would never have guessed. You don't look anything like I expected."

"Oh? How did you expect me to look?"

"More like Caro, small and redheaded. I wouldn't have looked for an elegant dark girl."

"Elegant? I think not."

"You will be once you buy whatever modish wonder your maid has discovered. Are you sure you wouldn't prefer to go straight to the mantua maker?"

"I'm not sure I should go anywhere. I'm staying with Lady Windermere and she will be worried."

Marcus hastened to weaken her resistance, which seemed to have been raised by his casual compliment. "What a coincidence. I know Windermere but I haven't seen him in years and I never met his wife."

"Windermere went abroad soon after their marriage."

"Shall I escort you to Hanover Square instead?"

"The bookshop will do very well." Her manner softened infinitesimally. As he watched her take her selection to the attendant and order it delivered to Windermere House, he pondered their recent exchange. Whether she was haughty or merely deeply reserved remained to be discovered.

Anne had been pleased at knowing Lithgow's identity. She'd grown up hearing about Caro's friends, who always sounded such fun. Her own life had been spent in the country with her elderly grandfather. A year after the latter's death, she'd come to London, staying first with Caro and now with Cynthia, Lady Windermere. She still lived quietly, aside from an occasional evening party. Lithgow was the most interesting person she'd met in months.

But Anne was naturally cautious, especially

when it came to single gentlemen. The prospect of the Camber acres did strange things to unmarried men.

It had been too much to hope that a man she liked would also be a suitable match. Lithgow was hopelessly ineligible, despite his recent succession to a viscountcy. As long as she resisted any flirtation, she could enjoy the acquaintance. Where was the harm?

Feeling agreeably daring, she set off down the street on his arm, her maid trailing behind. After their first meeting she'd been unable to give Cynthia a satisfactory report on his appearance, having been overcome with delight by his ability to tell the difference between a Greek original and a Roman copy. Now she took inventory while he kept up a flow of inconsequential chatter. His straight brown hair, worn longer than the new fashion in London, suited a rather handsome forehead. His nose was likewise straight and well-shaped, his chin firm; and his cheekbones prominent. When he turned to listen to a reply she determined that the eyes were a catlike green. How had she missed that?

To her disappointment, Hatchard's didn't have Mr. Warner's book. "I'll have to order it," she said to Lithgow.

"Since the printer is in Bath it could be weeks before you receive it. I know a bookseller in Soho who makes a particular point of carrying such books. Walking shouldn't take more than a quarter of an hour, unless you prefer to go by hackney."

She told herself that she really wanted Mr. Warner's *Illustration of the Roman Antiquities Discovered at Bath.* Now. To read that very evening; nothing else would do. "It's a fine day and I like to walk."

Anne's maid did not. The middle-aged dresser sent heated glares into Anne's back. Not that she could see Maldon's sullen expression, but the woman had attended her for most of her life and they knew each other very well. By the time they passed Burlington House, awareness of Maldon's resentment and sore feet distracted her to the point of spoiling the conversation. It would be unkind to make Maldon walk farther, yet Anne was enjoying herself. Just for once she didn't want to do the right thing.

"Maldon," she said firmly. "Please return directly to Hanover Square and tell Lady Windermere where I have gone."

"I shouldn't leave you, miss."

"I wouldn't wish Her Ladyship to be worried, and Lord Lithgow will look after me."

Her unwonted strength of command cowed the dubious maid and rendered her obedient. *I pay her,* Anne told herself. *I may have no control over my money but it is mine. I should be allowed to do what I wish.* A startling thought.

"I'm confident of my ability to keep you safe," Lithgow said, once the maid had turned into Sackville Street, "but I would hate to expose you to gossip. My reputation is not of the best," he continued with a wry twist of the lips, "and Caro would have my head if I hurt her dearest Annabella. Perhaps I should take you home at once."

"No," she said. "I will be safe with any friend of Caro's. I want that book."

The streets grew narrower and dirtier, the houses shabbier, and the passers-by poorer. As she picked her way gingerly through piles of rubbish, she reflected that Maldon was going to have something to say about the state of her shoes. Frogsham's turned out to be a small shop on a road little wider than an alley. When she entered with some trepidation, the first thing that struck her, once her eyes grew accustomed to the gloom, was an enormous stuffed owl, perched high and regarding the shambles below like an unblinking tutelary god over a bewildering mélange. Pictures, tapestries, statues, and Lord knew what else lay higgledy-piggledy on shelves, hanging from the walls, and heaped on the floor.

"Is this really a bookshop?" she whispered.

"Frogsham sells books and so much else," Lithgow replied.

The proprietor, a wizened little fellow wearing a tasseled velvet hat like a nightcap, greeted him by name in an odd accent. Anne could scarcely understand him, but the essence of his inquiry seemed to be "Are you looking for something in particular, or just looking around today?"

"I thought you might have a book on Bath by Richard Warner," Lithgow said.

"Third shelf down." Frogsham pointed into a corner. Behind the tall figure of a turbaned Moor, Anne perceived a small, neatly arranged collection of books.

Her eyes flew to Lithgow and he nodded his

encouragement. Edging round the lowering Othello, she peered at the row of books and found not only the desired volume neatly bound in calf, but an intriguing quarto on the antiquities of Northamptonshire that must surely be worth a look. Alas, the author apparently believed antiquity to begin with the reign of Elizabeth. Finding nothing else she *had* to have among the books, she turned her gaze on the confused miscellany around her.

"Do you have anything Roman?" she asked the shopkeeper.

"There's a basket of heads over there."

Despite this alarming statement, she discovered nothing but a group of decapitated miniatures—men, women, and children in marble or terra-cotta, sporting the unmistakable hairstyles of the classical past.

"What do you think of these? Are they Roman or Greek?"

Lithgow studied them gravely. "Roman in style, but whether they are ancient I couldn't say. I've seen forgeries by the thousand in Italy, produced for the tourists."

"I shall take the risk and buy one." She decided she liked this shop, an adventure compared to the modish emporia of Bond Street. She selected a pretty child, not sure if it was a boy or a girl, and a rather handsome young man. Then her eye caught an item in weathered bronze on the next shelf. "I think it must be a pendant," she said, "judging by the loop at the top, but I can't imagine what it signifies." The curved cylindrical column had a slight bulge at the bottom and matching spheres on either side at the top.

"I have no idea." Lithgow smiled. "Roman jewelry can be very odd."

"It's rather ugly so I won't take it. But I will buy the book and the two heads."

"Let me handle Frogsham," he said softly.

In Anne's experience a price was a price. If she decided she wanted something, she paid whatever was asked. Lithgow and Frogsham, however, commenced an extended bargaining session over what was, in the end, quite a small amount.

"Oh dear," she whispered at the conclusion of the negotiation. "I don't have any money with me."

Marcus had foreseen this. He'd escorted rich women all over Europe and found one thing they had in common, regardless of nationality: They never carried ready cash.

"Usually when I go shopping the merchant sends me the account," she continued, "but I've never been in a shop quite like this."

"Frogsham is not a man to issue credit, but allow me to take care of this trifling sum."

"I shall repay you, of course."

"No need."

"I insist."

Marcus never expected to see those few shillings again. Wealthy ladies tended to forget insignificant debts and he had no intention of dunning her. The excursion had been a success. Frogsham, the rogue, had happily overcharged him for the Warner that Marcus had himself placed on the shelf the day before. But he'd beaten the man down on the heads, one of which probably was Roman. Thank God Miss Brotherton had decided against the pendant. She might not recognize a phallus, but he didn't count on the same innocence from Lady Windermere.

With a wrinkle of her aristocratic nose, she accepted the package crudely wrapped in newspaper. Miss Brotherton had no notion of life outside the rarefied confines of Mayfair though she had, he fancied, quite enjoyed the exposure to Frogsham's specialized pawnshop.

He let her precede him into the narrow lane and guided her to the broader thoroughfare of Warwick Street. A gentleman should always walk on the traffic side, to protect his lady from the dirt cast up by passing vehicles, but she got ahead of him, just in time for the appearance of a coalman's dray careering at excessive speed. The cart hit a bump and lurched onto the pavement for foot travelers, within feet of the oblivious heiress. Marcus threw his arms around her and dragged her to safety. "Take care," he yelled at the disappearing tradesman.

She trembled in his arms. "That man nearly hit me," she said. "I could have been killed."

"I trust it wouldn't have come to that." He held her closer, discovering a slender waist under the sensible cloth of her winter redingote. Very nice. He stroked her back to soothe her, barely resisting the temptation to explore the curves of her hips and behind.

"Thank you for saving me."

The driver of the cart, hired in advance and alerted by Frogsham's errand boy, had performed his task with impeccable timing. She clung to him and he made no effort to relinquish her. One object of the charade had been to get this skittish virgin accustomed to his touch.

Yet along with satisfaction at the success of the ruse came the thought that if he should, by a miracle, succeed in winning Miss Brotherton's hand, it wouldn't be the worst thing in the world. He didn't want to let her go. Along with the promised half crown, that coal hauler was going to win a rebuke for doing his job too well. Any closer and Marcus would have been too late. Anne Brotherton could have been badly hurt, and the notion annoyed him far beyond the threat to his plans.

Silky hair, revealed by a bonnet knocked askew, tickled his face, and a clean lemon scent filled his nostrils. Virtue and innocence were qualities he rarely encountered, and he had the absurd urge to protect them. To protect her. Absurd because he himself posed the greatest threat. He strengthened his embrace.

She was the one to break away. "My parcel!" she cried. It lay in a pool in the gutter.

With considerable damage to his boots, Marcus waded into the muddy swill and retrieved the sodden package.

"I don't think you want to carry this," he said. "My gloves are already ruined so save yours." Gingerly he lowered his nose. "And it smells. We'd better return to Frogsham and have it repacked."

"My book!" she wailed. "It will be all wet."

"Don't despair. It'll dry off and be readable, if not beautiful."

"I hope so. I am so eager to read it so we can talk about our impressions."

His poise restored after the ridiculous attack of sentiment, he smiled winningly. He trusted that when she struggled through Mr. Warner's dry prose she'd think of Marcus sacrificing his boots so she could enjoy it.

Chapter 4

Lord Algernon Tiverton took his punctilious leave from Lady Windermere's drawing room, allowing Anne and Cynthia to succumb to the giggles they'd repressed during an endless fifteen-minute morning call. The younger son of a marquess, he'd been introduced to Anne by his aunt Lady Ashfield.

"He can barely restrain his passion," Cynthia cried dramatically.

"Hah! His only passion is for his own ancestry. Like every other man in London he looks at me and sees gold, and not interesting Roman gold artifacts. Just piles of dull modern guineas."

"The man's a fool if he fails to see what you are really like."

Anne looked affectionately at her loyal—and deluded—friend. Cynthia was a pretty woman with delicate features in a heart-shaped face. Fair hair fell in a cascade of curls from a deceptively casual knot. Without extraordinary elegance, she made the most of her small, rounded figure. Even in a morning dress of light worsted over an impeccable pleated chemisette and ruffled collar, Anne judged her alluring. Her own appearance was much less satisfactory. Clad in a heavy gray twill, designed for winter in the freezing corridors of Camber, she looked dowdy. There was nothing she could do about an angular body and a small bosom, but a skilled dressmaker could work wonders.

"Do you want to go shopping?" she said.

"If you mean Hatchard's," Cynthia said warily, "I'll let you go alone and visit the furniture warehouse instead." Cynthia spent an inordinate amount of time and money on both furnishings and her wardrobe.

"I need a new gown or two, for the winter."

"My dearest Anne! What has brought about this miraculous reversal of habit? No, don't tell me. I can guess. You have fallen in love with Lord Algernon! Fear not. Clinging skirts and a revealing bodice will penetrate his aloofness and he will sweep you into his arms and carry you off to whatever country fastness he occupies to live happily ever after."

"A garment such as you describe would more likely send him scurrying out of town, alone."

"An excellent result, but I don't think that's the real reason for your unprecedented interest in fashion." Cynthia gave her a hard look. Further interrogation was forestalled by the appearance of servants delivering the post.

Anne tore open a missive from the Duchess of Castleton. Cynthia, evincing little interest in her own correspondence, fiddled with the arrangement of white hothouse roses that filled a large Meissen vase on the mantelpiece. "What do you think, Anne? Do they look better this way?"

Anne glanced over the top of the letter. "Yes."

"Or maybe with less of the maidenhair. I'm not sure I like it."

"Definitely."

"You aren't paying attention."

"White roses are always pretty and I detest maidenhair. Why did you buy it?"

"Denford sent them. To celebrate becoming my next-door neighbor. He takes up residence at Fortescue House today."

Lady Windermere's air of disinterest was unconvincing. Anne couldn't ignore the opening, despite an innate reluctance to interfere in the affairs of others.

"Caro isn't pleased to hear that the duke is back in London and paying you marked attentions."

"Pish. Caro always worries about me and Denford."

"Listen to what she writes. *I do not trust Julian's motives in pursuing Cynthia and I fear for her tender heart. She is less worldly than she likes to appear.*"

"I know what I'm doing." Cynthia finished removing the despised fern and stepped back to regard the flowers with a satisfied smile. "Denford and my husband are at odds. I don't know why and I don't greatly care."

"Although Lord Windermere is abroad, he may still hear gossip."

"I hope so," Cynthia replied with a brittle

laugh. "I know quite well that Denford is using me as part of a scheme to embarrass Windermere and I intend to use *him* for the same reason."

"I wish you would be careful." What more could she say? Cynthia was both her hostess and her senior. It wasn't Anne's place to read her a lecture.

"I think the pot calls the kettle black, Miss Annabella. Admit that you have a tendre for the wicked Lord Lithgow. I knew it as soon as you mentioned new gowns."

Anne made a play of shuffling the pages of the letter. "I don't *think* so. I find him agreeable company. Very easy to talk to. And he is a man of substance too."

"You find any man substantial who will talk about Roman ruins."

Anne smiled at Cynthia's teasing and as usual said less than she felt. There was something about Lithgow's company that added a pleasant frisson of danger. When she tried to analyze it she could only suppose it was due to his somewhat unsavory background. Yet even when he'd embraced her to save her from the runaway cart she hadn't felt he was taking advantage. She felt safe in his presence, safe from the pressure of courtship. He never lavished her with the overblown praise that she loathed in her suitors. Aside from that one time when, ridiculously, he'd called her elegant, he was friendly and sincere. Perhaps he meant it. Perhaps he did find her elegant.

If so, he'd find her even more so if she were more fashionably dressed.

"What else does Caro have to say?"

Anne turned over the page. "She wants us both to come to Castleton for Christmas."

"We could do that, I suppose." Anne feared Cynthia's lack of enthusiasm stemmed from the fact that Denford was unlikely to be invited.

"She writes a lot about Castleton's twin sisters."

"I know she's happy to have sisters. I've always wished I had them myself."

"She is like a sister to me." Though they hadn't spent much time together, she and Caro had always been each other's dearest friends. While she shouldn't resent her cousin's happiness, she felt a certain abandonment. The prospect of achieving a warm family life with a suitor of her guardian's choosing seemed remote. A sliver of jealousy, selfish and irrational, chilled her heart. Ashamed, she shook her head, returned to the letter, and gasped.

"What?"

"Speaking of Lord Lithgow, listen to what Caro writes. *While I am on the subject of my old friends—* underlined for emphasis—*I want to counsel you to beware if you come across Marcus Lithgow. I cannot tell you what happened between us without breaking Thomas's confidence and revealing secrets about his family, but I am quite disillusioned with him. Marcus has behaved very badly to me and Castleton, who dislikes him very much. Do not trust a word he says.* Underlined again. *I wish I could tell you everything but it is not my secret.*"

"Goodness! How very dramatic!"

"Caro has always enjoyed a drama," Anne said, a little sourly.

"What can he have done?"

"No doubt he did something to annoy Castleton, which wouldn't be difficult. Since they left London every letter is 'Thomas did this,' 'Thomas says that.' Evidently he's managed to turn her against her old friends."

"You must be right," Cynthia said. "I still don't understand how Caro can be happy with Lord Stuffy. They are so different." This was an old and oft-repeated conversation. Neither of them quite fathomed their lively friend's attachment to the poker-backed duke. And they both missed her.

"Another thing. Lithgow hasn't made the least effort to charm me. I've had what feels like every man in London making up to me and he doesn't behave like any of them."

"Still," Cynthia said, "there must be something there to make her write like that."

It was ironic, Anne thought, that Cynthia gave any credence at all to the warning against Lithgow when she refused to listen to Caro's admonitions about Denford. "It's unlike Caro to be cryptic. How can I find out? Could you ask Denford? Since you are so close."

"Or *you* could ask Lithgow."

With mixed feelings Marcus discovered that the Duke of Denford had moved in next door to Windermere House. Julian disclaimed any interest in the Brotherton heiress. He'd spent several months making up to the wife of his former best friend, Windermere, for some unexplained and doubtless nefarious reason. But Julian was quite capable of playing more than one game at the same time, and it seemed logical that a man who found himself with a title, a couple of huge mansions, and very little ready money would solve his problem by courting the heiress next door. A friendship of more than ten years had taught Marcus that trying to outfox Julian was fruitless. One reason he never played cards with him.

When he called at Windermere House a couple of days after their Soho adventure—never appear too eager was one of his hard rules of seduction—Julian was cozily ensconced in the drawing room, amusing both ladies greatly. Anne Brotherton rose to greet him with a shy smile he found encouraging.

"Miss Brotherton." He took her outstretched hand and held it a bare second longer than necessary. She made no effort to pull away. "I came to inquire after the health of a certain book."

"Thank you. I am glad to report that the volume is dry, though its scent may never be suitable for polite company. Cynthia refuses to let me read it downstairs. I have to keep it in my bedchamber."

"I trust it wasn't so dry as to send you instantly to sleep."

"The content is perhaps more fascinating than the prose. Nevertheless I am grateful and will think of your gallant rescue whenever I consult it."

With a more worldly lady, Marcus would have offered a saucy double entendre. Anne Brotherton's words were flirtatious but her expression remained grave. He wondered if she ever played games of chance. She would have the advantage of being hard to read.

"It's a fine day," she said. "I do believe the sun is struggling to emerge from those clouds. Would you care to see Cynthia's garden? It's quite fine."

Intriguing, especially since the sun seemed likely to fail in its efforts. Following her downstairs, he listened to her observations on the history of Bath, showing she had indeed been reading the evil-smelling volume, much more carefully than he had when it was pristine. She collected her pelisse and did not flinch when he placed a careless hand on the small of her back to guide her down the steps into the garden, which was a decent size for the middle of London but not, in its early winter barrenness, of any special beauty.

In the bleak surroundings his companion seemed more animated than usual, a leftover late rose among dying leaves. Her dark hair set off delicately pink cheeks and a sweet red mouth. An invitation to a deserted garden usually presaged a kiss at the very least and Marcus was willing, even eager, to take it.

Without saying a word, he stood in the light breeze, letting her make the next move. He read hesitation in the hazel eyes, more blue than brown in the dull light. A quick nod, a deep breath, and she spoke.

"I had a letter from Caro today."

No kiss then. How disappointing. But he had been expecting this and he was ready. "How is she?" he asked.

"She warned me against you, said I shouldn't trust you. Because of what happened between you and Castleton."

Tempting as it was to entirely blame the duke, he'd already planned to tell her as much of the truth as was politic, slanting it to his own advantage. That Anne had jumped to the conclusion that Caro's grievance had something to do with her husband was an unlooked-for benefit.

"Caro is angry with me, and rightly so. Let me explain, though the story does not redound to my credit."

She nodded and perched on a stone bench. He remained on his feet, looking down at her with his best troubled look.

"As you know, I have made my living by my skill at cards and dice, since I was sixteen years old. I had no choice. I have no fortune and it's all my father taught me. He was a rogue. Lately I became aware that gaming was no way to spend my life. I returned to London this year, determined to find a more respectable means of support. The first thing I did was to raise some capital by collecting a few debts."

"Caro?" She was quick.

"Robert Townsend lost a large sum to me just before his death. I didn't want to dun Caro, and I never would have after Robert left her in such straits. Once she married a duke I thought she could afford it."

"Did Castleton refuse to pay you?" she demanded with a convenient air of disapproval.

"He was under no obligation to pay another man's gaming debt, and neither was she. I behaved badly." Badly as in trying to steal Caro's most precious possession from under Castleton's precious nose. He saw no need to go into details.

"Did you apologize? Caro is the most forgiving person in the world. She would never hold a grudge."

"But her husband does. He's a distant connection of my mother's and we had a childhood quarrel. He dislikes me."

"This is terrible! I always thought the Duke of Castleton was a man of principle."

"I have no reason to believe otherwise. Yet even the most upright of men can be ruled by his passions."

"Do you know that Caro used to call him Lord Stuffy? And then she married him. I know she loves him but they are an unlikely couple. He used to disapprove of her circle of friends, but I thought he had come to accept them."

"The others perhaps, but not me. We have too much history between us. My dear Miss Brotherton, believe me when I say I'd do anything to mend the rift."

"I shall write to Caro on your behalf."

Marcus, who had been standing over her with folded arms, ventured to sit beside her. "Your sympathy means so much to me." He took her hand and stroked the smooth white skin, skin never marred by a minute of work, and bestowed a light kiss on the knuckles. "Thank you for listening and giving me the benefit of the doubt, which I fear I do not deserve."

Her cheeks grew pinker and she didn't pull away. Raising her eyes to his, she looked like a woman waiting to be kissed and he wanted to oblige her. He wanted to taste those lips much more than was sensible for an adventurer with a scheme. As Lewis Lithgow had instructed him from an early age, genuine desire or even liking for a mark was a weakness that led to carelessness and exposure. Summoning his resolution, he let her go. Side by side on the bench, each looked straight ahead. He wished he knew what she was thinking.

She recovered first. "I honor your ambition to find a new occupation and I know it's difficult for a man without fortune or connections. What would you wish to do, if you had the choice?"

"Don't laugh, but I think I would enjoy being a land steward. A brief time I spent at Castleton was a pleasure. I wished I could live in the country and was all the sadder when my father and I were ejected. I also visited a great-uncle's house in Wiltshire and loved it there." Which was sort of true. He hadn't hated it. "But I have no experience. I've been reading a few books on the subject of estate management."

She shook her head as though bewildered by the problems of such an unconnected man.

"Enough about my vain ambitions. I'd much sooner talk about you than me. Tell me about Anne Brotherton. What has she been doing all her life?"

She looked doubtful. "I've led a very dull existence compared to you."

"Perhaps, yet I envy you that dullness. There's much to be said for having an established position in a family and society."

"I am lucky, I suppose." She shook her head and continued slowly. "But I confess I don't always feel that way. My good fortune is an accident of birth and nothing to do with me. I've always felt"—she paused—"like an empty vessel, the unwitting repository of the Brotherton future. My father and mother both died when I was an infant. I lived at Camber with my grandfather and my governesses and later my companion. Nothing much happened, except when Caro came to visit."

"Livened things up, did she?"

"What do you think?"

"It's impossible to be bored when she's about. Robert was a lucky man, and so is Castleton. The loss of her friendship is one of the great regrets of my life." He'd never spoken with more sincerity.

"She'll come round." A light touch on his arm squeezed at his heart, though never was sympathy less deserved.

"I hope so. Now go on. Did you have friends? And admirers. I'm sure you always had the latter."

She wrinkled her nose. "My grandfather's health was poor so we neither visited nor received many people. Felix was with us a good deal of the time, my second cousin, the heir to the earldom."

"Was he your playmate?"

"Hardly, since he was a decade elder, but he was always kind to me, even when I was a little girl. He didn't seem to mind too much when he proposed to me."

Although he knew all about her former engagement to Felix Brotherton, Marcus feigned surprise. "A lady should expect a stronger sentiment from a husband than mere tolerance. I should hope you sent him about his business with a flea in his ear!"

She gave a little giggle, more animation than he'd yet seen in her. "Of course not! I always knew we would marry. We were betrothed when I was seventeen."

Poor little heiress. In some ways she had even less choice in life than Lewis Lithgow's son. He at least had traveled the world and made his own luck. He beat down pity and with it compunction.

"What happened?" he asked, well aware of the answer. "I hope you came to your senses and sent him to the right about."

"I accepted him. He died of a lung fever less than a year later."

He gathered her hands in a light clasp. "I'm sorry. Did you love him?"

"We were comfortable. We knew what to expect of each other."

"Did he ever kiss you?"

"No." The answer was more a breath than a word.

Her eyes grew large and lovely and her lips parted, just enough to emit a breath. Gently he cupped her cheek, warm and smooth as an Italian apricot under his palm. He lowered his head and brought his mouth to hers, soft as a whisper, frightened she might melt away. He found her as pliant yet firm as he'd suspected, and every bit as sweet. Instinct told him to surge in and take possession, and only years of practiced control held him back. His reward, after a second that lasted an age, was a perceptible movement. In her inexperienced way she kissed him back.

It wasn't much of a kiss, little more than a mingling of breath, and he wanted more. His fingers found the wild pulse at her temple, threaded into the hair she wore firmly coiled about her head. It was soft and fine. Closing his eyes, he let her scent and taste and the texture of her lips wash over him. She felt clean and pure, and that very fact lent a faint erotic charge to their contact. He wanted to pull her into his arms, to discover the body hidden by ill-fitting layers of wool, and most of all to kiss her properly, until she was gasping and crying out for more.

Her innocent enthusiasm touched him, and shamed him too. A man like Marcus Lithgow had no business with this artless girl.

Too bad. He needed her and he couldn't afford scruples.

He opened his eyes and hardened his resolution, gauging her reaction as though she were a hand of cards. He knew the moment when the crescendo of pleasure halted. Her mouth lost its pliancy and her entire body stilled. Before she could succumb to panic he ended the kiss himself, inching his face away and letting his hands drop to her shoulders. She gaped at him, then averted her eyes.

"I shouldn't have done that," he said. "I do beg your pardon, but the temptation was more than I could resist." He smiled his most ingenuous smile, a little humorous with only a hint of ardor. "For a rogue like me, there's only one thing to be done with a pretty girl in a garden."

Half expecting to have his face slapped, he gave her credit for poise. Wrinkling her nose, she made no effort to pull away. "Well," she said. "I've never been kissed before and it had to happen sometime."

"I am honored." He meant it. "I hope the experience met your expectations, otherwise I truly would be a villain."

She now shook off his touch, but not sharply. "What do you want of me?"

"Anne—Miss Brotherton, I'm not in a position to want anything. I know how disparate our positions are. You will make a great marriage, sooner or later, and there's no place in your life for a man like me. I will settle for liking."

She regarded him, clear-eyed, for some moments while he maintained the sincerity of his expression. There wasn't a gamester in Europe who could read what he was really thinking. He wasn't even sure himself. When he expressed regrets at his lack of eligibility, he had an uneasy feeling that he meant them. He'd kissed Anne Brotherton to render her flustered and yearning for more. He couldn't tell how he'd succeeded with her, but he'd certainly managed to confuse himself.

"I hope we can be friends. That is all," he said,

pulling himself together. "You needn't fear that I will ask for more. I will never do such a thing again."

"I would like that," she said with a nod. "Friends. We all need friends."

Chapter 5

Anne thought about kissing.

She thought about kissing her dinner partner, Lord Algernon Tiverton. To distract herself from what was coming out of his mouth, she concentrated on the shape of it. Quite pleasant, she concluded. Neither too plump nor too thin, a healthy color, and a nice little dip in the middle of the upper lip. She'd never paid much attention to mouths before, but now found she noticed nothing else. About gentlemen, that was. And more specifically she considered what those mouths would feel like on her own.

She wondered how Lord Algernon would taste. Then he drew breath to insert a forkful of cabbage and she shuddered. She hated cabbage. Trying to be fair, she acknowledged he wouldn't always be eating cabbage. Even Marcus Lithgow's kisses would be less than ideal if he'd been eating cabbage. Or fish.

Lord Algernon swallowed a morsel of haddock. The past two days had been spent trying not to think about kissing Lord Lithgow. Since that proved impossible, she compromised by thinking of kissing in general and assessing the possibilities of other men. The dinner party at Lady Ashfield's had come as a welcome opportunity to extend her investigations beyond footmen and shopkeepers. Unfortunately, her hostess seemed to have selected her guests with the aim of making Tiverton, her nephew, appear attractive in comparison. Poor Cynthia's expression was one of barely concealed horror as she listened to an elderly general with giant gray whiskers.

"Are you staying long in London, my lord?" Anne asked.

Tiverton took her polite inquiry as encouragement. "As long as necessary, Miss Brotherton. I look forward to pursuing your acquaintance. I expect we shall meet often at such assemblies as are planned, despite the dearth of people in town."

"I hardly find London empty. I cannot set foot outside without entering a crowd. I read in the *Morning Post* recently that the population exceeds a million."

"I see you are a young lady who values precision," he replied. "An excellent quality. I should have made myself clear that I refer to a scarcity of people worthy of notice. But you are quite correct in stating the capital holds an abundance of the lower orders that is impossible to avoid. In the country it is different. At Locksley, my Derbyshire place, I go weeks without encountering a soul beyond those neighbors of a proper rank."

"Really? How uncomfortable it must be to live without servants." Anne tried to avoid Cynthia's eye lest she burst out laughing.

"A jest, Miss Brotherton," he said. "Most amusing."

No, the conversation of Lord Algernon Tiverton was not enough to keep Anne from thinking about Marcus Lithgow and *his* kiss. Especially since he required nothing from her but an occasional word of agreement as he droned on—though *droned* was the wrong word for his clipped and slightly high-pitched voice—about his own interests, which interested Anne not a whit. The branches of Lord Algernon's family tree were extensive, ancient, and unpolluted by scandal. A murderer or pirate would have enlivened the tale.

Or a gamester.

That got her thinking about kissing again. Her new gown was of whisper-soft silk with an overdress of gauze that caressed her shoulders and arms. She'd let Cynthia persuade her to buy new undergarments of linen so fine as to be almost transparent. The touch of the delicate material gave her a new awareness of her own skin. All over. These thrilling and not altogether comfortable sensations seemed to be connected to the kissing business. But not Lord Algernon.

"What do you think, Miss Brotherton?" He was actually asking her opinion? "Do you think I should quarter my personal escutcheon with that of my mother's family? I would also, of course, be willing to do the same with my wife's."

He had his beady eyes on the Brotherton coat of arms.

"I know little of heraldry."

"I shall be happy to instruct you." And off he went again, leaving her sure that she would never, under any circumstances, wish to kiss him. She'd rather listen to Marcus Lithgow talk about laundry than endure another hour of Tiverton's company.

After three interminable courses, Lady Ashfield led the ladies out and invited Anne to her boudoir to tidy herself. Since none of the others received this privileged invitation, Anne expected the ensuing tête-à-tête.

"Lord Algernon admires you very much," the countess said.

Anne sat at the dressing table and pretended to tweak her neat plaits, arranged so tightly by her maid that not a hair was out of place. "I don't know what to say." Not without being impolite to the gentleman's cousin.

"I have written to dear Lord Morrissey and I am happy to say he favors Algernon's suit."

"A younger son?" she replied, not letting a twinge of panic show. This was unwelcome news, suggesting that her guardian was becoming serious about finding her a match. If she wasn't careful her days of freedom would soon be over. The thought caught her by surprise. She hadn't previously seen her unmarried state in that way. Rather the opposite, since she couldn't conceive of a husband who would be *more* autocratic than her late grandfather or her current guardian.

"Lord Algernon is no fortune hunter," Lady Ashfield said. "He has a very easy competence of his own and no need to seek a rich wife. Besides, he has far too much principle."

"My guardian has always wished me to look higher."

"There's nothing wrong with Algernon's birth and connections. His position makes him an ideal custodian of the Camber estates because he won't be distracted by his own responsibilities."

Anne bit back the retort that he was more likely to be distracted by his own conceit.

"He's even willing to add the Brotherton name to his."

"Do you mean to say that if I married him I would be Lady Algernon Brotherton-Tiverton?"

"A trivial matter. I know half a dozen people with sillier names. I daresay Morrissey will exert his influence with the king to have the earldom of Camber revived for him."

For *him*. For a pompous creature who cared nothing for her person or her interests. Anne wished quite desperately that she had not been born an heiress. Then there would have been some chance she could be an individual. Her heritage and her duty to marry oppressed her.

And then there was the matter of kissing. That marriage involved kissing—and a good deal more—could no longer be ignored. She had a lowering suspicion that the least eligible men were the most kissable.

"There's another thing I must mention," Lady

Ashfield said. Anne wished she wouldn't. As a close friend of her guardian, the countess felt she had the right to favor Anne with her trenchantly expressed opinions on every subject. "Lithgow."

"What?"

"I heard a report that you walked from Berkeley Square to Piccadilly on his arm. It will not do."

"My maid was with me." Until their unplanned excursion into Soho.

"I don't care if you were followed by an army of footmen and the Prince of Wales himself. Marcus Lithgow may have somehow fallen into the peerage but he never was and never will be suitable company for any young woman of reputation. Do you have any idea who his father was?"

"He didn't choose his own father."

"None of us chose our fathers, yet our course in life is determined by our birth. A man like that must do much to atone for the faults in his ancestry and upbringing, and nothing I've seen or heard of Marcus Lithgow suggests that he's done anything at all. Quite the opposite."

"I find Lord Lithgow pleasant and well-informed."

"Very likely, but he's not the kind of man you marry."

"It's a wide leap from conversation to marriage. I wasn't thinking of wedding him."

"I should think not! Neither should you be seen with him, now. Later he may be an agreeable companion for a married woman, as long as you are discreet about it."

Could Lady Ashfield possibly mean what Anne

thought she meant? Anne had at first been shocked by the looser morals that pertained among Caro's friends, but many of them were artists. She hadn't expected a friend of her guardian's to advocate postmarital flirtation. Such hypocrisy!

"It would be rude to cut the acquaintance. He's one of my cousin the Duchess of Castleton's oldest friends."

The feathers adorning Lady Ashfield's gray curls quivered and she waved a dismissive hand. "Duchess or not, Caroline Townsend is a flibber-tigibbet and always was. I don't recommend you take her advice when it comes to the ways of the world. After her first marriage she moved in a fast set, and association with Robert Townsend's friends will do you no good. I don't even like to see you living with Lady Windermere. She is not good *ton*."

"I don't quite understand you, Lady Ashfield. Is a chance encounter with Lord Lithgow at the circulating library, after which he kindly lent me company to a bookshop, enough to damage my reputation? I had not thought it so fragile."

"Come, come, my dear," she replied, taking Anne's hand. "You suffer the lack of a mother, or a responsible older lady to guide you. I know you mean no harm. Anyone can see you are painfully innocent and naïve. Now you have been warned, you will know to keep Lithgow and his ilk at a distance. I repeat, such company will do you no good."

"You mean it will render me unmarriageable?"

"Nothing," Her Ladyship said with an indul-

gent laugh, "can render so great an heiress as
yourself unmarriageable. That doesn't mean all
matches are equal. With the right husband you
can become a leader of the *ton*, influential in fashion or in politics should you so choose. But the
freedom to pursue your own desires comes only
when you wed a man of substance, and that de-
pends on your own reputation as much as your
fortune. There will always be men who will overlook any blot on your name if it means laying
hands on the latter. But men of principle will think
twice, and Algernon would dismiss the match out
of hand. I assured you he is not a fortune hunter
and that proves it. Not all the Brotherton wealth
would make him ignore the whiff of scandal. It is
of the greatest importance now that you behave
impeccably."

Anne smiled. "Thank you, Lady Ashfield. You
have given me much to think about. And thank
you for this delightful occasion. I appreciate the
chance to know Lord Algernon Tiverton as he
really is."

Become a Brotherton-Tiverton? Never!

When Morrissey had proposed she marry
the Duke of Castleton, Anne had been willing
enough. He seemed a decent man, and so what
if they had little in common? They would have
their duties and their children to hold them together and pursue their own interests when they
had time. She didn't feel the same way about Lord
Algernon Tiverton.

She needed to find a way to thwart her guardian's plans, and she doubted her powers of resistance once Morrissey returned to England and brought his forceful personality to bear. He'd summon the authority of her late grandfather, remind her of her duty to the Brotherton lands and name, and she'd give in.

Her views of marriage had changed. She wanted more than a manager for her fortune. Her guardian had been wise to keep her immured in the country. Exposure to the greater world had made her question her destiny.

Cynthia sat quietly beside her in the jolting carriage, a married woman but not a happy one. Anne counted her a friend and they'd shared a house for months, but she knew little of what went on behind Cynthia's pretty, smiling face. Bred to reserve, it had never occurred to Anne to inquire or even to wonder.

"What do you think makes a good marriage?" she asked.

In the light of the swinging carriage lamp, anguish disturbed Cynthia's serene features. She rarely spoke of her husband, who had gone abroad a month after their marriage. "My dear Anne, I'm the last person you should ask. What do I know of marital bliss?"

"Why did you marry Windermere?" she asked.

"The match was arranged by my uncle."

"Were you willing?"

"My alternatives were worse. What do I have to complain about? I am rich and healthy and live in a fine house in the best part of London without the inconvenience of a spouse."

Anne's heart bled for her bitterness. "Were you always so cynical?"

"Only because my husband has taught me by his actions. I used to be as innocent and stupid as a newborn lamb."

Anne took her friend's hand. "You deserve better."

"We all deserve better, but when do we get what we deserve?"

"Morrissey wants me to accept Lord Algernon."

"Don't do it, Anne. Don't give in. Without a penny of my own I had no option but to obey my uncle. With your wealth you can make your own choice. You come of age in two months."

"But not into my fortune. If I marry without permission I could be penniless. Morrissey has complete discretion over when to turn over the estates to me or my husband."

"Truly?"

"Unless I keep my pin money. I have seven hundred and fifty a year according to my grandfather's settlement."

"There was a time when I would have been ecstatic at such an income."

Anne shrugged. Though to most people her wealth was her defining characteristic, she rarely thought about money. "I think I keep it were I to marry without permission, but since I never considered doing so, I never asked. To tell you the truth I don't even know if I spend my allowance. I just send my bills to Thompson and they are paid. No one has ever objected to my expenditures."

"Does Lithgow know?" Cynthia voiced the question that had been buzzing at the back of her own mind.

"I don't know."

"You should tell him. It will settle the matter of his intentions."

"I'm not looking to marry to disoblige my guardian, merely to choose my own husband. Besides, Lithgow doesn't appear to be courting me." If one discounted the kiss, which she decided not to mention to Cynthia.

She didn't want to think ill of him. She wanted to take his profession of friendship at face value. "He tells me he is looking for a steady occupation and is studying estate management."

Cynthia looked a little dubious. "You have plenty of estates. Could he be seeking your patronage?"

"As though Morrissey would listen to me! He decides and I obey. That's why I'm so terrified of what will happen when he returns from Ireland. The only way to drive off Tiverton before then is to soil my reputation, just a little."

"I'm not the person to advise you on the ways of the beau monde. My uncle made his money in trade, and in Windermere's absence I have no standing in the *ton*. But what you suggest sounds dangerous to me."

"Lady Ashfield assures me that only a stickler like her nephew will care. For most people my fortune washes away all sins. Even if it doesn't,

I have no aspirations to the kind of social leadership she describes. She also says if I pursue Lithgow's acquaintance it will shock Lord Algernon. In her words, *Not all the Brotherton estates would make him ignore the whiff of scandal.*"

"Her Ladyship is very full of opinions," Cynthia said, smiling at Anne's imitation of the old beldame's tones. "That's the answer then. You should be seen in Lithgow's company. It's just what I've been doing with Denford. I daresay neither Denford nor Lithgow is fully to be trusted but they have their uses. We can enjoy them, as long as we proceed with care."

Anne squeezed Cynthia's hand, delighted with a solution that so perfectly aligned with her own inclinations. "I'll ask Lithgow to escort me around London, only in daylight and in public places so I shan't be in any real danger. Everyone will talk and Lord Algernon will cut my acquaintance."

"But, dearest Anne, guard your heart. As I must too."

"You may not be of the *ton*, but you couldn't give me better advice. I am glad Caro introduced us and proud to have your friendship."

At Hanover Square Cynthia went straight upstairs, exhausted by the tedious delights of Lady Ashfield's entertainment, but Anne was restless, her mind swirling with the evening's discussions. Slipping out to the garden, she was drawn to the spot where she'd received her first kiss. Her lips seemed to have developed a permanent state of sensitivity and she wanted to dwell on the moment. Thinking about it gave her little thrills of pleasure.

Not that it could happen again. Since she intended only to see Lithgow in public, and chaperoned by her maid, there wouldn't be a chance. Besides, one didn't kiss friends. And if one was wise, one didn't kiss possible fortune hunters or potential stewards.

Even without kisses, she keenly looked forward to spending time with Lord Lithgow. How splendid it would be to visit the British Museum with a knowledgeable companion. Communicating her wishes posed a problem. She couldn't simply write him a note and ask him to escort her, could she? Such an invitation might be misinterpreted as a desire for further kisses and she didn't want to give him the wrong idea. They were friends, that was all.

Kisses were out of the question.

They would merely share fascinating conversations about the wonders of the ancient world. With his wide experience, he had much to teach her. But not about kisses.

Well, doubtless he could provide an education in that area too, but it wasn't going to happen.

Kisses were for husbands.

Marry Marcus Lithgow. The idea popped into her head out of nowhere.

Ridiculous. It could never happen. Yet the seed once planted sent insidious tentacles into her mind.

His past was a little tarnished but he now held a peerage. Apparently wealth and high rank were not essential in Morrissey's mind, only the ability to take care of her estates. Lithgow was studying the subject, and she was certain he was a capable man. And she employed plenty of people who actually did the work. She fancied he was quite shrewd enough to oversee them.

An enticing vista opened in her mind: life with a husband whose company she enjoyed and whose kisses—and other things—she would like even more. Why not? Since she had to be married for her money she might as well get something from the bargain. He wouldn't treat her enthusiasms with disdain. She pictured herself searching for Roman remains on all the thousands of acres of her inheritance with a husband who would aid and encourage her rather than complaining about the waste of land. And he would introduce her to new wonders, guiding her around Italy. Rome!

Ruins by day, kisses by night. And more.

In gathering wonder, she contemplated the strange restlessness that had possessed her since she met Lithgow, dissatisfaction with her dull existence and a yearning for something more. Could she possibly be in love?

Love wasn't anything she'd expected or allowed herself to aspire to. It was for other people, not plain Anne Brotherton with her millions and her common sense, her odd passion for Roman remains, and her sensible, unmodish wardrobe. Yet tonight she wore flimsy gauze and silk over a fine lace-trimmed shift. If her wardrobe had changed, she had too.

A weight in her chest threatened to erupt into

joy. Cynthia's warning to guard her heart came too late. If not in love with Marcus Lithgow, she was well on the way, and it was wonderful.

She celebrated the realization with a few little dance steps on the rough garden path.

But could he love her in return? She thought he might. He had kissed her sweetly, then spoken with sincerity of the disparity in their positions. She must inform him of the way her fortune was settled, but she didn't believe that would deter him.

Dealing with her guardian was another matter, an obstacle that made an invitation to an antiquarian outing a mere bagatelle. Persuading Morrissey to consent to the match would be difficult, if not impossible, but a surge of optimism seized her. Her will had been muffled in a coat of passivity and she hadn't even known it until she shook it off. Her brain felt sharp with a new determination to fight for what she wanted.

She shivered in her heavy cloak with its fur-lined hood, and buried her free hand deeper into the matching muff, but not because of the chill of the November night. Heat warmed her cheeks, flowed through her veins, and settled low in her belly. She'd never experienced such a peculiar physical reaction. She felt overdressed.

Another buffet of wind put paid to that sensation. She scurried for shelter and discovered, by the light of her lantern, a rusty gate. Behind a tree, almost hidden by the thick ivy that covered the bricks on that side of the garden wall, it appeared to have been unused for years. Anne remembered that the house on that side belonged to the Duke of Denford and wondered if generations of children had used the gate to meet for play. Or—and before she came to London, it wouldn't have occurred to her—whether a pair of illicit lovers had used it for discreet trysts. Through the foliage she heard steps approach, an aromatic smoke penetrated the wintry odor of decaying plants, and voices drew nearer. Male voices.

One particular voice revived the fluttering in her heart. Lithgow must be spending the evening with Denford, whose deep tones were unmistakable. She toyed with the fantasy of slipping through the gate and displaying her new gown.

"Good cigar, Marcus. You can't find such tobacco in London."

"I still have a dozen or two left of those I bought when I was last in Spain. Lord knows when I'll get more. After the devilish time I had getting here from Italy, I suppose I'll have to remain for the moment."

Her governess had stressed that listening to conversations was dishonorable and cautioned her that eavesdroppers heard only ill of themselves. She didn't care. Stowing the lantern against the wall so the light wouldn't seep through the gate, Anne pressed her ear to the bars to make out Lithgow's pleasant baritone. She wanted to hear about Lithgow's travel plans. After all, they might very well include her.

"The French have inconvenienced those of us who find the shores of England limiting."

"Lord, Julian. How excited we were in '89.

Being able to see the Revolution at first hand was well worth getting kicked out of Oxford. What a time the four of us had in Paris. And now Robert is dead and Damian is God knows where."

"Persia, I believe."

"Exactly. Do you remember how wooden-faced the respectable English became over the whole affair?" Anne smiled to herself, remembering her grandfather expressing himself strongly on the subject. "Afraid the infection of liberty and equality would spread here. As though the fat, stolid English would ever take to the streets. I miss Paris. Pity things got out of hand."

"That's one way of putting it."

"You were the last of us to leave. You witnessed what happened in the Terror."

"Some of it," Denford answered curtly. "I don't talk about it."

"You never did. Was it a woman?"

"It was long ago and I never think of it."

The men fell silent for a minute or two and the scent of tobacco grew stronger. Fearing the smoke might set off a cough, Anne inched back and waited.

The duke broke the silence. "And what are you up to, Marcus? My spies tell me you haven't been gracing the gaming hells of London with your presence."

"I'm a reformed character. My valet undresses me and puts me to bed early, then I rise with the dawn and fill my days with useful study." Although he spoke carelessly, Anne was pleased by evidence of Marcus's sincerity. Soundlessly she mouthed the word. *Marcus.* She liked it. A noble Roman name.

Denford emitted a short, derisive laugh. "I'd like to see that. Almost I am tempted to invite you to live at Denford House. Almost. And only for the cigars."

"Thank you, Julian, but I'm quite content in my own rooms."

"I'd believe you if I hadn't seen them. Your lodging is a slum."

"In St. James's? I don't think so. As Lewis always said, the address itself is what matters."

"A slum is in the eye of the beholder, and to this beholder you live in a pigsty."

"You insult my servant. Travis would be desolated to hear you say so. Or he might agree." She could hear his smile.

Boots crunched on gravel and the voices grew faint so she could barely make out their idle banter. She'd heard nothing she shouldn't. Huddling in her cloak, she was about to leave when the volume rose and Marcus's words became clear again. "Your house is conveniently placed. Think how much beauty resides beyond that fine wall."

"And how much wealth."

"I wondered if your ultimate aim was to win the heiress," Marcus said with a short laugh. "Flirting with her hostess is a clever stratagem to get close to a girl who strikes me as excessively reserved. Toying with Damian's bride may amuse you, but I doubt you will succeed there and I'm sure you know it. Lady Windermere strikes me as a proper chit under the veneer of worldliness."

"You underestimate me."

"Never that. But judging by the state of your house you could use a fortune, and marriage is the easiest way to get one. I'd expect you to take advantage of Miss Brotherton's proximity."

"I make it a point never to do the expected. The Brotherton lucre is yours. If you can bring it home, which I doubt. How goes your pursuit of the lady?"

The sixth sense that had kept him alive and relatively prosperous in an occupation fraught with hazards told Marcus not to answer, to deny mercenary motives toward Anne Brotherton. Yet his instincts hadn't been much use to him lately and might be as flawed as his luck. Julian wouldn't betray him. He might try to outwit him. He might be in pursuit of the same end, no matter what he claimed. But there was truth to the adage about honor among thieves. Or in their case rogues. Neither he nor Julian had ever been a common thief.

Since meeting at Oxford they'd shared a kinship, based on their lack of fortune and birth, when compared to Robert Townsend with his handsome estate and Damian, Lord Kendal, heir to the earldom of Windermere. Marcus never entirely lost the feeling that he needed to sing for his supper and Julian felt the same. Their jokes were wittier and more frequent, their schemes more outrageous when the object was, as usual, to shock the sedate. And the sedate, duly shocked, always blamed them because what could they expect from a pair of young men with such disreputable sires, each a greater disgrace to their distant but nonetheless noble families.

There'd also been a competitive element to their roguery. The old feeling of wishing to outdo Julian made Marcus boastful. "Spoiled heiresses need careful handling," he said. "I believe I progress with the amiable Miss Brotherton. The poor girl is beginning to trust me. Two steps forward and one back. You know how the game is played. I kiss her, and apologize for the liberty. Next time I shall declare myself unable to resist her. It won't be long until she's begging for my attentions. As long as her guardian stays away for a few more weeks I'm confident I can bring home the prize."

Anne choked back tears as her maid unlaced the lovely gown. Maldon, approving greatly of the addition to her mistress's wardrobe, gave the silk a shake and laid it reverently over the back of a chair. Anne wanted to hurl it onto the floor and stamp on it.

Fool, fool, fool that she was to believe he wanted her for herself. How stupid to delude herself that a handsome young man with a reputation as a scoundrel could have been attracted to a quiet, plain heiress for any reason but the obvious one.

Maldon helped her out of her fine new petticoats and shift and held up the new nightgown Cynthia had persuaded her to buy. The fine white cotton shimmered like satin and was trimmed with beautiful Brussels lace.

"Not that. It's impractical for winter. Fetch one of my old ones."

She lay in the dark in the high-necked garment of thick flannel, suitable for warding off chills. But the sturdy cloth had been softened by washing and offered none of the physical discomfort she needed to match her inner anguish. What she deserved was a hair shirt, whatever that was. Better yet, sackcloth.

Spoiled heiress, was she? Beg for his attentions, would she?

She'd show him.

Chapter 6

Marcus was in a splendid mood, not just as a result of Julian's excellent claret. The morning had brought delivery of a letter that pleased him beyond its significance to the success of his stratagem. He looked forward to an enjoyable day. The idea of winning Anne Brotherton and actually marrying her had taken hold of his mind, and not solely for material reasons. The money would be splendid, of course, but the bride that brought it evoked an unaccustomed tenderness. There was a lovely woman beneath her reserve, one who deserved to be introduced to the finer things of life, such as passion and even love.

"Travis, I need your advice," he said, fired with enthusiasm for the task ahead.

"Yes, sir?"

"Miss Brotherton has asked me to show her some of the sights of London."

"Very good, sir."

"I think so too. But how shall I do it? I don't like to ask if we can use one of Lady Windermere's carriages since she does not offer. Should I take her in a hackney?"

"Certainly not. I believe the best course is to hire a town coach and driver from a first-class livery stable."

"That will cost a pretty penny."

"And a footman too. To wait on you, and for propriety."

"She will be bringing her maid."

"Anything less than a footman would appear shabby. Ideally there should be two."

"One is quite enough. I've escorted ladies before, but they always provided their own carriages. Or boats, in the case of the Venetians. I fondly recall the contessa's well-appointed gondola. Velvet cushions and a brocade curtain for privacy. I wonder if such a thing is to be found in London. On wheels, of course. It might be worth the expense."

Travis's bushy eyebrows flew comically north. "Miss Brotherton is a virtuous young lady!"

"All the better."

Travis's features relaxed into benignity. "Your Lordship does enjoy a joke. There's one matter I'd like to bring up, my lord." *My lord* usually presaged an unwelcome demand. "Your hair."

"My hair? What's wrong with it?"

"Nothing, of course. Except that gentlemen now are wearing Brutus crops. You will wish to appear in the latest mode for Miss Brotherton."

"Judging by Miss Brotherton's attire, her notion of the latest mode dates to before the Revolution. My hair is fine. I like it long and always have."

"Not even a little curl?"

"Especially not that. Help me dress."

"The green coat, I think."

"By all means. It matches my eyes."

"And where are you intending to take the young lady?"

"The British Museum, where else? I've sent a boy to obtain tickets, which are, I am glad to say, free of charge. I daresay she'll be hungry after all that antiquity."

Travis looked doubtful. "It isn't usual for a lady to take refreshments in a public place in London."

"Good Lord, how uncivilized."

"I suppose a lady, duly chaperoned, might dine at a posting inn, or other well-appointed and discreet establishment."

"Somehow, Travis, I don't think you and I have the same notion of the definition and uses of a discreet establishment." Not that Miss Brotherton was ready for seduction. But another kiss in the carriage, definitely. "Are you sure I need the maid if I hire a footman?"

At eleven o'clock sharp, Marcus drew up in Hanover Square in what he considered a very decent town coach with two better-than-average job horses. The hired footman—he'd drawn the line at two—sprang down and rapped on the door of Windermere House. A stately butler admitted Marcus and informed him, with a faint odor of disapproval, that he would inquire whether Miss Brotherton expected him. After twenty minutes there was no sign of either the servant or the lady.

"Will she be much longer?" he asked the footman on duty. "If so I should tell the driver to walk the horses." He hadn't taken her for the unpunctual sort. Though what lady was not? He hoped it meant she was taking special care with her toilette, just for him.

The footman disappeared and Marcus kicked his heels in the black and white marble hall, examining a vast and ugly Chinese urn. Lady Windermere's purchase, most likely. He couldn't see Damian tolerating such a monstrosity. Denford's feelings about his inamorata's taste in furnishing must cause him considerable pain. Marcus wasn't nearly as sensitive as Julian when it came to art, but even he shuddered at a particularly horrible Dutch still life prominently featuring a variety of dead game birds, well painted but gruesome.

Hearing steps on the stairs, he turned and found that Miss Brotherton had finally appeared, unfortunately accompanied by her maid.

"Miss Brotherton, you look beautiful. What a very fine bonnet."

"Lord Lithgow," she said, offering her hand with an air of condescension and making no apology for her lateness. "Shall we go?" As he handed her into the carriage, she eyed the scratched leather seat with unmistakable disdain. "I don't believe I've ever been in such a vehicle. Is it hired?"

"It's my pleasure to offer you a new experience." Marcus smiled at her.

"Where are we going?"

"I have obtained tickets for the British Museum."

Her mouth fell into a pout he hadn't seen before. "I've already been there, several times. You promised me a new experience. I should like to see Sir Ashton Lever's Museum in Albion Street."

A discussion with the driver revealed that the new destination lay in Surrey, just the other side of Blackfriars Bridge, and Marcus would be paying for the longer journey.

He settled beside her in the despised carriage, which he'd selected for its cozy dimensions. "I've never heard of this place. Is Lever a collector of Roman antiquities?"

Miss Brotherton sat bolt upright and looked forbidding. "I'm told his museum is extraordinary. Oh look! There's a donkey. What a dirty creature."

She was not to be drawn on the topic of the delights ahead. Instead she kept up a disparaging litany about the smells and dirt and the unsavory appearance of the people in the streets.

"So many beggars and vagrants! They should all be transported to the colonies."

To Marcus they looked like the ordinary people of London, of all ranks and occupations, going about their affairs. The drive went through the busiest part of London at the busiest time of day so she had plenty of subject matter for her observations and endless time to make them. Her illiberal attitudes surprised him, but perhaps they were typical of the political opinions of the very rich. Back in his naïve youth he and his friends had been fired by the ideals of the French and cheered the storming of the Bastille. Later he decided that a man who lived by his wits hadn't the luxury of deeply felt principles.

"A city is never at its best on a gray day. At least we are in a carriage and not walking through the dirt and fog."

Her answer was to run her fingertip down the window glass and stare disdainfully at the resulting mark on her glove.

"London in damp weather is dirtier than any city I've visited, though in many other ways the public facilities here are superior."

She waved her solid hand dismissively. "Of course they are. Foreigners have no notion how to go on."

Marcus gritted his teeth and refrained from commenting that since she'd spent most of her life in Buckinghamshire she was hardly in a position to cast judgment on the citizens of the greater world. He muttered something soothing and hoped this new and unappealing facet of the heiress's personality would recede.

"The odor of the river is making me unwell," she said as the carriage turned onto the bridge. "I fear I cannot speak."

Good, he muttered beneath his breath.

Unfortunately she exaggerated her powers of silence. "The Thames is disgusting," she said with a handkerchief pressed to her nose and mouth. "All those idle villains we saw should be put to work cleaning it."

"And how would they do that?" he asked curiously.

"That's not for me to say. But I hate to see people idle. A man without a useful occupation is a disgrace to his sex." He winced and wondered if this crack was aimed at him. If he was seeing the real Anne Brotherton emerging from the reserved exterior, he'd prefer to remain in ignorance of her character.

Anger carried Anne through the journey to Albion Street, enabling her to speak as she never had in all her life. Once the carriage stopped she judged it time to abate the torment—for the moment. She had every expectation that misery in plenty awaited her dastardly suitor beyond the walls of their destination. As he helped her alight, she favored him with a smile. "I do beg your pardon for my ill temper, Lord Lithgow. Carriage travel makes me peevish. I am so delighted to be here."

"I too," he said, his beautiful, lying mouth curving into the false smile that no longer gladdened her heart.

She enjoyed his displeasure—hastily concealed but she was watching closely—when he had to pay two shillings and sixpence apiece—including her maid—for their admission. One of the reasons she'd picked this obscure gallery. A dimly lit hall, dominated by a couple of gargantuan hexagonal stone pillars, contained several glass cases. She bustled over and squealed with pleasure at a collection of firearms.

"Listen," she said, reading from a label. *"A gun which burst in the hand of Lord Grey's gamekeeper,*

without his receiving any hurt. A remarkable circum-
stance considering how greatly the gun was shattered."
She shook her head in wonder at the shapeless
lump of metal. "I should have been so frightened
to see it. Isn't it amazing?"

He tried to conceal his astonishment at her
interest in this ridiculous object, and failed. "Incredible," he said.

"I'm so glad we came here. Thank you! I shall
look at everything!" She concentrated fiercely on
a case labeled "Remarkable Horseshoes." "The
shoe of a Tuscan mule, fancy that. You've been to
Italy. Can you tell me what is special about it?"

"It looks like a perfectly ordinary horseshoe to
me. But then blacksmithing is not one of my talents. Shall we move on to the next room? Perhaps
the displays there are more interesting."

She agreed, but only once she'd finished looking over a case full of rusty weapons. "Plants and
animals next."

"Not even whole animals," he said. "I wouldn't
mind seeing a stuffed elephant or tiger."

Anne pored over a case full of bits of birds. "It
says here that the beak of the rhinoceros hornbill
bird is remarkable for the curious appendage on its
upper mandible." Darting over to another case, she
rhapsodized over a curious fungus, a nicker-nut
(whatever that was), parts of fishes, cotton pods,
a rolled-up armadillo, several complete homes
of white termites, and a dismal exhibit labeled
"Sundry Seeds, Leaves, and Other Parts of Curious
Unknown Plants Brought from Botany Bay."

"Have you ever been there?" she asked brightly.

He deserved to be transported to the colony for convicted criminals.

"I've never traveled beyond Europe."

"You must have seen so many exotic animals."

"Very few. My time has mostly been spent in cities. There are few armadillos roaming the streets of Berlin, Paris, and Naples."

"How disappointing. I thought you must at least have met a tiger. Or a hippopotamus."

"I did join the King of Naples's wild boar hunt. Other than that, I've never had my courage tested by a wild animal." He smiled winningly. "Should we meet one in these chambers I trust I would be capable of fighting it off."

When she ignored this attempt at flirtation, he managed to show dogged interest in case after case of minerals and sponges and who knew what else. After half a dozen rooms his façade was crumbling and he couldn't hide the fact that he was thoroughly bored. So, unfortunately, was she.

"I believe your maid is tired," he said gently, reminding her that they weren't the only ones suffering.

The eyes of the middle-aged woman, who had trailed them patiently for two hours or more, gleamed with relief.

"Oh, Maldon! I'm sorry. Your feet must be hurting you," she said guiltily. Then, lest her fish think he was off the hook, "Perhaps we could come back another day, Lord Lithgow."

"I should be honored. But it grows late and I wouldn't wish Lady Windermere to be worried."

"I must confess," she said, "that I am a little

tired. Cynthia won't worry when I am in your care, but I yearn for some tea."

"Are you sure? I wouldn't wish to endanger your good name."

She waved off his objection. "Maldon is quite capable of protecting me."

"I assure you, madam, that you need no protection from me."

"Of course not. You *are* a gentleman."

He directed the driver to take them to a coaching inn, a little way beyond the bridge. If she was any judge of the matter he was in dire need of refreshment himself, preferably something stronger than tea. Good. She'd like to drive him to drink.

The courtyard of the inn was thronged with people, not all of them respectable. Half a dozen passengers, laden with baggage, spilled from a stagecoach. Delivery carts brought meat and bread. A sad mongrel rummaged for scraps in a corner. Above them, on a second-floor gallery, the shrill quarrel of a pair of maids cut through the cries of ostlers, the impatient snorts of horses, the purposeful chatter of travelers. Never having visited a London inn, Anne looked around her with interest, forgetting her supposed scorn for unwashed humanity. When a young man in a smart curricle eyed her with curiosity, she remembered that she wanted word of her outing to reach the ears of the *ton*. She smiled at him and he tipped her hat. Perhaps he genuinely admired her new bonnet.

"Let's go inside," Lithgow said, guiding her by the elbow.

So much for Marcus's hopes of whispered compliments and slightly warm jokes in front of statues of naked Romans. There was something about the contents of the Leverian collection that dampened dalliance.

He decided to hire a private parlor, another drain on his purse but it couldn't be helped. In the public coffee room there was too much risk of her being recognized. By the time the wrath of Lord Morrissey descended on him, Miss Brotherton must be so enamored that she would be prepared to defy Morrissey and demand consent to marry the unsuitable Lord Lithgow. Things hadn't gone nearly far enough.

She proved a little petulant. "I want to watch the people."

"They smell," he said firmly, and led her into the small parlor.

A fire lent cheer to the dim chamber, and a waiter appeared promptly.

"Tea for the lady," Marcus said.

"And for my maid too." She smiled at the shivering Maldon. "Sit by the fire, Maldon." At least she was kind to her servant.

"Are you hungry?" he asked, positioning a chair for her. "Biscuits or cake, perhaps?"

"Both, and some bread and butter," she said. "Be quick about it," she ordered the waiter.

By the time the waiter returned, she'd removed her mantle and gloves and was seated at the table, across from Marcus. She looked over the plate of confectionery and wrinkled her nose.

"I find I'm ready for something more substantial."

"We have a good steak-and-kidney pudding," the waiter suggested.

"Just the thing. And a slice or two of ham. And cold beef. And some cheese."

"Might I also recommend an apple tart with cream?" The waiter scented a large bill and a fat tip.

She clasped her hands with a girlish giggle. "Perfect." Marcus thought of the tally and gulped down a draft of ale. Her eyes lit on the tankard and narrowed. "I find I'm not in the mood for tea, after all. I'd prefer a glass of wine."

"We have an excellent Chambertin, miss."

"My grandfather's favorite wine!"

And one of the priciest vintages in the cellar, Marcus silently wagered, sure that in this case he'd win the bet.

"Right away, madam," the servant replied.

"And some braised mushrooms. And buttered carrots." She smiled at Marcus, innocent as a lamb. "My governess always made me eat my vegetables."

"We wouldn't want to endanger your health." He forced a smile and hoped he had enough money.

When the meal was delivered by a team of inn servants, Miss Brotherton wasn't rude. She simply behaved as though they didn't exist and the numerous dishes had appeared by magic, as was her right. Marcus poured wine for them both—if he was going to pay for it he might as well enjoy it—and raised his glass. "To a most enjoyable day and an excellent dinner. May it be the first of many."

She prodded her plate with a fork. "I believe the beef is overcooked."

He'd had enough. The girl who had touched his steely heart had vanished, and he doubted she'd ever existed. How could he have mistaken her character so badly? Disappointment was capped by fear that his ability to judge a person had disappeared along with his luck. If that was so he really was in trouble.

There was more than one reason to accelerate the pace of his wooing, but the one that exercised him at present was the desire to get the better of this spoiled brat. With any luck he'd be offered the bribe to leave her alone and never have to see her again. By that time he'd *deserve* the money.

Time to soften her up for the killer blow.

Hunger fought with Anne's desire to be as contrary as possible. She'd been doing a good job so far, considering her lack of experience in behaving badly. All her life she'd exercised the quiet good breeding her governess had taught her. The rudeness she'd exhibited today made her giddy. Each time Lithgow suppressed his annoyance—so subtly she wouldn't have known had she not been looking for it—caused her a stab of satisfaction. But anger at him and disappointment in her own stupidity, having carried her through the long day, was fading a little in the cozy parlor with the enticing smells of a well-cooked dinner that made her mouth water.

She looked up from the unfairly maligned beef to find him gazing at her with the look of deceptive candor that had almost borne her to disaster. Against her better instincts she still found him attractive. She'd be safer if she could continue to behave like the spoiled heiress he'd called her, but her strategy was not to drive him off. He needed to believe he charmed her, so it was time to let herself be charmed.

"You should have let me choose the menu. I enjoy feeding women."

Against all judgment she wanted to respond to the deceitful, caressing words. She helped herself to carrots and a tiny spoonful of the pudding. "What do you find they like?"

"Have you ever tasted truffles?"

"I don't even know what they are."

"Black gold from the ground."

"Like coal?"

"In a way. A kind of mushroom that grows underground in France and Italy. Ugly but with a rich taste and scent. I wish I could feed you with veal as it is cooked in Turin, rich in wine with the sublime aroma of the precious *trufelle* sprinkled over it."

"What else do you think I would like?"

"There's nothing like food you gather yourself. I'd take you for a walk through a French wood, with dappled light through the old oaks revealing *fraises du bois* on the forest floor, like sweet, tart treasures."

Almost tasting the tiny wild strawberries, Anne hooded her eyes. Also to avoid Lithgow's green ones fixed on her face with a sensual glow.

"Then there are the southern fruits. Peaches and apricots as soft and blushing as a maiden's cheek. A trite observation, I grant you, but nonetheless true. And oranges straight from the tree."

"We grow them in the orangery at Camber but they are sour and a little dry."

"Stunted trees forced in pots are all very well. You should see Seville at Christmastide. The streets are lined with trees loaded with fruit, brightening the winter gloom."

"How pretty! May one pick them?"

"The Seville fruit is bitter. You would prefer," he continued, "oranges from groves near Simione on Lake Garda, where the villa of Catullus lies."

"That I would like to see," Anne said.

"But you haven't truly tasted an orange until you've picked one warm from the tree and eaten it in the sun with a view of the Bay of Naples, the juice dripping over one's hands." He put a forefinger into his mouth and sucked on it.

She couldn't look away. Blindly she forked something into her own mouth—a carrot—and licked a stray trace of butter from her own lips. Her face grew warm. She imagined seeing these fabled spots with a guide as knowledgeable as he. And as appealing. If he wasn't a scoundrel.

"Nothing in England can equal the experience."

"Are you not happy here?" she asked. "Surely it is your home?"

"I've never had a home here, or not since my

mother died when I was seven." It was impossible to believe that the sadness in the back of his eyes wasn't genuine. Her own parents having died when she was very young, she was susceptible to pity in this instance.

She put down her knife and fork. It was time to pull herself together before the snake had her dazzled into infatuation again. "I'm surprised," she said, summoning the condescending tone of Lady Ashfield's depressing pretension, "that you are seeking a position here. It's the war, I suppose, that drove you back to England and its unsatisfactory food."

"It was, but now I am glad. Otherwise I wouldn't be sitting here with you. Try the mushrooms," he coaxed. "They are very tasty."

They were indeed but Anne ate only one, offering silent apologies to the excellent cook. She had decided that ordering a lavish dinner and then eating like a bird was the kind of thing a *spoiled heiress* would do. So she barely tasted each dish and claimed she didn't care for half of them. Needing to keep her head clear, she only sipped at her wine and noted with satisfaction that Lithgow drank most of the bottle.

Driving him to drink.

"Thank you for the meal," she said cheerfully, as though her behavior had not been abominable. "We'd better get back before it's entirely dark. Where shall we go tomorrow? I'd like to climb to the top of the monument commemorating the Great Fire. The view is said to be very fine."

Chapter 7

"**I**'m exhausted!" Anne sank into a chair in Cynthia's drawing room. "I looked at every single rock, fossil, and specimen in that place."

"The British Museum? I thought you loved it."

"We had a change of plan. I made Lithgow take me to see the Lever collection instead."

"When you found it in *The Picture of London* you said it sounded tedious."

"Far, far worse than tedious. Poor Maldon thought I'd gone mad. So did Lithgow. He pretended to be fascinated but I'm happy to say he's not as good an actor as I. He doesn't like my political opinions either."

"Do you *have* political opinions?"

"If I do they aren't the ones I claimed today. I spouted every diatribe I've heard from Lord Morrissey, who believes half the population of the country deserves the gallows and most of the rest should be transported."

Cynthia burst out laughing. "You wicked girl. Do you think Lithgow suspects?"

"If he did he would have taken me straight home. Or abandoned me the other side of the Thames, which is probably what I deserved. He *acted* like a perfect gentleman intent only on my amusement, but I could tell he was annoyed. You should have seen his face when I ordered a full dinner." She stopped laughing. "The worst thing was having to treat the servant at the inn arrogantly. My governess would have scolded me roundly for such hoydenish manners."

"I think that's the least thing your governess would have disliked about the expedition. Is this wise?"

"Wise, no. But despite the tedium I enjoyed the day. You have no idea how entertaining it is to behave badly."

Cynthia looked away with a coy smile. "I have some idea."

On her way into the house Anne had met the Duke of Denford leaving. She didn't want to inquire what form Cynthia's bad behavior had taken.

"Take care, Cynthia, and do not fall in love with the duke. I am protected by the knowledge that Lithgow is nothing but a shameless rogue."

She couldn't admit out loud that despite everything she still found her worthless suitor attractive. There had been moments during the afternoon when she forgot what she knew of him and wanted to relax into the pleasure of his company. When he'd talked about eating oranges . . . Her lips tingled and stomach fluttered. Perhaps she should let him kiss her again. If she was going to make use of a scoundrel for her own purposes, she might as well enjoy herself.

Then she recalled that moment in the dark, damp garden, hearing the words that dashed her newborn hopes. To Lithgow she wasn't a person but a prize, a shining pile of gold in the lottery of life. Every word he'd spoken to her had been false, and she would make him suffer for it.

Marcus would have enjoyed the Raphael cartoons at the Queen's Palace had the entrance fee not been ten shillings and sixpence each. Boydell's Gallery in Cheapside was a shilling, but the cost of carriage hire was mounting. Climbing the monument required only a sixpenny tip to the boy who led them up the three hundred and eleven stairs. The soles of his boots suffered. Travis would have to take them to be mended, another expense. He looked forward to Westminster Abbey. It cost nothing to enter a house of worship. He hadn't counted on paying sixpence for entrance to each of the kings' tombs and there were a devil of a lot of them. English monarchs had been buried in the abbey with regrettable frequency and Miss Brotherton was enthralled by each and every one.

The investment would have seemed worthwhile if she had behaved more pleasantly. The modest, slightly shy girl he'd first encountered had vanished, to be replaced by a capricious tyrant. She kept changing her mind about her preferred destination, usually involving a drive that retraced the route just taken. She was haughty and dismissive with Marcus's hired footman and with the attendants at places they visited. He found himself wanting to do nothing less than put her over his knee and give her a good spanking. If her upbringing had been strict—which he had cause to doubt—it had failed to teach her manners and kindness toward her perceived inferiors.

What he couldn't decide was if those perceived inferiors included him. Most of the time she seemed to like him and appeared gratified by his increasingly lavish compliments. Yet there were moments when he sensed barely concealed contempt. She was attracted to him; he wasn't mistaken about that. Confusingly, he couldn't help finding her appealing in his turn. He'd wooed many women and even loved a few in a temporary sort of way, but he'd never found one as baffling as Anne Brotherton. The uncertainty was exciting, like holding a good hand against a first-rate cardplayer who might, or might not, have the means to defeat him.

Just when he was deciding that she was playing him for a fool and making use of him as a handy escort (and open purse; she never carried money) she'd throw him a smile that warmed him to the core. Practiced trickster that he was, he couldn't for the life of him guess what her game could be. It made no sense. There was no reason for a young woman like her to risk her reputation being seen in company with a man like him except attraction.

He was getting ready for another outing when a caller knocked. In Travis's absence he went to the door, not unduly upset about being late to pick up the heiress. It would do her good to wait for a change. A large, glaring man filling the threshold.

"What an unexpected pleasure," Marcus said to the Duke of Castleton. "Last time we met you were naked. You'll forgive me for saying that I prefer you fully dressed."

His visitor appeared to be striving for control. "I advise you, Lithgow, not to refer to that occasion, unless you wish me to tear you limb from limb."

"You are welcome to attempt it." The duke might outweigh him by two stone, but Marcus was confident of outfoxing him, even in a confined space. "I'd be delighted to send you back to Caro with a broken nose."

Peace, or rather absence of overt hostilities, hung in the balance. Marcus tilted his head in provocation, spoiling for a fight. Fists clenched, the duke glared, then collected himself, relaxing—if that was the right word—into his usual state of formality.

"I've come to talk to you, Lithgow, not to soil my hands," he said.

"I have no idea why you do me so much honor."

"Like hell you haven't. Let me speak plainly."

"When do you not?"

"Never, I thank God. I don't have your talent for lies and dishonesty."

"I do my humble best. Won't you sit down?" The remains of his breakfast sat on the plain wooden table. Marcus was suddenly infuriated that Castleton, lord of mansions and countless servants, should see him in his lowly surroundings.

"This isn't a social call," the duke replied, not even favoring the room with a glance. It was quite simply beneath his notice. "I won't beat about the bush. Leave Anne Brotherton alone."

"Don't be a dog in the manger, Castleton. You had your chance with her before."

"That you should even raise your eyes to a decent young woman is a disgrace. You are and always have been a wart on the nose of humanity."

Marcus had been the recipient of worse insults, but somehow this stung. "I'm curious, Castleton. When we were boys we were friends, of a kind. You taught me to ride when I visited Castleton House." He wouldn't admit that one long-ago visit to the ducal estate has been one of the happiest of his life, giving him a glimpse of a civilized and gentle world in contrast to the grubby contrivances of life with Lewis Lithgow.

"You fed Caro with some nonsense about me being responsible for the injury to a horse and blaming you. My father threw you out because your father was a thief."

"I was eleven years old." He despised himself for trying to excuse himself.

"And you've proven yourself a thief since," was the pitiless response. "So leave Anne alone. She is my wife's cousin and under my protection. I will not let you ruin her life."

Resentment surged through Marcus's veins. While he couldn't justly blame the duke for all his woes, he felt like blaming someone and Castleton would do. At the very least he was responsible for the loss of Caro's friendship.

"Did Caro send you?"

"Caro is none of your affair."

"I've known her far longer than you have."

"She's put all that behind her."

Marcus reassembled his bravado. "What? You aren't going to invite me to Castleton for a family reunion?"

"My wife is a grown woman and I trust her to make her own decisions. But I will not willingly let you breathe the same air as my sisters. And I repeat: leave Anne Brotherton alone or you will regret it."

Damn Castleton. If he'd married Anne Brotherton as he was supposed to, Marcus might still be poor, but at least Caro would still be hosting her friends at her cozy Conduit Street house and he wouldn't feel alone. Nor would he have to deal with Miss Brotherton's maddening whims.

Lithgow was quiet in the carriage that afternoon on the way to Westminster. Anne had expressed a fancy to observe the House of Commons in session, mainly because the entrance to the gallery was two shillings and sixpence. The supply of quips and smooth compliments seemed to have dried up and she missed the battle of wits.

Their exchanges resembled a dance in which she would curtsey, take his hand, and gaze coyly into his eyes, letting him believe she succumbed to his cynical advances. Then the music would change and she would escape his grasp with a waspish set-down. He was a much more experienced dancer than she so the exercise tended to make her dizzy and confused. And she had to constantly fight the attraction that would surface at inconvenient moments.

Now, for instance, she was conscious of a certain pique that he made no effort to charm her. Sitting beside her, he stared straight ahead, still and self-contained. He wasn't a man who expressed himself much in gestures or body movements. The thought took her by surprise for she was not in the habit of studying her companions. She tended to take people as she found them. But Marcus Lithgow fascinated her. She wanted to know what was going on below his glib surface, despite the certainty that the handsome exterior covered a core of pure deceit.

"Why do you allow me to spend so much time with you?" he asked suddenly. "It will be the talk of the town when we appear in such a prominent location. Do you have no fear for your good name?"

"I don't care," she replied with her best shrug of disdain.

He smiled faintly. "I applaud your courage."

"No courage needed. I don't concern myself with the opinions of fools."

"How fortunate to be able to ignore them."

"Do you care what others think of you?"

"I have to, my dear. How else am I to succeed?" She felt a twinge of unwelcome sympathy. What else was he to do in life but cozen and cheat? No, that was wrong. Bad luck when life was meting out its advantages should not force a man into villainy.

She employed her most sickeningly sweet expression in preparation for the sting of the lash. "I think you succeed very well."

"Here we are at Westminster Palace. Shall we apply for admission and see what pearls of wisdom we may garner from our nation's representatives?" He alit and offered his hand to help her out.

"You know," she said. "I find I no longer wish to listen to a parliamentary debate. I daresay the speakers will all be rogues and radicals."

A sharp intake of breath greeted this latest capricious change of plan. "Where would you like to go?" he ground out.

"Don Saltero's Museum of Curiosities," she said. "I believe it is in Chelsea."

He ordered the coachman to head west. As he took his seat again he appeared barely to restrain his temper. Finally she'd penetrated his self-control. "At least we are already partway there," he said. "I'm grateful you haven't taken a fancy to cross London again."

She'd thought about it and was glad she'd chosen the closer destination. Traveling at close quarters with a man in a towering rage might not, it occurred to her, be wise. Lithgow clenched his fists as though he'd like to punch the walls of the carriage—or toss her out of it. Folding his arms, he stared out as the landscape turned to green fields, punctuated by spanking new terraces.

Time to reel him in again.

"I do enjoy our outings," she said, laying her hand on his arm. "You like all the same things I do. What do you suppose Don Saltero has in store for us?"

"I cannot imagine," he said curtly.

She'd gone too far, perhaps driven him off with her whims. That was not what was supposed to happen. She intended him to dance to her tune until she was done with him and could leave his lying soul rotting in the ditch of rejection.

"But I shall be sure to find it fascinating in your company," he continued more softly.

As she suspected, he would tolerate any nonsense she cared to serve up in pursuit of his ends. She smiled at him again.

Chapter 8

"**G**ood morning, my lord!"

Marcus groaned. "For the last time, Travis, could you try not to sound so damn cheerful in the early morning."

His headache was among the worst he ever suffered. He should know better than to drink gin. What else was there to do of an evening? Most of his London acquaintances were interested only in play. And Marcus couldn't join them and risk his rapidly dwindling funds. The hostesses of London were not impressed by him, despite his title. So he sought quiet corners of seedy taverns and prayed for a miracle in his cups.

Damn England, damn the English, and triple damn to Lady Luck.

And all he had to look forward to was another day touring the moldy backwaters of London in company with a cantankerous heiress. If he had any other option he'd drop her fast. But he had too much time and money invested and no reasonable alternative when he had mouths to feed, his own and that of the incorrigible Travis, who stowed an enormous amount of food in his lanky frame. He wondered if his valet had a tapeworm.

He accepted the cup of tea and a couple of letters from Travis with singular lack of enthusiasm. The one on top was in the neat, well-trained penmanship he'd learned to know and dread. He'd almost lost his temper yesterday, a huge mistake. Marcus was not given to anger. It was another emotion he had never been in a position to afford. A cool head was vital to his well-being. But Anne Brotherton made him crazy like no other woman—or man—he'd ever met. How could a girl, pretty and agreeable when pleased, turn into such a witch, with little or no warning? She'd nearly found her pampered little bottom parked in the gutter outside Westminster Palace.

Better find out what treat she'd planned for him today. Hm. A reading of French comedy by Monsieur le Texier, whoever the hell he was. He felt the hair at the back of his neck bristle, usually an augury of bad news. "Do you have yesterday's *Morning Post*?" he asked.

Travis produced the paper and it didn't take long to find the announcement of the remarkable recitation by the famed performer late of Paris. And the fact that Monsieur charged half a guinea per person for the pleasure of hearing him perform Molière solo. Marcus had seen the best French actors at the Comédie Française and he was not impressed.

"Hand me that other letter," he said.

Via the Salisbury mail. Intriguing. Marcus had

almost forgotten his inquiry to his great-uncle about the purported treasure his father had left for him. With the closest thing to a prayer since his distant childhood at his mother's knees, he removed the seal. A quick glance told him the letter wasn't from Mr. Hooke but one Joseph Oakley.

We have been trying to find you for some months, not knowing you were in England. Your letter to Mr. Hooke gave us your direction.

Incredulously, Marcus read that his uncle had died and left him his estate.

Hinton Manor is in a poor state, your uncle having much neglected the place in recent years due to poor health. You will no doubt wish to dispose of the property for what little it is worth.

"Travis," he said with jubilation, "pack up everything. We're going to Wiltshire."

"What about Miss Brotherton, sir?"

"She can go hang," he said with a lighter heart than he'd felt in months. "I'm a man of property now."

Travis appeared unconvinced and with reason, though he knew nothing of Hinton Manor. Marcus didn't know much more. He remembered an old house, dark and gloomy. At the age of eleven he hadn't been in a position to judge its condition, but he wasn't surprised to hear it was in disrepair. He didn't know how many acres of land went with the manor house. Still, assuming it wasn't mortgaged, it should sell for enough to relieve him of his current embarrassment.

"How long will we be out of town?" Travis had no sympathy at all for the misery Marcus had endured of late. "It isn't wise to leave a lady for too long when one is courting."

"Are you an expert in the art of wooing?" Marcus asked, rather unkindly given the valet's plain features and unwed state.

"No, sir."

"Then keep your advice to yourself."

"Very good, my lord." Marcus sent him a threatening look at the use of the honorific. "But I do trust, *my lord*, that you intend to take a mannerly leave of Miss Brotherton. You wouldn't wish to upset the young lady."

Actually Marcus wouldn't mind tossing her out of a window. Failing that, he'd enjoy telling her that he was leaving, forever he hoped. So two hours later saw him announced to Lady Windermere.

"I daresay Anne will be down in a little while," she said. "I hear you're taking her to hear some French poetry. Or maybe it's German drama. I know it sounds quite dreary." She waved languidly from her chaise longue where she was draped in the latest fashion for Grecian-inspired muslins, most unsuitable for London winters.

Marcus hadn't paid much attention to Anne's hostess before. In contrast to her ghastly taste in furniture and pictures, her personal adornment was perfect, artfully chosen to display her blond prettiness.

"She always chooses the most unexpected places to visit," he said noncommittally, not wishing to spill the beans and miss the moment when Anne learned that today's treat was off.

"Indeed. I don't know how she comes up with them. But Anne is very resourceful and you, Lord Lithgow, so *very* kind. I know she is *very* grateful for your devotion to her amusement." Marcus had the feeling the lady was laughing at him. He could hardly blame her, given the absurdities he'd been reduced to in pursuit of her wealthy friend. He suddenly despised himself. Not for hunting a fortune but for being prepared to humiliate himself doing it.

As a rule Anne Brotherton kept him waiting for a minimum of twenty minutes while he fretted about the horses. Today he'd come on foot so of course she breezed in promptly.

"Lord Lithgow," she said, offering him her hand. "I cannot tell you how much I look forward to Monsieur le Texier's recitation. I do hope you were able to obtain tickets!"

"I come with bad news. Our expedition will have to be postponed."

She gave a huff of annoyance and her mouth set into her discontented look. Lady Windermere, with better manners, asked if anything was amiss.

"My great-uncle has died."

Miss Brotherton had the grace to look abashed. "I am sorry. My condolences on your loss."

"As to that, I hadn't seen him in several years. But I must leave for Wiltshire at once."

"Will you be in time for the funeral?"

"Mr. Hooke died some months ago. The executor was uncertain of my whereabouts and only now have I learned that I am the heir to his estate. So my tidings today are good, except for the very great sadness of being deprived of your company. I don't know when I shall return to London. I trust it won't be too long."

He gave her his most languishing look and hoped she would be devastated by his desertion. Instead she looked alert as a pointer. "Mr. Hooke? Mr. Hooke of Wiltshire?"

"Yes. Of Hinton Manor. Have you heard of him? I doubt he left the place in years. He was a gentleman of great obscurity."

"I read an account of a Mr. Hooke of Wiltshire who found two Roman villas on his land. Could it be the same man? It's not such a common name. You should have told me you were related."

Marcus searched his memory. No such excavations had been in progress during his brief sojourn at Hinton. "It's possible," he said. "My uncle had scholarly inclinations."

"Lord Lithgow, you are a lucky man. I would so like to see Mr. Hooke's discoveries."

"If they exist," he said, "and if I decide to keep the estate, I should be happy to show them to you."

Never in a thousand years, he swore. Now he had something Anne Brotherton wanted and he'd take the greatest pleasure in denying her.

Chapter 9

Marcus knew little of Hinton Manor. As his post chaise slowed down to take the winding lane toward the sizable brook and a lengthy drive that separated his uncle's house from the nearby village of Hinton, he recalled the former brief visit. Abandoned by his father after only a day, he'd soon afterward been sent to school by Uncle Josiah Hooke. He had never returned.

"Nearly here, Travis."

"I confess, sir, that it will be a relief to be still." The valet had suffered silently but obviously each time the chaise hit a bad patch of road.

The alteration in the sound of the wheels told Marcus they crossed the bridge. Soon the house would be visible. Despite a light rain, he lifted the window flap and stuck out his head in time to see the worn sandstone building loom out of the mist.

Following a few weeks' stay in the splendid surroundings of Castleton House, Hinton had seemed unimpressive to the eleven-year-old boy. But the adult Marcus, who had stayed in palaces and hovels, now saw a modest but solid manor house, a couple of centuries old, nicely proportioned, with rows of tall mullioned windows on the first two floors topped by three gables. The drive was weedy and lined with shrubbery that looked close to expiring, but that might be the season. Marcus knew nothing of gardening. Neither was he in a position to assess the condition of the stonework.

Not so bad. And then, as the carriage drew to a halt before a battered front door set in a rather handsome stone arch, *Mine.*

It was a startling thought. In all his twenty-eight years, he had never owned anything more substantial than the clothes on his back and in his trunk—and not always the latter when things went awry. Without waiting for the steps to be let down, he jumped onto rough, moss-covered flagstones. This piece of the earth, crowned with a confection of stone and glass and slate, belonged to him and no other. In the twenty years since he and his father left his mother's cottage, he'd never had a place to truly call his own, a home instead of temporary dwellings in a dozen countries where he'd unpacked his bags but never felt any connection. His eyes blurred in the afternoon drizzle and his boots felt rooted to the ground. Blinking, he scanned the façade, scarcely noticing cracked panes of glass, chipped and loose stonework, a bird's nest clinging to the eaves beneath a broken slate. This was his house and it was damn fine.

The door opened with a creak.

"Lord Lithgow?" A short, stout bewhiskered

man, whose clothing and demeanor proclaimed the country attorney, greeted him with a bow that made his old-fashioned periwig quiver.

"Oakley, I take. Good of you to be here. I trust you haven't waited too long."

"Not at all, my lord. You made good time."

"Will you have the servants bring in my bags while I pay the post boy?"

Oakley's chin quivered. "As to that, we have a difficulty I will explain inside. Can your own man handle the matter?"

Travis clambered out looking green.

Marcus rolled his eyes and shook his head. "Even if he wasn't carriage sick, he's not strong enough to manage the trunk. Give me a hand with it, will you, Oakley. Travis, you bring in the hand luggage."

With some huffing and puffing on the part of the solicitor, the trunk was deposited in the hall, throwing up a cloud of dust. Marcus looked around at the scarcely remembered interior of his new possession. Ignoring the muddy floor, ponderous unpolished furniture, and faint odor of mold, he saw lovely carved paneling in dark wood and a low strapwork ceiling aged from white to a rich chalky color like the foam on a tankard of ale. Beneath a patina of neglect he sensed the presence of generations of Hookes, witnessed by the solid oak staircase whose broad, shallow steps were worn at the center by the passage of a thousand feet.

As his chest tightened with excitement, a chunk of the ceiling fell onto his head.

"I told you the house was in poor repair," Oakley said apologetically, brushing scraps of plaster from Marcus's shoulders. "If you care to come into Mr. Hooke's study I will tell you how things stand."

In an office only marginally less filthy than the hall but warmed by a small fire, Marcus did his best to follow the estate accounts presented by Oakley. "If I understand correctly," he said, "the revenue from the tenants comes to a little under eleven hundred pounds a year. A decent income for a gentleman, if not lavish."

"Indeed. But Mr. Hooke neglected the land in recent years."

"How did he spend his income? Was he given to personal extravagance?"

"Certainly not. He was a gentleman of frugal habits."

"So there must be an accumulation of monies."

Oakley sighed. "There was indeed, and a nice sum in the funds, but he left it all to the Countess of Sandford's evangelical sect. In recent years Mr. Hooke became an ardent adherent."

"Was it much?"

"The clergy of the congregation received some fifteen thousand pounds by Mr. Hooke's will. Why he decided to leave Hinton Manor and its land to you I cannot say. Perhaps in the end blood was thicker than water." Oakley spoke with approval of such a sentiment.

"Let me get this clear. There is no ready money."

"Quarter day has come and gone since Mr.

Hooke's death. The Michaelmas rents are on hand."

"More than two hundred and fifty pounds," Marcus said. Better than nothing and there'd be another quarter soon.

"Not as much. Floods last year reduced the arable acreage, necessitating a reduction in rents. And the servants needed wages and board." Oakley shuffled through some paper. "One hundred and eighty-five pounds remains. Just enough to put the house into fair enough condition to sell it for more than a song."

Marcus's half-formed vision of settling here and becoming a country gentleman suffered a fatal blow. Still, he had expected a pig in a poke. Whatever sum the estate could be sold for put him ahead of where he was. And yet . . . "Supposing I keep the place. What would it take to return the estate to productivity?"

Oakley hemmed and hawed and made calculations modified by lawyerly hedging. Finally he named a sum that might as well have been the income of a prince for all the chance Marcus had of laying hands on it. "If you remained here and did much of the work yourself, it might be managed for less. But I doubt you wish to become a gentleman farmer."

"I'll think about it. I shall stay for the moment and assess the situation. In the meantime, where are the servants? How many do we have?"

Oakley shook his head mournfully. "After Mr. Hooke's death, not knowing how long it would take to find you, I reduced his household to a minimum."

"By a minimum, I assume you mean more than none."

"The housekeeper, one indoor manservant, and two maids were kept on. Country folk are much given to superstition, and a month or so ago they decided the house was haunted and left."

"You can't be serious."

"I fear so. Only old Jasper, the stableman, agreed to stay. He has quarters in the stable block and has served as caretaker for the house. He's a stubborn fellow, not likely to be frightened by specters, but he's nowhere to be found. When I arrived today I had to stable my own horse and light the fire."

If Marcus had any sense, he'd take the one hundred and eighty-five pounds—three times his present worth—and return to London to wait out his luck. He hadn't tested it since Oakley's letter arrived, hadn't even thought of it. But it might augur a change of fortune. The alternative was to remain in a falling-down house with whatever ghost the servants had fled.

His gamester's instinct, unreliable as it had become, urged him to stay. He envisioned the office cleaned and tidied, the film of dust on the windows removed to admit the gray afternoon light, warmed by a blazing fire. A cozy spot to read, or to study the business of managing his property with real intentions, instead of the lie he'd fed Miss Brotherton. And he had a servant. Finally Travis could make himself useful and repay the debt he insisted he owed.

"My valet and I will make do for now. Perhaps

when the house is inhabited the local people will see reason. Show me the rest of it."

When Oakley left, Marcus found Travis in the master's chamber, putting fresh linens on the bed. "How are we to get the trunk upstairs, sir? I need to unpack your clothes so that you can dress for dinner."

"I assume someone named old Jasper will appear at some point and help me carry it. Dressing for dinner is the least of my concerns. I'd prefer it if you set yourself to ridding the house of some of the grime. I have reason to believe it hasn't been cleaned for over a month and, if I'm any judge of matters, for much longer."

"Surely there are maids."

"Not one. You are the only indoor servant at Hinton Manor."

Travis's Adam's apple wobbled. "No staff? In a house of this size?"

Marcus smiled and crossed his fingers behind his back. He wasn't about to mention ghosts to Travis and his shaky nerves. "We'll hire more soon. In the meantime I'm putting you in charge of cleaning."

"Me? I am a valet. The purview of a gentleman's personal servant is a gentleman's person."

"My person is going to be busy with matters other than adornment. You kept the rooms in St. James's neat."

"And I shall do the same for your rooms here. I cannot be responsible for other parts of the house. It would not be correct."

Since the man received no pay, Marcus was arguing from a position of weakness. He could dismiss him but that hadn't worked in the past. "I don't suppose you can cook." Travis dignified the question with another horrified stare. "In that case, if we are not to starve, I'd better find the kitchen."

It was better than he had dared hope, given the state of the house. Old Jasper might live in the stables but he used the domestic offices of the manor. The brisk fire heated a small range and oven, as well as an open grate over which hung a rusty spit that Marcus had no intention of using. No roast meats on the menu until he acquired a cook. Hot water was piped in from a copper boiler in a well-equipped scullery. Best of all, the larder was stocked with staple foods, eggs, milk, and half a flitch of bacon. Tonight, at least, they need not go hungry.

The floors, on the other hand, offended a soul he never regarded as fastidious. Discovering a broom and a tub of fuller's earth, he'd made progress loosening a thick layer of greasy dirt from the flagstones when the back door opened, letting in a blast of chill wind and rain that sent the dust pile flying.

"And who might you be?" The belligerent question was spit from the gap-toothed mouth in a face as brown and wrinkled as a walnut shell.

"Old Jasper, I presume," said Marcus, looking with disfavor at the damp filthy coat and shapeless hat, pulled low over the ears, of his new servant. On the other hand he *was* a servant, perhaps a more willing one than the fussy valet upstairs. "I'm Lithgow, your new master, and I'm doing your job."

Jasper plunked a large loaf of bread on the table. His vehement denial knocked off the hat to reveal straggling gray locks. "I'm an outdoor man," he said, continuing to shake his head. "Stables and garden only."

"Sweeping floors is a much cleaner task than mucking out stalls," Marcus said, holding out the broom. "It will make a nice change for you."

Jasper folded his arms. "Master always said you were a cozening rascal."

"I do not believe an insult is a good way to begin an acquaintance. Besides, I'm a reformed character."

"Fair words butter no parsnips."

"True, alas. The proof of the pudding is in the eating."

"Handsome is as handsome does. Master said there was never a prettier man than Lewis Lithgow, nor one more rebukeful."

"There he was right, I grant, but I think you have me confused with my father. I am Marcus Lithgow, now rejoicing in the title of viscount."

Jasper muttered something to the effect that he didn't hold with lords.

"Splendid. You may address me as sir. I wish you could persuade Travis to my way of thinking. Speaking of which, despite your disinclination for indoor work, could you bring yourself to help me carry a trunk upstairs?"

Having servants was just one long negotiation.

Lewis Lithgow had always said he who traveled alone traveled fastest and Marcus tended to agree. It was also how he knew how to cook. During the years Lewis had dragged his only son from pillar to post, Marcus had fulfilled the duties of man-of-all-work instead of studying his Latin grammar, like other boys of his age and class.

With a good deal of panting and swearing, during which Marcus added some colorful country terms to his vocabulary, the trunk was delivered to Travis, who had deigned to dust the master bedchamber and dressing room. Marcus also learned that the manor boasted a vegetable garden, a stable containing a pony and gig but no carriage horses, a small home farm with chickens, a breeding sow, a couple of pigs almost ready for slaughter, and a milch cow.

"Good Lord, Jasper! You look after all of those by yourself? I take back any aspersions I may have cast on your readiness to work."

Jasper seemed pleased. "I can cook a pease pudding with bacon and a cabbage soup," he volunteered.

Marcus thought of the ingrained dirt on the old man's hands, the powerful odor of the barnyard that hung about him, and the unappealing bill of fare.

"I shall cook," Marcus said, "until we hire some female servants. Is there a woman in the village, and perhaps a maid or two, who could be persuaded to return?"

"Chickenhearted. They don't like the ghosts."

"You seem a sensible man, Jasper. Do you

credit that Hinton Manor has suddenly become haunted?"

"I've heard strange noises," the man replied with a cunning look. "Don't bother me in the stables, but the females couldn't abide it."

"What kind of noises?"

"Chains clanking like some poor devil was tied up in a dungeon."

"Don't expect me to believe a house this age has a dungeon."

"It has a cellar. And then there's the powerful thumping and cries like a soul in agony. Women ran out of here like Old Nick himself was after them. Came hollering to me in the stables."

"Didn't you tell them it was nonsense?"

"No use arguing with females. Better without them," he said with a shifty look. Jasper had described the ghostly incursions with a good deal too much relish.

"I shall have to get to the bottom of it," Marcus said sternly.

A cursory search of the house revealed no traces of the supernatural—if ghosts left traces, which he doubted. But disturbances in the veil of dust that covered every surface suggested that someone quite corporeal had gone before him. Particularly around any closet, cupboard, or drawer. He thought of the "treasure" his father claimed to have left at Hinton Manor. While he didn't believe the ghost of his sire had returned to haunt the place, it seemed possible that Marcus was not the only recipient of Lewis's confidence. Though Oakley had denied any knowledge of whatever

Lewis had placed in Mr. Hooke's care, Marcus thought, with rising excitement, that there might be something of value hidden in this tumbledown house.

The November dusk fell early, making any organized search impossible. He returned to the kitchen to prepare dinner for his odd little household. In the glow of a lamp the utilitarian chamber became a warm cavern as the three men sat down to bacon, cheese, fresh bread, and in Jasper's honor, a dish of parsnips swimming in butter. The fare—simple enough—seemed more delicious than any Marcus could remember. Perhaps food tasted better in one's own house.

He wished he could say the same for his company. The fastidious valet and the filthy groom-gardener regarded each other with suspicion, hardening to dislike. As they ate in hostile silence Marcus conceived a plan to solve his labor problems. It was risky, but he was feeling lucky.

"Let's play cards," he said once the food and dishes had been put away.

Travis looked pained but Jasper's eyes gleamed. "I'd sooner dice," he said. Marcus recognized the look of a gamester. When the old man produced a set of knuckles from his pocket, Marcus examined them carefully and cast them a couple of times. They were well worn but clean.

Ever one to start cautiously, Marcus proposed chicken stakes and won a couple of farthings from each.

"Paltry," he said after a while. "I propose different stakes. If I win, Travis will do the scullery work and clean the entire house until we hire more servants."

"And if *I* win?" Travis was getting into the spirit of things.

"What do you want?"

"Your Lordship will permit me to cut and curl your hair."

Marcus wasn't one to shrink from a wager when the winnings outweighed the potential loss, but there were limits. "Cut only," he said firmly.

"I won't do indoor work," Jasper said.

"I wouldn't ask it. If you lose, you go down to the village and tell everyone the ghost has been exorcised by the new owner and the maids can come back to work. Now, pick my stake."

Jasper grinned. "Ten shillings." A healthy sum, more than a week's wages.

"Too much," Marcus said. He'd get no respect if he didn't haggle. "Half a crown."

They finally settled on five shillings and six-pence and Marcus counted himself a good negotiator to get the wily old devil down so low. Not that he expected to have to pay. Fortune had turned his way at last. That optimistic glow in his veins had rarely let him down. It was to be a simple match, best of three tosses against each man.

Lady Luck was a fickle wench, drawing him in only to throw him out of bed.

It was over very quickly. Old Jasper pocketed his plunder and cackled his way off to the stable quarters. Travis fetched his scissors.

Chapter 10

Anne was furious that Lithgow had withdrawn from the fortune-hunting lists and left town. How dare he? How dare he cynically pursue her for his nefarious ends and then drop her like a burning coal when something better came along? She wanted him abject, groveling, and grinding his teeth as he obeyed her most outlandish demands. She wanted to lead him on for weeks and then turn down his eventual proposal with all the scorn the mercenary wretch deserved. She wanted to kick him somewhere painful and break his heart.

Instead, she was left behind with empty days stretching ahead without a man to torment, while he inherited a fine estate with—the greatest insult—a wonderful excavation that she'd give anything to explore. And he didn't even care! All his purported interest in the classical past had been feigned, like his admiration for the plain but fabulously wealthy Anne Brotherton. So plain that the moment he had another option he took off with every appearance of relief.

Cynthia went out that evening with the Duke of Denford, and Anne was not invited to accompany them. She was left restless at home with Mr. Warner's account of Roman Bath for company. The trace odor that suffused the pages reminded her of the day she acquired it, before she discovered the perfidy of its donor.

She rose the next morning determined to forget him. She'd spend the day at the British Museum and immerse herself in the unruffled enjoyment of her own passions, before her well-ordered life was interrupted by the machinations of a louse.

Unfortunately a well-ordered life seemed unspeakably dreary. Aside from the pleasure of Cynthia's company she might as well be back at Camber. To cap her misery, the post contained a letter from her guardian.

The first several pages of the fat missive covered the usual report on dispositions of her estates. Since she had no say in the matter, their management being entirely in the hands of trustees, she read the account with dutiful boredom. The sting was in the tail, as though he thought the item of most interest to her was the least important.

> *Lord Algernon Tiverton is a suitable match. I expect to be back in England in the new year, weather in the Irish Sea permitting. At that time we shall settle the betrothal. Meantime, I hear no very good account of Lady Windermere. I have arranged for you to reside with Lady Ashfield where*

you will have ample opportunity to forward your acquaintance with your future spouse.

She put down the letter in a panic and hurried into the hall. She didn't care that it was far too early for Cynthia to be awake. She needed moral support. It was one thing to resist Morrissey's demands at a safe distance, but once he brought his forceful presence to bear she'd be bullied like his Irish subjects. Unless her reputation was already sufficiently tainted, she risked ending up a Brotherton-Tiverton.

It was all Lithgow's fault for disappearing before his job was done.

"Miss Brotherton!" Lady Ashfield's familiar and unwelcome voice stopped her as she placed her foot on the bottom stair.

Suppressing a sigh, Anne turned to face her would-be jailer.

"Have you heard from your guardian?" the countess demanded once Anne had dutifully led her back to the morning room.

"Lord Morrissey writes regularly."

"I had a letter from him this morning but I suppose you haven't yet received his instructions."

"What did he have to say?" Anne said cautiously.

"He wants you to come to me. Immediately."

"I cannot leave Lady Windermere alone. I promised I would remain with her until her husband returns."

"Lady Windermere's affairs are not yours. I've spoken before about what an unsatisfactory chaperone she is. She is not in a position to procure you invitations to the right houses and she keeps you on a long leash. She has no business letting you be seen with Lithgow."

Anne shrugged. "Lord Lithgow has been kind enough to show me some of the sights of the capital."

"My dear girl. While there's nothing amiss about visiting Westminster Abbey with a gentleman and your maid, you can do so much better."

Westminster Abbey? Anne couldn't believe she'd trailed around all those tedious places, and the only one to reach Lady Ashfield's ears was the abbey.

"Lord Algernon will be delighted to take you anywhere you wish in the next week. Then we shall leave for Sussex."

"Uh . . ."

"A few weeks in the country will give you and Algernon ample time to improve your acquaintance."

The threat of a month or more of Tiverton's undiluted company restored Anne's voice and wits. "I am grateful for the invitation and I would have enjoyed it immensely. But Lady Windermere has invited me to the country for a visit before we go on to the Duke and Duchess of Castleton. I prefer to spend the Christmas season with my cousin."

"Morrissey wishes you to come to me."

"Until I receive a direct command from my guardian, I believe I must honor my existing arrangements."

The letter containing the fatal command

seemed to emit a special glow from the writing desk in the corner. Anne forced her eyes away from that part of the room.

"As soon as you hear from Lord Morrissey let me know." Lady Ashfield seemed put out, but what could she do? She couldn't bodily drag Anne out into Hanover Square. "In the meantime, Lord Algernon will be at your disposal tomorrow."

The minute Lady Ashfield left, Anne tore upstairs into Cynthia's bedchamber without waiting for a response to her knock.

"Cynthia," she called into the darkened room. "I'm sorry to waken you but . . ."

"It's all right. I'm awake." The few words communicated her distress.

"What is it, Cynthia? What has happened? Shall I ring for your maid?"

"Wait. Could you let in some light?"

Anne pulled aside one of the curtains in heavy embroidered brocade, just enough to dimly illuminate the room. Cynthia sat up in the big silk-draped bed, looking forlorn in her linen nightdress, fair hair untidy over her shoulders. "Oh Anne," she said. "I'm afraid I am infatuated with the Duke of Denford and will not be able to resist him. The only answer is for me to leave town before I succumb."

She stared in bewilderment when Anne smiled.

"I'm sorry," Anne said, collecting herself. "I know you're upset but this is too convenient. I came up to tell you the same thing. I took the liberty of informing Lady Ashfield that I was leaving for the country with you almost immediately."

"I don't understand," Cynthia said. "Lithgow has already left. You're in no danger from him."

"I'm in danger of having to spend a month in the same house as Lord Algernon Tiverton."

Dear Cynthia understood at once and set her household bustling in preparation for their departure. She remained in poor spirits, however.

"Do you truly love the Duke of Denford?" Anne asked. A flirtation with the duke was one thing, but Cynthia was, after all, a married lady.

"I don't know. I don't think so, yet he fascinates me. I never meant for things to go so far. The thought of being at Beaulieu oppresses me. It's where Windermere and I lived after we were wed. I came to London to escape it. Besides," she added with a touch of defiance, "it's where he expects me to remain while he gads about the world and I am not inclined to oblige him."

"I have another suggestion," Anne said. "What I really want to do is visit Hinton in Wiltshire."

"Hinton?" Cynthia looked baffled.

"Hinton Manor is the house Lithgow just inherited."

"Anne! That is shocking."

"Please listen. I have a plan. First of all we'll stay at an inn nearby. With you as my chaperone and several servants in attendance there can be no great objection."

"Perhaps."

"In fact, we can even let most people—Lady Ashfield and my guardian, for instance—think I am at your house. I have not yet been indiscreet enough to deter Lord Algernon Tiverton, but a little sojourn in the vicinity of a rogue should take care of that. If he proves persistent I shall give him a hint about my shocking behavior. I see it as insurance."

Cynthia shook her head. "There's something I don't understand. Why on earth would you wish to see Lithgow again? My example should be warning enough to leave the rogue alone."

"I'm not going to fall in love with him, I promise, but he has something I want: a Roman settlement on his land. He said he—"

"My dear Anne! You cannot dig up antiquities in December!"

"Oh stuff! I never feel the cold. You may stay indoors. I shan't ask you to join me."

"If you do I shall certainly refuse. If you dig, you dig alone."

Anne grinned. "I don't think so. I shall make Lord Lithgow help me. He said he'd be happy to show me the place and I shall take him up on the invitation."

"Poor man. I almost feel sorry for him."

"Not I. I have not yet finished bedeviling his life."

Chapter 11

Marcus explored his new possession. He walked every inch of his land and spoke with his tenants, a downtrodden lot who seemed pleased to have a landlord take an interest, but without much hope that he could improve their lot. They were in no position to pay higher rents and provide enough income to undertake the needed improvements to the land. As for the manor house itself, it had the potential for beauty, with fine paneling and handsome plasterwork in every room. He essayed a few repairs, but he needed skilled workers and craftsmen. Everywhere he turned he saw a problem that required money, a great deal more than he had in his ever-dwindling account.

He thought of Anne Brotherton. A tiny portion of her rents would make all the difference to Hinton Manor, yet he dismissed the notion of continuing his wooing. He could just imagine her turning up her nose, failing to see the beauty beneath the neglect and dirt. For dirty it was. True to his word, Travis had rendered Marcus's own bedchamber spotless. But he refused to wield so much as a duster elsewhere, and the rest of the house was, to put it mildly, disgusting. Marcus had swept a couple of floors but he needed a legion of maids armed with mops and buckets and polish to render the place habitable by any form of life higher than the porcine.

His father's treasure was ever in his mind. Since a search of Josiah Hooke's papers revealed nothing, the only recourse was a room-by-room hunt, which he undertook methodically, removing dustsheets from solid old furniture, rifling through drawers and cupboards full of insignificant rubbish. He found broken door handles, candle stubs, scraps of paper, a box of assorted buttons, some tangled embroidery silks: the kinds of items someone might hesitate to throw away in hope they'd be useful someday. As he'd noticed before, someone else had been there, perhaps Jasper, or a hopeful thief who had broken into the empty house looking for valuables. There was little there that was portable or easily sold. His half-acknowledged dream of keeping Hinton dimmed.

At the end of the first week he came in from a morning spent trying to dam a stream that had flooded a field. He was wet and dirty and his muscles ached. Never in his life had he done so much physical work. Every night, after another simple dinner in the kitchen, he fell into bed exhausted. Lady Sandford's sect, he had learned, did not approve of strong liquor, so the wine cellar was empty and small beer from the larder barrel was all the stimulation available. Even without the soporific aid of wine he slept heartily until woken by the gray dawn, then shrugged into his clothing and set to work. He should go into Salisbury and buy the sturdy wardrobe of a country gentleman: His European garments, purchased to impress on potential pigeons that he was a man of fashion, would not long survive rough treatment.

Another call on his purse. Perhaps it was time to cut his losses and move on. The enormity of his problems as a landowner weighed on his shoulders.

He stripped off his boots and coat, and handed them to Travis. "I'm wet and cold and need a bath," he said, heading out of his bedchamber for the kitchen, where the bathtub and hot water resided.

"We're running out of shirts, my lord." The valet's tone heralded a complaint.

"There's a laundry next to the scullery. If you can't manage with that there must be a washerwoman in the village. As long as she doesn't have to come to the house I daresay she won't turn away my custom."

"A country laundress! I wouldn't wish to entrust our linens to a yokel."

"In that case you'll have to do the washing yourself. Or is that beneath you, like dusting?" Marcus had never been so tempted to throw the man out on his ear.

"I have inspected the facility, my lord. There appears to be a leak in the pipe leading to the copper boiler. And cold water will not do."

Marcus sighed. He'd planned to spend the afternoon searching the bedrooms. "I'll have a look at it. Perhaps it's something simple. No point changing into clean clothes, especially if I don't have any."

At the top of the stairs he heard a carriage approach the house. Aside from Oakley, no one had come to the manor since his arrival. He considered his stockinged feet and shrugged. If a member of the neighboring gentry had deigned to call, he would have to take Marcus as he found him.

The door knocker sounded as he descended to the hall. He opened the front door and stared at a familiar female figure waiting at the foot of the shallow steps.

"Lord Lithgow," said Anne Brotherton. "I've come to see your Roman villa."

The gall of the woman, to come to *his* house in *his* county and make demands! He stared down at her warm traveling dress made from first-quality wool trimmed with fur, at the impeccably clean boots, the shining hair, the arrogant countenance. She reeked of wealth and well-being while his house was falling down about his ears. His first impulse was to send her about her business with the same courtesy she had extended to him. Then he thought.

Well, well, well. A lamb had entered the wolf's lair, and as the wolf it was his duty to fleece her. Compromising her would be pitifully easy, and not even the strictest guardian would deny the necessity for marriage. But she was on his ground now and she'd play by his rules. She no longer held all the cards, and Marcus knew he could out-play her. A couple more animal metaphors came to mind. The pigeon would be plucked, the shrew would be tamed.

Lithgow had cut his hair. Anne wasn't sure she preferred it that way, for a moment, then decided the crop suited him. In the days since she saw him last she'd forgotten how handsome he was. But something was wrong: He wasn't glad to see her. Far from a beguiling smile, his mouth was set in stony displeasure. She'd expected him to welcome her with honeyed words and false blandishments. He didn't even invite her inside.

Judging by the dilapidated state of the house and grounds, he hadn't come into a fortune. On the contrary, possession of a rundown estate made a man more anxious to marry money. Why then, instead of assailing her with his lethal, specious charm, did he look down his shapely nose as though she were something the cat brought in?

She resisted the instinct to squirm. He should be embarrassed, answering the door himself, and in a state of undress. She'd never been at close quarters with a figure like Lithgow's unswathed by the many layers of a gentleman's clothing. Perhaps it was the extra advantage of height from the doorsteps. Or the uncompromising way he folded his arms that made his shoulders appear broader in the folds of his shirt. Or the way his unbuttoned collar revealed his neck, so different from a woman's and not usually open to inspection. Tilting her head to find steel in his cat's eyes, she inwardly quailed and looked down to find that without a coat his breeches revealed the lithe muscularity of his thighs. And she noted that he wasn't wearing any boots.

She could think of one reason for a man to be half dressed and unshod in the middle of the day. Her cheeks grew warm. The rake!

"I beg your pardon," she said. "You must have company."

He knew exactly what she meant and smiled, but not amiably. "I do now. I was just thinking I needed a lady to enliven a dull afternoon. Won't you step inside?" His lips widened into a wolfish grin.

"I'm not alone."

"Of course. The charming and ever accommodating Miss Maldon. I believe she likes me."

Anne backed away half a step, then summoned her courage and the arrogant tones of the heiress. "Lady Windermere is with me. I would hardly call at a gentleman's house without a chaperone."

His arms dropped to his sides. "Well, you'd better both come in out of the cold," he said in his normal voice. He'd been baiting her and she had no idea why.

Glancing back she found Cynthia, halfway out of the carriage, staring at Lithgow with amazement. Then she realized something else. His buckskin breeches, waistcoat, and shirtsleeves were spattered with mud. Little as she knew of seduction, it seemed an unlikely costume. He'd probably been outside and was in the middle of changing his clothes.

"I'm sorry to interrupt you," she said, chastened. "We'll be glad to wait while you complete your . . . business."

"You haven't interrupted anything." He opened the door wide and ushered them into the shabbiest hall Anne had ever seen. A thick coat of grime on the windows excluded most of the light, which was probably fortunate. If the rest of the house was in a similar state he feared she'd leave with her clothes as soiled as his.

It was worse. She and Cynthia were ushered into a room in which every surface was gray with dust and festooned with cobwebs.

"Won't you sit down?"

If the manor had any servants they were remarkably lazy. Anne stiffened her backbone and risked her gown on an old-fashioned chair. She was dying for tea, but doubted it would be forthcoming. The glib charmer, determined to please no matter what discourtesy she threw at him, had vanished. He remained standing, feet apart, solid and dignified despite his informal costume and dirty house. Clearly he had no intention of breaking the silence. She cleared her throat.

"You no doubt wonder why we are here."

"You told me yourself. You want my villa."

"Do you have a villa, or rather two?"

"You're the one who told me about it."

"I read a report in an old issue of the *Journal of Antiquities*. I suppose there may be more than one Mr. Hooke of Wiltshire." If so she'd made a fool of herself.

"There may."

"But is there?"

"I'm new to the county. There could be half a dozen other Hookes for all I know."

"Have you found such a structure on your land?"

"As it happens I have. Such remains as my uncle uncovered have been largely filled in by the passage of time but I suppose it's still there under the earth."

"May I see it?" she asked eagerly. "The report said he found a mosaic pavement. It must be recovered. To lose such a treasure would be a tragedy."

Instead of offering her carte blanche and every accommodation in exploring the site, he regarded her for a while, giving the matter deep consideration.

"No," he said, finally. "I'm busy. I can't waste time on such a trivial matter. Besides, only a fool or a madman would attempt to dig up a field at this time of year."

"I agree that summer would be better. But I'm eager to get started and I'm not afraid of a little dirt." She raised her eyebrows and nodded at his breeches before looking away in confusion. It wasn't a part of the male figure a lady was supposed to stare at. "You wouldn't have to do anything. I'll do it myself and direct the outdoor laborers."

"I don't have the staff available."

"I'll hire some local men," she said with more confidence than she felt. She had no idea how much it would cost and no desire at all to apply to her man of business for funds for such a purpose.

"Supposing I don't want my villa to be dug up?"

"But you must! It's of great historical importance."

"So you say. All I know is that it's of great importance to you and none at all to me."

So much for his vaunted interest in Roman history and art.

"Could I at least visit the site? I've only ever read accounts of such remains and it would mean so much to see one." She hated to beg this despicable man, but to be thwarted was not to be borne, not after she'd dragged Cynthia all this way.

He *pretended* to consider the matter. "No." He shook his head. "I already told you. I'm too busy."

She looked to Cynthia for support, but the latter merely shrugged. Anne was on her own, baffled, and at a temporary standstill.

Lithgow ambled over to an ancient oak cabinet and opened a drawer. "Here. You may look at these. I assume they are something my uncle found."

Anne almost snatched the small wooden box from him. "Do you realize what these are?" She examined the little tiles with trembling fingers. "Parts of a mosaic pavement. We must go and find it. It would be tragic if it were permitted to be further damaged."

"I doubt the condition will decline further in the next year or two. Once I have attended to more vital matters, like the state of the land and the prosperity of my tenants, I might think about having a look at it."

"I'll buy the estate from you!" A rash offer. Lord knew how she would persuade Morrissey and the other trustees to invest in a wretched little property, but she was prepared to try. Just for once it would be nice to gain some personal benefit from her wealth.

"Hinton Manor is not for sale."

"You mean to remain here?" she asked. She cast her eyes around the dirt, the crumbling plaster, the cold, soot-encrusted fireplace.

"I haven't decided what I shall do in the long term, but—" He broke off, stroked his chin, looked around the room and up at the ceiling until Anne was ready to burst. "But we could come to an arrangement satisfactory to both."

"Name it," she snapped.

"I will allow you to explore the Roman site, without any help from my servants—"

"I accept!"

"On one condition."

"What?" She hoped she had enough money on hand.

"You must come to the house every morning for a couple of hours and do some cleaning."

"Is this a joke?"

"Certainly not. Thanks to the superstitions of the local populace, especially the females, who believe the place is haunted, I am unable to hire any maids. You may have noticed that the house is in need of work and you are female, and very likely a maid."

Cynthia gave a choke of laughter but Anne was flummoxed into silence. Setting aside his aspersions on her virtue, he actually expected her to act as his servant. Not even for a mosaic pavement would she tolerate such an insult.

"Come, Cynthia." She rose and brushed a smear of dust from her skirt. "Lord Lithgow is playing me for a fool. My lord, I shall have to decline your offer of employment. I've never cleaned anything in my life so I am not qualified for the job."

"You show unwarranted modesty, Miss Brotherton. I expect to provide training for an inexperienced servant. An intelligent girl like you should pick up the necessary skills quickly."

Anne gathered her dignity, not helped when a large spider chose that moment to descend from the ceiling onto her bonnet. She swatted it away with a shudder. "We are staying at the Hinton Arms for a day or two. Should you change your mind about my other offer, Lord Lithgow, send a message to me there."

"I don't care if you stay there all winter. I'm afraid, Miss Brotherton, that there are some things in life money cannot buy."

"The gall of the man!" Anne was fuming as they climbed into the carriage and rattled down the rutted drive. "And you were no help at all, Cynthia."

"I don't know what I could have done. He certainly snubbed you handsomely."

"Accusing *me* of caring only for money! When he's nothing but a fortune hunter."

"He didn't act like one today."

It was true. His actions made no sense at all, unless his goal was to infuriate her. She would have expected him to accede to her every wish, or try to sell her the estate for an outrageous sum. His parting shot had stung. She had been brought up not to vulgarly flaunt her fortune. Could he be getting back at her for her behavior in London? "I am very wealthy but I don't think I can buy everything," she said defensively.

"But you take your wealth for granted. You have no idea what it is like to have little or nothing."

Anne shifted on the bench and looked out of the window, thoroughly deflated. She'd been looking forward to seeing the villa and, yes, to crossing swords with Lithgow again. Well, swords had been crossed and she had been routed.

The carriage descended a gentle slope, heading for the river that separated the manor from the village of Hinton. Romans built near a source of water to supply their baths and heating systems. She leaned out of the window and surveyed the meadow. A couple of hundred yards away, at the top of the rise, lay some untidy mounds, partially grassed over.

"Stop the carriage," she ordered, banging on the ceiling. She scrambled down and ran across the field, tripping over hummocks and caring nothing that her skirts and jean half boots were soaked in the wet grass. The outline of the first structure was clear. It was huge, some hundred feet wide. The bases of stone pillars emerged from the ground along the length of the front.

Another building, perpendicular to the first, had been abandoned partially uncovered, but might be even larger. Falling to her knees, she grubbed in the dirt around one pillar, but it was fruitless without tools and she succeeded only in ruining her gloves. A light drizzle chilled the nape of her neck, exposed as she bent over. What did she care when faced with such a glorious sight?

"Do you have any idea how to sweep a floor?" she asked when she returned to the carriage.

Cynthia edged away from her muddy sleeve. "You cannot mean to accept Lithgow's offer. He doesn't even have any servants. No one would believe you weren't engaged in an *affaire* with him. Your reputation truly would be ruined."

"The lack of servants is an advantage. No one to gossip."

"And what of Lithgow himself? He could claim to have taken your virtue and force a marriage."

"I don't care. I won't marry him and I don't much care if I never marry anyone. All I want is the chance to explore a real Roman settlement. It's vast, Cynthia. Wait till you see it. I can't wait to dig up the whole thing and discover what's inside."

Chapter 12

The next morning, after an hour on his knees on a cold stone floor, trying to patch the rusty, leaking pipes of the laundry copper, Marcus began to think he was mad to have turned down Anne Brotherton's offer to buy Hinton Manor. Let her struggle with the myriad problems offered by a neglected old hovel. Or rather let her pour her thousands into the bottomless well of disrepair. How idiotic to let pride overcome sense and risk driving her away when he should have been coaxing.

Still, her response to being offered a job as a housemaid was priceless. A damn bad one she'd make. Even more incompetent than he was a plumber. He gave another wrench to the leaking joint and rusty water spurted into his eye.

"Travis!" he yelled.

No answer. The valet was doubtless rearranging his stockings. Marcus possessed the world's most organized wardrobe in the world's most broken-down house. He wiped his eyes and thanked Providence that the roof didn't leak. Yet.

Then the sound of the bell clanged from the hall. At least something in the house worked.

Better still, two women stood on the front doorstep. Things were looking up and he wasn't about to suggest they go around to the back door. He'd take a pair of maidservants any way they cared to enter. The younger of the two wore a particularly ugly brown cloak of some hardy stuff. And a rather expensive bonnet. Only then did he look at her face.

"Are you going to hit me with that?" The genteel tones of Anne Brotherton carried a certain anxiety.

He lowered the large spanner he still carried. "I'm not likely to drive away additions to my household staff. Am I to gather, Miss Brotherton, that you have decided to accept my offer?

"Yes, since you've proved unreasonable. Maldon and I would like to come in out of the cold."

"Excellent," he said, ushering them into the hall. "Two for the price of one?"

"Maldon is here to lend me countenance. She is a lady's dresser. Perhaps you don't understand these distinctions, but she does not do rough work."

"Believe me, I understand only too well. She'd better go round to the kitchen then. It's the only warm room in the house. Unless you're afraid to be alone with me." The maid looked alarmed. "Don't worry. I believe I'll be able to resist the urge to force my attentions on your mistress in that fetching ensemble. Come with me. You'd better come too, Anne, and I'll show you where the brooms and dusters are kept."

"Miss Brotherton to you, Lithgow."

"In this house junior servants are addressed by their Christian names." Marcus was beginning to enjoy himself. "You may call me *my lord*."

"It's all right, Maldon," she said to her maid, who looked as though she might faint. "Once Maldon is settled, *my lord*, we will discuss the terms of our arrangement."

Marcus showed her where to hang her cloak and bonnet and wondered just how far he could push her before she exploded. He loaded her arms with a dustpan, rags, and other paraphernalia from the broom cupboard.

"Aren't you going to carry anything, *my lord*?"

"Just this once, Anne, I shall carry the broom and save you a second journey. Be sure to note where everything is kept. They must be put away when you've finished."

She followed him in a steamy silence to the drawing room. "The clock says ten past four. Is it wrong or has it stopped altogether?"

"Both. Don't worry. I shall let you know when you've worked for two hours."

"I don't think two hours each day is fair. I'll give you one. And I'll start from when I walked in the door. I checked my watch and it was exactly nine o'clock." She pulled a dainty jeweled timepiece from her pocket. "Quarter past now. I leave at ten."

"One and three-quarters and we'll count it from when you removed your cloak."

He respected her for bargaining. Even in a cheap gown of a dull green cotton, she looked unmistakably a lady and an aristocrat. Perhaps it was because her tall, smooth forehead, defined cheekbones, and straight nose beneath flawless glossy braids wound around her head made him think of a portrait of a Tudor queen. Apparently centuries of breeding and privilege left their mark. As she argued, her hazel eyes snapped with golden lights, and he'd rarely seen her so animated, or looking prettier. If being thwarted made her so appealing, he'd be happy to provide further occasion.

They finally agreed on an hour and a half, measured from her arrival.

"You may start in here. Sweeping and dusting should be enough for today. The windows need washing but they will wait. Do you know how to wield a broom or shall I demonstrate?"

"How difficult can it be? I may as well get started. Lord knows there's plenty to be done." She stuck her nose into the air and took a derisive sniff. Then blanched when her eye caught the forest of cobwebs draped from the mantelpiece. "There are spiders in here." Her voice wavered.

"My dear Anne. There are spiders everywhere in the house. Just sweep them up. They rarely bite and I don't think there are any poisonous ones in Wiltshire."

"I know that." She sounded brave but doubtful.

"Surely you aren't afraid of such tiny creatures."

"Of course not."

"Call if you meet a particularly large one," he said with exaggerated concern. "I'll come and save you."

She glared at him, snatched the broom, and started swishing it over the floor in a haphazard fashion. He left her alone without any confidence that the drawing room would be cleaner by half past ten.

Sweeping seemed easy enough, but after about twenty minutes Anne examined her aching hands. Aside from the slight bump of the middle finger of her right hand where she held her pen, her hands were kept perfect by Maldon's nightly application of a lotion. Now her palms and fingers bore angry red marks that could develop into sores. The dull wooden boards looked little better because there were little streaks and heaps of debris all over the room. With a sigh she stretched her back and tried pushing them into centralized piles. Her broom kept driving them into the edge of the carpet, which exuded further clouds of dust and a goodly population of moth. The carpet had once been handsome but the colors had faded and the worn pile was punctuated by large holes. When she bent to move a corner aside she found it heavy with dirt. Her eyes itched from sneezing. After extensive trial and error she managed to maneuver most of the dust from the floorboards into the dustpan, set it near the door to the hall, and surveyed her handiwork. Her shoulders ached but she felt a degree of satisfaction in a completed task.

She could do this. But the more she looked, the more she found to do. The floor needed polish. Moth had attacked the curtains as well as the carpet. The fireplace enclosed by Ionic columns would be handsome were it not for the soot that clogged the elaborate carving. The stone mullions on the windows were likewise blackened. She'd never thought much about the dozens of servants who kept Camber in pristine repair and felt a dawning respect for them.

Her terms of servitude had said nothing about the quality of work expected from her. Yet if she was going to undertake this humiliating labor she might as well do it well. In the time remaining she decided to assault the mantelpiece, spiders and all.

Holding her breath, she swiped a rag the length of the shelf, shuddering with loathing as the sticky cobwebs clung to her hands. When she realized one still contained its resident, an enormous brute with dozens of thick black legs, she could not restrain a shriek that competed with the crash of a porcelain vase shattering on the floor. Shaking her hand in panic, she dislodged the horrible beast.

"I'll kill you!" she cried, and chased the speedy little monster over the floor, vainly slapping at it with the broom and knocking over the dustpan. Filth spewed over the threshold. On the brink of despair she stared at the ruination of her morning's work.

A figure loomed out of the dark hall. "Is everything all right? You were making a terrible din."

"Fine," she said. She was absolutely not going to cry in front of Lithgow.

He came in and surveyed the wreckage. The hearth, on which she'd expended such effort, was strewn with cobwebs. Refusing to hang her head, she tilted her chin and awaited his well-deserved scorn.

"I should have dusted before I swept the floor," she said, acknowledging her stupidity before he could.

"Never mind. You're new to the job and it already looks better in here."

His encouraging tone deflected her defiance. "I don't think so," she said despondently. "I knocked over the dustpan chasing a spider."

"Better than a mouse, perhaps?"

"I'm not afraid of mice. Nor of spiders either," she added hastily.

His lips twitched but the expected sarcasm didn't materialize. "Here," he said. "I'll hold the pan in place while you sweep the dust into it."

He knelt at her feet, wet hair clinging to his forehead, the muscles of his shoulders and arms outlined by a damp linen shirt. Unwillingly she felt the stir of attraction return. He raised his cat-green eyes to her, watchful and serious. Her chest tightened. It had been easier to deal with him when he was ordering her around.

She'd wondered why, on her arrival at Hinton, his manner had been so different from the ruthless charmer of London. When she'd decided to accept his offer there'd been a certain equality in the transaction: an impersonal exchange of his needs and her wishes. She was confused by his switch back to amiability. Was he still playing a game, designed to win her over? She wished she were more experienced at reading the behavior of others.

She flicked the brush and drove as much dust

over his shirt and breeches as into the pan. "I *do* beg your pardon." It was safer to believe the worst and treat him with due disdain.

"I see you want me to be as dirty as you."

She drove up another cloud of dust. "So sorry. You'll have to return to your bath. I'm so glad you were occupied in comfort while I worked."

"I have spent the last hour mending pipes, successfully I may add. Do you think you might get a little of this dirt where it belongs? Or do you intend to leave it until tomorrow?"

If she wanted that villa she would have to return and it was pointless to repeat work. Without saying another word she finished the job. About to consult her watch, she caught sight of her cloudy reflection in a mirror across the room and gasped. Her face was smudged and her hair a fuzzy rats' nest of cobwebs. Luckily she didn't care what Lithgow thought of her.

Marcus, fresh from his triumph over unruly plumbing, had expected to find a sullen Anne who'd made little or no effort to attempt the admittedly gargantuan task of getting his house in order. When he found her almost in tears, whether from the terrifying spider or the spilled dustpan he wasn't sure, he'd wanted to offer comfort. For a sheltered miss who'd never attempted anything more taxing than embroidery or dirtier than flower arranging, she'd impressed him with her zeal.

She'd quickly climbed back onto the high ropes again and, having covered him with dust, was favoring him with what he dubbed her heiress look.

"I've done as you asked. Now it's time I went down to the villa."

He nodded. "I'll show you the way."

"Where's Maldon?"

"Your maid has agreed to help my valet with the washing, now that the copper is working."

"Really? She sees to my—er—delicate attire, but I can't see her agreeing to help with the heavy laundry." Her cheeks flushed faintly beneath the smudges.

"She and Travis have taken a liking to each other. He's a very proper fellow." He saw no reason to reveal that the pair of them were already acquainted.

"She will do nothing but complain about the cold if I take her, so I'll leave her be. Will you lend me a spade?"

Marcus looked over the tools in the gardener's shed. He handed Anne a trowel, slung a spade over his shoulder, and a rake for good measure. "This may be useful."

As they approached the site of the villa, pale midday sunlight seeped through the massed clouds for the first time in a week. He breathed in crisp air and caught his companion's palpable excitement. "The place looks like a big wreck," he warned. "I don't know when my uncle first discovered it, but he lost interest a long time ago."

"The journal in which he reported the find was at least twenty years old, perhaps more."

"The soil has filled in most of it, I fear. It'll be hard work."

"But just think of the splendid things that we shall find. I want to explore the whole place and make a full report to the journal. This might be one of the most important villas in all of England." Her fine bonnet, jammed over disordered hair, slipped backward, and her cheeks were flushed as she hopped over a rut.

In this mood, if it lasted, wooing her would be a pleasure. Genuine enthusiasm tempered her arrogance and made her almost beautiful as she strode forward, her eyes sparkling with excitement. He wouldn't mind seeing her passions take a more earthy direction.

"What?" she said. "Why do you smile?"

"It's a beautiful day."

"It is. And *that* is a beautiful sight!"

No one else of his acquaintance would call this disordered mass of soil and stones and grass beautiful. Possibly Sir William Hamilton, who had conducted Marcus about the ruins of Pompeii. But a field in Wiltshire couldn't compare to the Bay of Naples. "Tell me what you see."

As she explained her theory about the probable location of the chryptoporticus and the courtyard and the kitchen and the hypocaust, the shape of a Roman residence took shape before his eyes. She had studied her subject and knew what she was talking about.

"Where shall I begin?" he asked.

"Are *you* going to dig?"

"I thought I'd help get you started. The ground is probably hard."

"I thought you were too busy for such foolishness." She was pouting again.

"I can give you an hour or two."

"I want to dig. I swept your floor and got horrid cobwebs all over me and now you want to have all the fun."

Shaking his head in wonder, he handed her the spade with an exaggerated bow. "Never let it be said I would deprive a lady of her pleasure."

She cast him a darkling look and accepted the heavy implement. Clearly she was as unfamiliar with garden tools as she was with domestic ones. After experimenting a little, she settled it to her satisfaction and stepped over a protruding section of foundation wall to the lowest section of the site. "Here. I shall start where there's likely to be the least amount of soil to remove." With a mighty swipe she thrust the sharp end of the spade into the dirt and almost fell backward with the force of the ground's resistance.

When he jumped forward to steady her she shook him off. "I can manage." My, she was a stubborn little thing.

She hacked at the hard ground for a few minutes without appreciable progress. "Why is it not working?" she groused.

"Very likely the soil has been packed down over the years. Would you like me to try? Come," he said coaxingly, not liking to see her so despondent. "I agree that you are in charge but I could loosen the surface for you."

"I suppose so. Gentlemen are stronger."

The ground wasn't that hard. She really wasn't very strong, and why should she be? Until this morning she'd never done a minute of manual labor in her life. Working steadily, he scooped off the grassy sod in an area about two yards square. Then, without exerting any additional force, the spade hit a soft spot and plunged in deep, hitting something hard with a crack.

"Stop!" she cried. "You could break something. Suppose you've cracked the mosaic pavement."

"Excuse me, Anne." He enjoyed addressing her thus, knowing it irked her. "I'm trying to help."

"Well stop it. Taking off the top layer must be done with the utmost caution and after that I believe I must use the trowel. Only by hand can I be certain nothing is damaged." She fell to her knees in the dirt and began to remove the loose soil in minute portions, feeling as she went with the fingers of the left hand. Her pricey gloves would be ruined in minutes.

"Found anything?" he asked after a few minutes. While he quite enjoyed having her kneeling at his feet, he was getting cold.

"I don't expect I'll find any objects, if that's what you mean. Anything in this part of the villa would have been dug up and taken away already. But I'm guessing this is the atrium and I may find the remains of the floor at any time."

He took up the spade again and started to remove the top layer from another area. She cast an occasional eye on him and seemed to find his method satisfactory. They worked away in silence for a while and he contemplated the mystery of Anne Brotherton. Spoiled willfulness wasn't incompatible with a total absorption in her chosen area of interest. She'd agreed to the lowly cleaning task because it was the only means to get her own way. Yet she hadn't needed to work so hard at it.

Then there were her capricious moods, swinging from the pleasantly shy girl he'd first encountered to the demanding witch. Unpredictable behavior was common among the wealthy women he'd encountered, but he couldn't think of another who made his head spin. While at times he wanted to kill her, right now his thoughts ran more toward kissing.

Recalling a moment in the garden of Windermere House, his attention wandered from his digging. Once again the spade went in too hard and hit something.

"If you can't be more careful you should stop," Anne said, scowling at him through the dirt liberally streaking her face. "I'm sure you have many more important things to do."

Back to Lady Haughty again, and he refused to tolerate it.

"Yes I do," he said, "I'll leave you to your grubbing and see to my estate. No doubt you'll come in when it gets dark. If I don't see you then, be sure to be here promptly in the morning."

Feeling a little sad, Anne watched Lithgow stride away in the direction of the manor. She'd enjoyed their conversation and appreciated his help. That was the trouble. The more time she spent with him, the stronger the return of her insidious attraction. He'd listened to her ramblings with every appearance of interest. Her grandfather, the Earl of Camber, had been dismissive when she'd begged him to let her explore some of the thousands of acres under his care. Acres that were now hers and might as well belong to the Man in the Moon for all the good they did her. She could just imagine Lord Algernon's attitude to her ruling passion. He'd refer with distant tolerance to her odd little enthusiasm, chide her gently for having dirty gloves, and start talking about his ancestors. The notion of him wielding a spade was absurd.

But Lithgow, after softening her up with his apparently genuine interest, had sent her senses whirling when he'd saved her from a fall. Then utterly disarmed her by doing exactly what she needed him to do. And looking very fine while doing it, a miracle of muscular efficiency. But some or all of it was part of his nefarious plan to win her and possess those very acres that seemed a yoke about her shoulders.

If he thought her presence in his house would lead to her being charmed or compromised into marriage, he mistook Anne Brotherton's strength of mind. She would not be wooed, she would not be manipulated, and by God she intended to dig up this villa. And if she had to do it entirely alone, so be it. Allowing Lithgow's participation presented too great a danger to her peace of mind. She understood now exactly why Cynthia had to flee London. Knowing a man was a scoundrel didn't stop one wanting him.

Chapter 13

Marcus had barely finished serving breakfast to his servants when he heard an impatient knock at the front door: Anne bright-eyed and ready to work.

"I've been thinking," she said, pushing past him into the drawing room. "Before I go any further we need to take out the carpet and the curtains."

"I bow to your experience in such matters."

"I have no experience. At Camber I direct the housekeeper, who directs the maids and consults the house steward if a task requires the strength of a man."

"I apologize for my ignorance of the running of an earl's household."

Sarcasm had no effect on her. "Any fool can see they are full of holes and if I attempt to clean them will merely fall apart. I'm not a fool and it's only fair that I uphold my part of our bargain and get your house into some kind of barely livable condition." Her snort of disdain was somewhat spoiled by a sneeze from the inhalation of dust. "I can't do it alone. Will you call in your gardener?"

"Jasper doesn't do indoor work." He sighed. "You'll have to make do with me."

Together they rolled up the filthy carpet. "At least," she said, panting lightly, "we don't need a fire. I'm hot. Now for the curtains."

He noticed, as they tore down the disintegrating drapes, that she avoided his proximity. Any time they came into contact by the casual brush of an elbow or hand she jerked away. What had changed to make her so wary of his touch? What went on in that neat head of hers? Not that she looked very neat now, in a floppy cap that protected her hair but was covered in dust.

"Oh look!" She peered at the paneling in the wide window embrasure. "There's a little cupboard hidden here."

"Let me look." How had he missed it before? Rather too eagerly he prized open the door and discovered an ancient pack of cards. How ironic.

"Did you expect to find something? Something particular?"

"Who can resist a secret cache?" He riffled through the pack. No markings that he could detect, which meant there were none. He'd feared for a moment that his father had been playing another joke on him.

"I expect an old house like this could have all sorts of secrets. What fun."

"If you find anything you'll let me know, won't you?"

"Of course I would. Why wouldn't I?"

"I suppose I've dealt with too many dishonest people in my life."

"I am not one of them." Her eyes blazed. "As though I had any reason to steal!"

"You want my Roman villa, and presumably anything you find under that mound of earth."

"My interest is that of a scholar. My discoveries will still belong to you. Besides, I offered to buy it from you."

"Does that offer still stand?"

She looked away. "Perhaps."

"Do you think I should sell the place? To you or to anyone else?"

"That would have to be your decision, Lord Lithgow."

"I would like your opinion. Is the house and estate worth restoring?"

"I can't speak for the land. I haven't seen it and I was never trained for estate business. My grandfather expected my husband would see to it."

"What about the house? What do you think of it?"

She gave the question due consideration before speaking. "It needs a lot of work. Yet I like it. It's a handsome old place with some fine features."

"I think so too." Ridiculous to feel a glow of pride.

"Take this room. The paneling and fireplace are lovely. I like the contrast between the dark wood and the white ceiling." She looked up at the strapwork, a more elaborate version of that in the hall, and shuddered. "But the cobwebs are terrible."

He grinned at her. "I'll get rid of them for you."

By holding on to the very end of the broom he reached up and swept away the dangling spiderwebs. "Watch out for falling creatures." Anne scurried out of the way.

"It's not a grand place, as you are used to." He shook a spider from his hair.

"It could be made very comfortable. At Camber it takes so long to get from one part of the house to the other and it's not as if I needed all those rooms. I spent most of my life in only three or four."

"Big houses were built for entertainment. Did you ever wish for more company? A lady in your position would expect to adorn the *ton*." He strove not to sound bitter. He could scarcely imagine what it was like to be welcomed everywhere, simply by reason of his birth and position.

"I'm not a hermit," she replied. "I enjoy the company of those I value but there aren't many. My grandfather and Felix, while they lived. A few neighbors, girls I knew when I was growing up. Caro, always. Now Cynthia. Is it not better to have a few true friends than a multitude of acquaintances?"

"We don't always have the choice."

"Do you still see any of the friends from your early youth?"

"After my mother died I lived with my father and we were constantly on the move and rarely stayed in one place long enough to establish connections. I went to school for a few years."

"I always envied boys their schools. Felix told me such tales of sport and pranks at Harrow. Besides, it's dull work learning alone."

He tried not to hate Felix, who was after all dead. "Mr. Pinkley's Academy was far from fun," he said. He'd been miserably lonely there while striving to fill the gaps in his education. The gaps that covered just about everything except waiting on his father, escaping angry debtors, and winning at games of chance. "Oxford was better. That's where I met Robert Townsend, and life became considerably more amusing. He gave me the entrée to interesting circles." He poked the broom into the last corner to dislodge an obstinate cobweb. The ceiling was now clean, as clean as it could be discolored by decades of smoke.

Anne had been observing his progress as they talked. "Much better." Now she was out of danger from savage arachnids, she didn't back away when he put down the broom and stood beside her. "Don't think I cannot enjoy an assembly, when the company is intelligent. But gentlemen can be trying with their insincere praise."

"You undervalue yourself, Anne. There are many things to admire about you."

The mild compliment, delivered without forethought or ulterior motive, was startling. "Much to admire about my fortune, you mean." Gone was the relaxed girl, swishing a broom, squirming at spiders, and chatting about life. Lady Haughty had returned. He was a fool not to have noticed before that she felt her fortune was her only asset. As a result she was terrified of fortune hunters, which would explain her wariness with him. She was, after all, no fool. But why had she come to Hinton, then? Despite the appeal of the villa, it made no sense for her to have delivered herself into his hands if she was aware of his motives.

"What time is it?" she said.

He didn't want to part with her like this. Since he knew that what he wished to do—put an arm about her and tell her she was a lovely creature whom any man of intelligence would want— would be repelled with disbelief, he decided to melt her into a state of steaming irritation.

"You have fifteen more minutes. Don't expect to dig up an ounce of soil until you've put in your full hour and a half."

She consulted her watch. "Ten minutes."

"Enough time to help me drag this carpet into the hall."

"If you insist."

"Excuse me, Anne. How are you supposed to address me?"

"If you insist, *my lord*." She was as good as Travis at making an honorific sound like an insult.

Shifting the heavy old rug was an awkward and dirty job. With a combination of pushing, tugging, and rolling they got it close to the front door when the knocker sounded. Leaving Anne panting on her knees, Marcus opened it to reveal a middle-aged man whose attire and red face suggested a country squire of sporting habits.

"I'm looking for Lord Lithgow," he said.

Marcus inclined his head. "At your service, sir."

The visitor regarded his shirtsleeves and dusty breeches in astonishment. "Good Lord! And I heard you were a dandy! Sir John Bufton from Winkley Stoke. Your nearest neighbor." He meant the closest member of the gentry, the inhabitants of the village of Hinton apparently not counting. Winkley Stoke was some three miles away. "Heard from Oakley you were here and thought I should call and say how d'ye do." His bluff tones held a distinct West Country burr, a more refined version of old Jasper's speech.

Marcus looked dubiously at his hand but Bufton, apparently not a fastidious man, seized it and gave it a hearty shake.

"Glad to make your acquaintance, Sir John. I'd offer you refreshment but as you see the place is at sixes and sevens."

"Never mind that." Bufton strolled around the hall having a good look around. "Haven't set foot in this house for twenty years or more and it looks like it hasn't seen a lick of polish or a broom since."

"You may be right."

"Who's this then? Oakley told me all the servants had left."

He doubted that Anne, standing behind him with her cap flopping over her forehead, would wish to be introduced as the Honorable Miss Brotherton.

"That's my valet's niece, who agreed to come and help out." She gave him a quick, reproachful glance, then lowered her eyes respectfully. Or at least discreetly. An imp of mischief seized him. "Make your curtsey to Sir John, Annie."

She hesitated, then bobbed clumsily. Bufton was examining her with a good deal of interest, more than that of a busybody countryman without enough novelty in his life. Marcus half hoped he would chuck her under the chin, just to see how she'd react.

"Where do you come from, my dear?" he asked.

"She's a little simple," Marcus said. Anne's face slackened into vacuity. "But a hard worker. Doesn't talk much."

"Nothing wrong with a quiet girl. Is she local?"

"She comes from the north of the county."

"Ah, other side of the plain," Sir John said, dismissively. "Pretty little thing." He moved closer. Anne backed away with a look of alarm. "Shy too. The simple ones often are. Still, you're lucky to get her. I heard the nonsense about Hinton being haunted."

"As to that, Sir John, I'd be grateful if you could put it about that there are no ghosts here and I am looking for servants."

"Credulous, the country folk. I'll stop at the inn on my way through the village and put the word out. Damn shame not to put the house in order. Josiah Hooke was a queer old fellow. Neglected the land too. Wasn't so bad before he took to religion." He shook his head. "Thirty-nine articles is all a man needs, not that I've read them, mind you. Leave that to the vicar. Church on Sundays. More than that makes a man strange. Always an odd one, Hooke, but a good neighbor. Used to make calls and dine out when your mother lived here."

Marcus's amusement at the man's blather turned to astonishment. "My mother?"

"Dashed fine girl, Ellen Hooke. You have a look of her. Often danced with her at the Salisbury assemblies."

"My mother lived here?" He'd had no notion, neither had he found any sign of her in his searches. Or perhaps one. The embroidery silks in a drawer were the only feminine items he could recall.

"For a number of years, after she lost her parents. Didn't you know?"

"I know very little about her. She died when I was a small boy." He hesitated. "Did you know my father too?"

"A little. He spent a summer here and courted Miss Hooke." Bufton pursed his lips as though he'd like to say more but refrained out of good manners. A common response to the mention of Lewis Lithgow.

Marcus stood in silence, lost in amazement. Uncle Josiah had never mentioned it; neither had Lewis. The knowledge enhanced his interest in the house. To think that his mother, whom he remembered only as a warm and loving presence, had walked these halls, sat in these rooms, played the spinet in the parlor. He wished he could recall her face.

"I'll leave you now but you must come and dine, meet the neighbors. Lady Bufton will be happy to receive you, as will my daughters. Charming girls."

"Now we're in the suds!" Anne said as soon as the door had closed behind Sir John. "When he stops at the inn he'll hear Cynthia and I are staying there. I know country people. They love to gossip."

"You'll just have to keep out of the way," Marcus

said, still distracted by Bufton's revelation. "It's not as though I invited you here. It's entirely your own fault if your presence causes talk."

"You did invite me, you just didn't say when. And it's not the gossip I'm worried about, so much as being asked to dinner."

"Delightful people, I'm sure. You'd enjoy it."

"Thank you, but no. I'm in Wiltshire for only one reason and that is antiquarian study. I shall leave Sir John Bufton and his *charming daughters* to you."

"It should be easy enough to avoid him since you spend all the daylight hours at the manor. Be sure to be here in good time tomorrow morning. There's plenty to do."

With a smile on his face, Marcus watched Anne stalk off with an infuriated little huff to find her hat and cloak. If he wasn't mistaken she'd shown symptoms of jealousy of the Misses Bufton. More importantly, however, when introduced as the witless Annie she'd enjoyed it. He'd seen them: a gleam in her eye and a twitch of her mouth, both over in a flash.

He began to doubt that the hardworking, antiquarian-loving, and sometimes cheeky maid could coexist in the same body with the haughty heiress. There was a real possibility that Anne Brotherton had been feigning the ugly side of her character.

He started to whistle the tune to a bawdy Italian song. Eventually he'd find out why.

Chapter 14

Anne's back ached—not as much as it had, she was getting stronger—but she forced herself to continue. She'd painstakingly cleared the top layer of soil from the atrium, making herself approach the task in a methodical manner. She felt a little lonely and would have enjoyed a companion in her work, even the dastardly Lithgow.

Especially the dastardly Lithgow. She must not let their pleasant morning weaken her defenses against him, or make the mistake of believing his interest in the ancient remains anything but feigned.

It was time to dig deeper and she could hardly wait. Her reward came quickly. A layer of sacking, rotten but stout enough to retain its shape, stretched over the ground six inches beneath the surface. Tearing off her earth-clogged glove, the better to explore by touch, she enlarged a hole in the burlap and found the unmistakable ridges of tiny tiles. Careful scraping with fingers, trowel, and her handkerchief cleared a section of mosaic about a foot square.

She scrambled upright to gain perspective. Staring at the pattern of black, brown, and orange tesserae, she thought she could make out the head of an animal and couldn't wait to test the assumption.

"It's a lion."

She jumped and spun around. "What?"

A gentleman sat on one of the grassy mounds, leaning forward on a walking stick. "My apologies for shocking you. I've been watching for some time and didn't want to disturb you."

"What makes you think it's a lion?" Anne asked.

"I saw it thirty years ago, before Hooke abandoned the work. The terrace was in quite a remarkable state of preservation, then." He rose to stand beside her, regarding the mosaic from her viewpoint.

"Let's hope it still is. At least someone had the sense to cover it."

Anne studied the newcomer. He was older than she'd first thought, a handsome middle-aged man with cropped salt-and-pepper hair, dressed in sensible country clothing, but with a certain air of style. She did some rapid calculations.

"Were you a child, then?"

"You flatter me, madam. I was quite grown up when I became acquainted with Mr. Hooke." There was something about his demeanor that didn't quite fit the country gentleman.

"Do you live nearby, sir?"

"A few miles hence." He waved in the direction of the hill behind Hinton Manor. "I heard a rumor that someone was digging again, and since I enjoy a good walk and the weather is uncommonly fine, I decided to investigate. I didn't expect to find such a pretty explorer. Do you work alone?" His smile was charming, his voice mellifluous. Too much so.

"For the moment," she said. "I have decided laborers may lack the delicate touch needed to excavate these fragile remains." She stepped aside to put more distance between them.

"Are you planning on making a lengthy stay, then?"

"My plans are uncertain. Lord Lithgow has kindly given me permission to explore the site."

"Lithgow, eh. Young Marcus. I heard about his good luck. A peerage and an estate, from different sides of his family."

"Are you acquainted with him?"

"My visits to Hinton were before he was born. I live mostly in town and saw little of Hooke in later years."

Despite her misgivings, Anne indulged the curiosity that had been raised by Sir John Bufton. "Did you know Lord Lithgow's mother?"

"Ellen? I knew her long ago. She was a beautiful young woman."

"I have the impression," Anne said hesitantly, "that Lord Lithgow may wish to meet those who remember her. May I tell him your name and direction?"

"Bentley. David Bentley from Nether Barton. I look forward to seeing how the delightful Miss

Hooke's son turned out. And whom do I have the pleasure of addressing?"

"I'm Miss Brotherton." She dropped a reluctant curtsey but he showed no particular reaction. There were other Brothertons, though it wasn't a common name. Her suspicions somewhat assuaged, she decided to see if he could be useful. "Please tell me, sir, anything you remember about the villa. It would help me plan where to look."

Mr. Bentley turned out to have a considerable knowledge of his subject and an excellent memory. As they walked around the site together, the shape and arrangement of the rooms came to life before Anne's eyes.

"I believe the remains of a hypocaust were found along that side of the building and Hooke speculated that the furnace lay at one end." He pointed out a corner that appeared never to have been touched. "But he kept trying new areas willy-nilly. He didn't proceed methodically, like you."

"As soon as I have cleared the terrace and the rest of the atrium I shall start on that area. I'm quite fascinated at the ingenuity of the Romans in heating their houses."

"I've always thought it a tragedy for the English that they lost the art. I must be off if I'm to be home before dark. May I come again and see your progress?" He held out his hand and reawakened her discomfort by raising hers to his lips.

"I'm usually to be found here from the middle of the morning onward," she said stiffly, snatching it away and tucking both hands behind her back. Mr. Bentley was a useful consultant but there was something about him she didn't like. Their encounter reminded her of her first meeting with Lithgow, though the latter's initial advances had been far more subtle.

"And does Lithgow join you?"

"When his estate doesn't keep him busy," she said, not anxious to confide her opinion about his incredible lack of interest.

As she stared in blissful admiration at the mosaic terrace, she forgot about the departed Bentley and thought about its owner. Surely anyone, even the ruthless Lithgow, would be thrilled by such an amazing discovery on his land. To tell the truth, she couldn't wait to show him.

Anne was bright-eyed this morning, no trace of reserve or arrogance about her. Marcus found her adorable as she burst out her big news.

"The terrace? That's wonderful!" he said. "I truly doubted you'd find anything of value."

"I knew it had to be there! I cleared almost all the earth away before the carriage arrived to collect me at dusk. I can't wait to see it in daylight."

"What are we waiting for? Let's go and look at it."

"Immediately?" Her lips pursed and she shook her head. "I'd rather do my work here first. Once I get to the villa I won't want to leave it."

"My dear Anne. A discovery like this is worthy of celebration and a celebration means a holiday.

No housework for you today. Besides, I want to see it too."

"Aren't you too busy?" She was halfway out of the door as she threw the words over her shoulder with a hint of a taunt but no bite in her sarcasm.

The chill mist failed to dampen her spirits. She hurried across the meadow, her skirts gathering water from the long wet grass. "I worried all last night that the rain might damage the tiles," she said, running the last fifty feet. "It's all right! The water has washed them. Oh Marcus! Have you ever seen anything so beautiful?"

The mosaic glistened wet under the gray sky in shades of brown, yellow, black, and white, forming the figure of a ferocious lion, fully four or five feet wide. Here and there a small section of tiles was lost but she was right. It was a fine example. Marcus had, of course, seen better. This couldn't compare to the intricacy and splendor of bright colors and gold under blue Italian skies. But none of those, he was certain, had ever evoked greater delight by its discovery. Anne gazed down at it, hands clasped and eyes bright with ecstasy.

And she'd called him Marcus.

"It's marvelous, Anne." He put his arm around her, a spontaneous gesture of congratulation and shared joy. "Who would think to find the king of beasts under a muddy field?"

She didn't pull away. "He's very fierce, isn't he? Perhaps he's angry about the cold."

"Maybe he wants to frighten away marauding mice."

"Or badgers."

"You deserve credit for uncovering him. It was a lot of work."

"I never enjoyed anything so much in my life." She looked it over with a critical eye. "I wonder if the border is undamaged all the way around, and how wide it is. There may be a great deal left to do."

"Shall we start?"

They knelt in the mud at either end of the terrace. Even Travis would never be able to clean his breeches, but to hell with them. As they scraped away, Marcus following the example of Anne's method, they speculated on the possible age of the villa, fruitlessly since neither had the knowledge to place it.

"We could make a drawing and send it to an expert," he suggested.

"Mr. Warner of Bath, perhaps?"

"Ah yes, Mr. Warner. How did you find his book?"

"Tedious beyond belief."

"I apologize for the recommendation then."

"Some of the content was interesting but I see no reason why scholarship has to be presented in such dull prose."

"I've often thought the same myself. When you write your report on the Hinton find you must make it as entertaining as a novel."

"How would I do that? I've never written anything except letters and I'm not at all amusing."

"I wouldn't say that. You have quite a ready wit under your prim exterior."

She looked up, always suspicious of compliments. "Oh no," she said. "I'm quite dull and

too prosaic for wit." Then she grinned. "Anyone
seeing us on our hands and knees, staring at each
other, might think us a pair of dogs fighting over
the carcass of our lion."

Our lion. He liked the implication of shared
ownership.

"He needs a name."

"A Roman lion should be Leo," Marcus said.

"Commonplace."

"Richard, for King Richard the Lionheart since
we're in England."

She shook her head. "He doesn't look like a
Richard to me."

"Leonidas? Lancelot? Lorenzo?"

"Or Lewis. Wasn't your father Lewis?"

"I think not," he said. "What was your father's
name?"

"I'm sorry to say that Brotherton eldest sons are
always named Chauncey."

"*No.*" They spoke in unison.

"F—" He was about to suggest Felix, a suitably
catlike name, but thought better of it. He didn't
want her thinking fondly of her late fiancé. "Frederick."

"Frederick." She tilted her head this way and
that. "Fred. Frederick. I like it. Frederick it shall
be. Well, Frederick, I think you're as clean as we
can get you when the ground is so muddy." She
scrambled upright and, after carefully stepping
away from the terrace, flung her arms wide and
her head back. "I do believe Hinton Manor is the
most amazing place in the whole world. You are
so lucky to own it."

This was the perfect moment to suggest it could be hers if she wed him. He was already on his knees. The words of a graceful proposal of marriage formed in his brain, but they felt wrong. There was something honest and true about the morning they'd spent with Frederick, and their conversation had been without either pretense or rancor. He wanted to maintain this new friendship. Besides, she'd probably turn him down and feel called upon to leave Hinton. With the worsening weather there'd be less and less time for digging and she'd surely like to escape her housecleaning duties. In fact he had precious little time to win her—or compromise her reputation beyond hope of recovery.

"I am lucky," he said instead. "And I thank you for improving my property this way."

"The pleasure is all mine, my lord. What shall we do next?"

"It's up to you. Your methods have been effective so far. Clearly you have a talent."

She might shrink from compliments to her person, but this kind of praise delighted her. "Thank you. It's the only useful thing I've done in my life and I was afraid of making mistakes. It seemed to me an orderly system is best."

"I like order." He'd never thought it of himself but it was true.

"On the other hand . . ." She looked longingly at the west side of the villa, several yards away.

"Yes?"

"Mr. Bentley said the hypocaust was over there and I would dearly love to see it."

"Who is Mr. Bentley?"

"I forgot to tell you. He's a neighbor who stopped and spoke to me yesterday. An interesting man. He saw the villa when Mr. Hooke originally found it. He knew your mother too."

"I expect I'll meet him sometime," Marcus said, relieved that Bentley wasn't a young man. "You know, Anne, method and order are all very well but don't you think occasionally one is allowed to follow one's fancy? If you want to look for the hypocaust next, I think you should."

"Since I have the permission of the owner, that's what we shall do."

Digging in ground softened by rain was easier and dirtier. Working side by side—Anne's shovel technique had improved—they cleared the accumulated earth from around one column of bricks, about three feet tall.

"Remarkable," Marcus said, hopping down into the hole to get a closer look. "Very similar to ones I saw at Pompeii. Which way now?"

"Mr. Bentley speculated that the furnace was over there. I'd like to find it and see if we can work out how the hot air was projected between the columns of the hypocaust."

"You're in charge."

Judging by the compacted earth, Mr. Hooke hadn't reached this section and they found it hard going. Anne fussed about causing damage and her care was proven necessary when Marcus's spade dislodged a small metal object, caked in mud.

He expected a retort but she was too excited to

chide him. "Let me see." She knelt beside the hole, leaning in precariously. "There are other things here. Perhaps we've found a rubbish heap." From her voice he gathered she couldn't imagine anything more thrilling. He admitted to some excitement himself.

"Careful!" Too late. Scratching at a protruding knob with her fingers, she lost her balance and toppled forward. His body stopped her descent. They ended up in the mud, with her half prone between his bent knees, her arms around his neck.

Her body heat seeped through their damp, filthy garments. Her scent, subtle and costly, pierced the ambient odor of earth and rain and rotting leaves. Her breath was warm on his chin.

"Uh . . ." She interrupted a long, fraught moment and he wondered if she was as stunned and incapable of coherent speech as he was. Was that his heart hammering or hers?

He freed a hand to touch her cheek, pink and tantalizingly smooth, and she shifted a little, stirring his desire. The fact drew a low crack of laughter from him. It was impossible to imagine less propitious circumstances for lovemaking.

"What?" Her lips parted. By God, she was a lovely thing.

"I was thinking how much I'd like to kiss you, and how ridiculous that is."

"Why?"

"Because we are lying in a mud hole and it's raining."

"When did it start?" She made no attempt to break away.

"I don't know either. So, Anne Brotherton. Shall I kiss you? Shall you kiss me?"

She looked at him for what felt like an age. *Say yes*, he thought, staring at the curve of her mouth.

"I don't know."

"Would you like it? Tell me you want a kiss."

Her silence spoke volumes. She wasn't reluctant but he could see the wheels turning in her mind. She liked to think things through, and he tucked the fact away as an addition to his dossier on Anne Brotherton.

Her mouth moved. To speak or to kiss? He waited in delicious anticipation.

"Good God! What is going on here?"

He groaned. A perfect moment for a negligent chaperone to make an appearance. Not that Lady Windermere, in a dusty pink ensemble that could have been made in Paris, resembled any duenna he'd previously had to dodge. There could be no guardian dragon less alarming than this pretty young woman, peering through the misty rain into their hole.

"Are you hurt, Anne?"

Anne clambered up, not without kneeing him rather painfully. That took care of that, at least. "Cynthia! I fell into the hypocaust but no harm done." Marcus winced. "What are you doing here?"

"I thought I'd come and see your mosaic for myself. It started raining on the way but luckily I had my umbrella in the carriage. Do you want to come in out of the rain? It's coming down harder."

Water flowed off the brim of Anne's bonnet.

"First you must meet Frederick. Our lion. Isn't he splendid?"

"Lovely, my dear. Can I look at him when it isn't raining?"

Anne felt obscurely guilty about driving off in the carriage, leaving Lithgow to trudge home in the rain.

"He was so helpful today," she told Cynthia. "And he seemed to be truly interested in the villa."

"I see."

"He didn't even make me do any housework. He gave me a holiday to celebrate finding Frederick."

"What generosity!"

"We want to have a drawing made of him— Frederick, I mean. I have no talent with a pencil. You draw, don't you?"

"I used to. I wouldn't mind, if it ever stops raining. Next time could you conduct your excavations in the summer?"

Why was everyone so leery of a little rain? Yes, her cloak was wet through, but it wasn't as though she would melt, and she never caught cold.

"What I want to know," Cynthia said, "is what you and Lord Lithgow were doing in that hole."

"Er, nothing."

"It looked to me like you were kissing."

"No."

Cynthia looked skeptical. "Really? It just happened that you were lying on him with your arms about his neck and your face on his?"

"That's exactly what happened. I fell in and my face wasn't on his." Not quite. "He didn't kiss me."

"You sound unhappy about that fact."

"We talked about it. He asked me if he should kiss me. If we should kiss each other."

"The wretch! He left it up to you so you couldn't blame him afterward."

It was wonderful to have such an understanding friend. "Why couldn't he have just gone ahead and kissed me instead of making *me* decide?"

Anne pursed her lips and thought about the kiss that wasn't and the kiss that had been, back in London before she discovered Lithgow's scoundrelous nature. Why *hadn't* he seized the opportunity to kiss her? The hours they'd passed together had been so delightful she hadn't thought ill of him once. He'd been offered the ideal opportunity to take advantage of her when her defenses were weak.

The truth was she wished with all her heart that he had done so. She had really wanted to be kissed and hadn't wanted to ask because that would have given him the upper hand.

Something was wrong with that thought. If she wanted to be kissed, surely she should have said so? Leaving the decision up to him so that she could blame him was dishonest. Yet making the advance herself put her in a position she wasn't ready to be in. Shouldn't be in.

"Do you know something, Cynthia? Dealing with men is complicated."

"You don't need to tell me that."

Chapter 15

As the days passed, Marcus wished he'd seized the moment and kissed her. He didn't get another chance, and his regret didn't merely arise from a lost opportunity to advance his plans. Anne Brotherton, in her rough maid's clothing, her single-minded pursuit of knowledge, and her quirky temper, was getting under his skin. They settled into a routine, Marcus, his little household, and his strangely distinguished guests. Lady Windermere now accompanied Anne every day, ostensibly to make drawings of the objects excavated from the villa, probably because she was taking her chaperone duties more seriously since the muddy hole incident. Travis and Maldon took charge of the laundry and condescended to ameliorate the condition of the household linens and other fabrics. Anne diligently performed her cleaning duties and Lady Windermere turned out to be a talented polisher of furniture.

Marcus spent much of his time with his tenants, helping them make repairs to their cottages to keep out the weather as winter closed in. The drainage of the fields was a continuing cause of concern; completely dry days had ceased.

Whenever it wasn't actually pouring, Anne insisted on poking around at the villa. Untroubled by cold, wet, and mud, her enthusiasm never flagged. Since the discovery of Frederick he'd stopped feigning indifference to the excavations and would have liked to share them, but the urgent estate work had become important to him.

He returned one afternoon, stripped off his topcoat, and went straight to the study, which Anne had commandeered as the center of operations for archaeological records. It was warm, clean, and smelled of beeswax. A tray of tea waited on a side table.

Anne's smile at his entrance dealt him a jolt in the chest.

"You're very wet, my lord." The my-lord title didn't annoy him as it did when Travis so addressed him for it felt like a tease. Her hauteur and sarcasm had vanished for the most part, reappearing only occasionally. When she remembered. She'd only addressed him as Marcus that one time.

"And you are quite dry. And remarkably well dressed for a housemaid."

"Maldon brought a change of clothes for me."

"And where is Lady Windermere today?"

"She believed the chambermaid at the inn when she told us the curl of her hair was an infallible sign of a deluge."

"I should think iron gray skies and a stiff wind were sufficient prognostications."

Anne's coif, presumably through the ministrations of the impeccable Maldon, was smooth and gleaming without a stray wisp. He'd seen it frizzed, he'd seen it rumpled, and he'd seen it wet. He'd like to see it down.

"I'm surprised she risked leaving you alone with me."

She ignored the sally save for a telltale blush. "Sit down and I'll pour you some tea."

The tapestry-covered armchair, ancient and well-used like all Hinton's furniture, embraced his weary bones. He settled back and stirred in sugar, trying to recall if he'd ever experienced a moment like this. Himself, a woman, a cup of tea. He'd drunk champagne with countesses and courtesans, served by liveried footmen or, on one occasion, sipped from the navel of an enterprising lady. But a cup of tea on a rainy day with a virtuous woman in his own house? This wasn't the life of Marcus Lithgow, gamester and rogue. This was what happened to proper gentlemen with estates and families and good reputations.

"What were you doing out in the rain?" she asked.

"Mending a leaking roof."

"Do you know how?"

"I'm learning. Mostly I stood on the ladder and handed tools to my tenant, Jack Burt, who does know. He has three children and wants to keep them dry this winter. My uncle neglected the cottages and I'm doing my best to make a few improvements. To get a better price when I sell the estate."

She looked at him curiously, as well she might since he'd refused her offer to buy the place, leaky cottages and all. Why hadn't he seized the opportunity to present himself in a good light as a conscientious landlord? His statement wasn't even true. The pinch-faced children shivering in the damp house had been all the incentive he needed to invest a part of his dwindling funds in slates and nails and to pick up a hammer.

"How about you? Did you uncover the furnace yet?"

Anne sat at the desk, picked up a small brush, and rubbed away at a dirt-encrusted object. He observed the care she took not to damage whatever it was that dwelt beneath its coating of dried earth. Behind her she'd cleared a shelf on which was arrayed a growing collection of miscellaneous items disinterred from the villa and painstakingly cleaned.

"I'm very close but I keep finding things. Digging them out without damage takes time."

"I'm waiting for something extraordinary. A statue of Venus perhaps. Or the head of an emperor. I apologize for the pedestrian nature of Hinton's Roman inhabitants."

"Oh no!" she said with charming earnestness. "Of course it would be wonderful to discover a work of art like that, but I like finding bits of pots and strange metal things. Cynthia and I have great fun speculating as to their use while she draws them."

In comfortable silence he watched her work for a while. Her complexion glowed from outdoor work, enhanced by her dark blue woolen gown whose severity was broken by a crisp white ruffle at the neck. The delicate hands were a little reddened in places.

She caught him looking, put down her brush, and examined her splayed fingers. "I'm afraid I pull off my gloves without thinking. It's so much easier to reach a dusty corner or prize a stubborn artifact from the ground without them."

He reached over and took one of the maligned hands, caressing the palm with his thumb. "Still soft."

"Maldon is in despair. Not even her special cream can keep my skin in the condition she thinks proper," she babbled. "She has a recipe she refuses to divulge to anyone. I think it contains lemons."

He replaced his thumb with his mouth. She allowed perhaps five seconds' contact before pulling away. "Don't."

"I was just curious about the secret lotion. It does smell of lemons."

She shot him a disbelieving look but he thought she was embarrassed more than displeased. She made a play of sitting up very straight in her chair and frowning. "I found a lot of new things today." She wrinkled her nose. "This is just another piece of broken pottery. But I want to show you what I cleaned before you came in. Very curious."

Her hand hovered over the litter of muddy lumps on the desk and found the object she wanted. "Do you remember that pendant we saw in the funny shop in London? This is the same shape, with the two spheres at the top of a long cylinder." She frowned in bafflement. "This form must represent something of significance to the Romans."

Evidently she was unfamiliar with the cult of Priapus. "I'm sure you're right," he said, his expression as impassive as though he were playing brag with a cardsharp.

"I wish I had my books with me. I have a volume on classical iconography but never had occasion to study it. It's a little longer than Mr. Frogsham's example but definitely the same design." She ran her forefinger the length of the metal penis. "And rougher too."

Marcus shifted uncomfortably.

"It has the same bulge at the end of the cylinder."

If she went on like this he was going to have a bulge in his breeches.

Her thumb caressed the ballocks. "Unrefined. Probably the work of a lesser craftsman."

He was feeling remarkably unrefined himself.

"Did you say something?"

"Not a word," he mumbled.

"Do you have any idea what this shape means?" She looked at him with clear-eyed innocence and he desperately wanted to kiss her. For a start.

"I'll be sure to let you know if I think of anything," he said, dismissing the notion with regret. Visions of stripping off that demure gown danced in his brain. He wasn't sure if he'd be able to stop himself from excavating *her* treasures. He stood abruptly and set down his teacup. "I'll leave you now. I need to go up to the attic."

"It'll be chilly up there."

Cold, preferably in a bath, sounded like an excellent plan.

On the way upstairs he asked himself what the hell was the matter. Never miss the opportunity to reel in a mark when the moment is ripe; that was Lewis's paramount rule and Marcus had always found it effective advice. He should be kissing Anne until she was dizzy. Instead he felt dizzy himself.

He'd put off searching the dark top floor of the manor thinking it unlikely his uncle would hide anything precious in quarters occupied by servants, but he'd had no luck downstairs and there might be something of value up here. Most of the garret bedrooms had been unoccupied for years, judging by the rubbish that had been thrown into them. Who knew what might be hidden among old broken boxes, heaps of discarded furniture, and old-fashioned clothing? Not for the first time Marcus wished he had any idea what he was looking for. He forced himself to undertake a methodical search, and as the light faded he was reasonably sure he'd neither found nor missed anything of value.

At the end of the passage there was a locked door that none of the household keys fit. The stout lock was beyond his powers to pick. Casting about he spotted another door he hadn't previously noticed. Tucked in a dark corner, it was merely a cupboard. He didn't find a key but the answer to one mystery: a rusty chain whose presence made no sense. Shaking it produced some satisfying clanking. Thumps and ghoulish cries would be easy for a man—or woman—of ingenuity to manufacture.

Marcus turned back to the locked door with heightened interest. Faint scratches around the lock suggested someone else had attempted to pick it.

Anne couldn't imagine her grandfather, or Felix, or even one of her stewards, superior and gently born retainers to a man, standing in the rain to help repair a roof. They had workmen to do that kind of thing. Part of her duty as the heiress, now owner, of Camber was to call on the Brotherton dependents. She found these ceremonial visits awkward. The bowing men and women were obsequious, the children quiet and still as though restrained by inner bonds, and everyone declared themselves honored by the condescension of Miss Brotherton. She always suspected they found her presence a burden. Better to do something helpful like mending a roof.

Marcus had looked weary. And wet. She wished he hadn't cut his hair because she could envision the longer locks clinging to his skull. She tried not to dwell on it. Or on his thumb and lips caressing her hand. She'd thought he might kiss her. He hadn't pressed and she wouldn't have minded being pressed. But she'd been the one to pull away, because she was stupidly shy. If she wanted to be kissed she should be bold enough to ask for it. She raised her fingers to her lips and caught a whiff of lemon.

Shaking off her foolish daze she turned her attention to today's bounty from the villa. Brushing off the dried mud, she found nothing as interesting as the curious piece she'd shown Marcus. The back of it had two prongs that must be intended to attach to something. A costume ornament of some kind, perhaps. She recalled reading about Roman belt buckles. It was a possibility. What was it made of? Certainly not gold or silver, as might be worn by a man of wealth. It had a greenish tinge. Was it bronze? She missed the great library at Camber. She cradled the piece in her palm, assessing its weight, which told her nothing. Gazing at it she had a notion. An appalling notion.

Though many statues of male figures she'd come across—mostly in books—were damaged, some of them still had intact male organs. Those balls were awfully similar. But the male part—she didn't know what to call it—was much smaller and looked soft, even when carved from marble or stone.

She sincerely hoped she was wrong because if not Marcus must have known and watched her stroking it. The idea made her hot and flustered, distracting her from her meticulous cataloguing of today's discoveries. She set them aside for Cynthia to draw and add to the sheaf of neat sketches.

Since the carriage would arrive from Hinton shortly, she'd better go and drag Maldon away from the fascinating company of Travis. Fearing blushes in light of her recent suspicion, she prayed Marcus would still be busy upstairs.

No such luck. However, consideration of male anatomy was displaced by surprise when she met him coming across the hall armed with a large axe.

"Good Lord," she said, eyeing the shiny, lethal head. "I often seem to meet you carrying dangerous weapons."

"I'm going to break down a door."

"Why?"

"Because it's locked and I can't find the key."

"What door?" Not really her business, but as the manor's only housemaid she took a proprietary interest. "I hope you won't make a mess that *someone* will have to clean up."

"It's in the attic. I want to know what's on the other side."

"May I watch? There could be treasure."

"Or a skeleton."

"Or a ghost."

He hesitated. "There'll be spiders," he warned. Thankfully there was nothing in his demeanor to refer to the recent and possibly indecent conversation.

"I rely on you to use the axe on them." Even the giant and vicious specimens that inhabited Hinton Manor would surely fall before such a massive tool.

Although she had the impression he wasn't eager for her company, he didn't object when she followed him up the main stairs, along the wide

central passage of the first floor, through a door
at the end, and up a narrow winding staircase to
the cramped upper floor. She caught herself staring at his buttocks and thighs, delineated by snug
breeches. About to lower her eyes she thought,
Why not? He'd never know and it was an interesting and not disagreeable sight. Not disagreeable
at all. Her stomach quivered in the way that often
happened when she looked at him.

"Here it is," he said.

"It seems a shame to destroy such a stout door."

"Its stoutness is why I need the axe. I'm not
strong enough to break the lock on my own. Stand
back."

He seemed quite strong enough to Anne as he
swung at the area of the door closure. Watching a
man exercise his muscles proved quite stimulat-
ing, until the axe hitting wood raised a shower of
splinters and she cried out and put a hand to her
face.

He stopped at once. "Are you all right?"

"Something hit my nose." She examined her
palm. "No blood. I'm fine. But you are hurt."
Blood trickled down his cheek.

"It's nothing. You'd better go downstairs, out of
the way."

"I have an idea. Did you try kicking?"

"No. I tried to force the door with my shoulder."

"Let me try."

"Really? Be my guest," he said with an exaggerated courtly gesture.

She thought about it, enjoying the puzzle and
determined to triumph over his skepticism. Then,

with a little run, she used all her strength to thrust the sole of her foot just below the lock.

"Ow!" She hopped up and down. "My half boots are too thin."

He laughed at her, the devil, but gave her a comforting pat on the back. "Mine aren't. And I think you have the right idea about where to apply force."

It took half a dozen kicks before the lock yielded and the door creaked open.

"We did it!" she said.

"Yes we did." She saw something in his smile that was new, a mixture of affection, admiration, and an unguarded pleasure. It had a different quality than the ingenuous look that had first beguiled her until she learned it was designed to deceive. She felt her mouth curve in response, and her chest tightened at the warmth in his eyes. "You're a clever little thing, Miss Anne Brotherton."

She looked away, made shy by the best compliment she'd ever received. "I'm not little. As a matter of fact I'm quite tall for a woman."

"You are right. There's nothing small about you. In any way."

Except for her revenge after she'd discovered him a fortune hunter. She didn't regret plaguing him with the dullest sights in all London, but the money she'd made him spend on her pricked her conscience. He could have used it to improve his tenants' cottages.

"Let me look at your wound." Holding his chin steady, she gently dabbed the blood on his cheek with her handkerchief. His green eyes regarded her without wavering as she took a good deal longer than necessary to clean a scratch. Her breath quickened and her heart raced and she stared at the mouth, inches away, and thought about asking for a kiss.

"Shall we see what's in there?" she mumbled instead. *Coward.*

"Of course," he said with a little shake of his head. "Lead on."

"You go first. It's your house."

He wasn't fooled. "Aha! The spiders."

They entered a spacious attic, dimly lit by the fading light through dirty dormer windows. The place was entirely empty except for a small traveling trunk in the middle of the rough floor. Anne fell to her knees and rubbed the dust from initials stamped on the lid: "E.C.H." She felt Marcus tense behind her. "Ellen Hooke? Your mother? What was her second name?"

"I don't know." The three words struck her as ineffably sad.

She looked over her shoulder at him. "Is it locked? Will you open it?" If it were hers she'd rip off the lid.

"It's not very large. I'll carry it downstairs."

"Supposing it's full of books? Or gold bars?"

He hoisted it onto his shoulder easily enough. "No gold bars."

Marcus stood alone in the drawing room. He hadn't wanted to open the trunk in front of Anne.

Whatever stolen or villainous thing his father had left him, he couldn't risk her seeing it. She'd departed in her carriage, her burning curiosity obvious but unexpressed, from good manners and a natural delicacy. Before she left she'd rested her hand on his and given it a little squeeze and left him alone in the unheated room. Far worse than the chilly atmosphere was a cold fear in his heart at what he would find.

He folded his arms and stared at the leather trunk, a plain but well-made piece with an arched lid and brass hasp. All he could think of was that he didn't know his mother's full name. Aside from a few distant childhood memories, he knew nothing about her. He didn't know if he dreaded more what he would find or what he would not.

He knelt and examined the closure. It wasn't locked. Considering the efforts he'd made to find the mysterious legacy his father claimed to have left at Hinton Manor, he couldn't understand his reluctance to look inside. His sense of foreboding was ridiculous. Pressing his lips together, he flipped up the hasp and raised the lid.

The contents had belonged to a lady. They were the kinds of thing a woman might leave behind when she left a house to be married. Nothing of value or importance, merely the remnants of an old life not worth packing for the new: some worn undergarments, a cracked embroidery hoop, a crushed bonnet. A handkerchief bore those same initials in a corner, figured in blue thread. Marcus raised it to his nose, expecting—hoping—to be wafted back to the long-forgotten scent of his mother's embrace. He smelled only musty linen.

At the very bottom lay a paper package, about the size of a novel. He recognized the handwriting of the inscription from the papers in the office. In his uncle's upright and resolute letters were penned five words.

"The Sins of the Father."

Most likely letters incriminating some rich and powerful person, blackmail material that, for whatever reason, Lewis hadn't felt were ripe for use. If so, Marcus wanted no part of it. Though a weakness in one who thought himself impervious to most prickings of conscience, he drew the line at extortion.

He untied the knot, and a collection of neatly folded squares tumbled out onto the floor. At a glance they appeared to be written in a lady's hand. What erring society dame's love letters had fallen into his father's hands? He expected a duchess at the very least. Resigned disgust had scarcely had time to settle when he noted that the addresses were all the same: to Josiah Hooke, Esq., at Hinton Manor, Wilts. When he opened one at random and scanned the closely written lines, his own name, Marcus, popped out at him. The letter was signed, *Your obedient niece, Ellen C. Lithgow.*

He learned when he had taken his first steps. The date told him he'd been a little less than a year old. He had no idea if that was early, or whether he'd been an unusually backward child. Either way, his mother's pride was patent. His father's reaction was not recorded.

Gathering up the letters, he carried them to

the warm office and settled down to read them in chronological order. His mother and her uncle had been on terms of some affection but she had not been obedient. Her marriage to Lewis Lithgow hadn't pleased him. She started out a happy new bride, excited by a move to London and a host of new experiences, eager to assure Josiah that he had been right when he reluctantly gave permission for the match. She made sure to inform him of her husband's many virtues.

The culmination of her happiness came with her son's birth. Marcus had no doubt that he'd never, in all his life, caused anyone so much joy as his mother felt at the mere fact of his existence. He knew nothing of maternal love. In fact he knew little about love of any kind, his relations with women having been casual, sometimes carelessly affectionate, and almost always carnal.

He read on. He had, apparently, been the sweetest, prettiest, and most precociously brilliant infant that ever lived. Every evidence of his childish wit, which seemed commonplace to him, was recounted in exhaustive detail. He was the source of her greatest satisfaction and quickly her only one. They'd moved to the small house outside town as being more spacious than their rooms in Harley Street and healthier for the baby. For a long time she defended her husband, cheerfully recounted his long absences as necessary for business and the well-being of the family. Then an uglier picture emerged. Reading between the lines Marcus guessed that Lewis had been a neglectful and faithless spouse. *Yesterday was Lewis's birthday so I had a fine dinner ordered. Alas, he was detained in town. I don't know where he stayed.*

The money troubles began. *I don't entirely understand*, she wrote, *but Lewis has tied up my dowry in some investments or funds and I fear I must request a small loan. He asks me to assure you that it will be only this once and you will be promptly repaid.* Once became three times and Josiah resisted. Ellen begged him to forgive her importunity and talked about Marcus's rapidly expanding feet and garments worn from outdoor play with the neighbors' sons. He had a faint recollection of a small garden, being dared to climb an apple tree. The next letter confirmed his memory. *I dare not disturb Lewis now with demands for new clothes to replace Marcus's suit, which is torn beyond mending. His affairs have suffered reverses.* Losses at the table, Marcus guessed. His father could never resist the big gamble, the chance for the spectacular win. When he had money he liked to throw it around, behave like the great man he wasn't toward people he wished to impress. These did not, it was clear, include his wife.

As the years passed the letters grew fewer. Josiah, it seemed, had tired of the Lithgows' sponging and Ellen refused to leave her husband and return home. And she became ill. As he read the very last letter, Marcus could hear the coughing that had been a constant refrain in his seventh year. His eyes blurred as he read the brief note. *My dear uncle*, she had written in handwriting sprawling and weak. *I am alone with Marcus. We have only one servant now, a poor little maid who has*

*gone to summon the doctor. I want to acknowledge that
you were right. Lewis never loved me. He only wanted
my fortune, and since it has all been spent he has no
use for me. I fear what will happen to Marcus if I die.
Please, Uncle, I beg you. Forgive me and take care of
my son. Your finally obedient niece, Ellen.*

Terrified, he had held his mother's hand as she
coughed her life away. Lewis had appeared hours
later, too late to say good-bye to his wife. Within
days the contents of the house were disposed of
and he and his father began their years of wandering. "We'll have a grand time, son," Lewis
had promised. And Marcus, excitement cutting
the dull misery of his grief, had believed him. At
last he had the attention of the father, previously
a dazzling, elusive figure who would swoop into
the house, full of charm, then disappear again.

He slumped in his chair, castigating the poor
fool that he'd been, worshipping a man whose
only consistent trait had been that of betrayal.
During their one short visit to Hinton, Lewis
must have persuaded Josiah to take Marcus off
his hands. Surely not because of any belated sense
of guilt for his son's nonexistent education, but because it was convenient to shed himself of the en-
cumbrance. And Josiah had acceded to his niece's
last wish and sent Marcus to school.

The wrapping that had contained the letters lay
in his lap. He snatched it up to read something
written inside. *I wash my hands of Marcus Lithgow.
He has proven himself his father's son.* It was dated
just after Marcus was thrown out of Oxford.

Josiah was right. Wasn't he exactly like his father,

hunting an heiress for her money? Yet Josiah had given him one more chance, by leaving him the manor. A chance to make something of himself, to lead a decent life. He wasn't sure he could do it. Supposing he persuaded—or tricked—Anne into wedding him. Supposing he made her unhappy, as miserable as his own mother had been. He had to let her go. A pity, because he thought he might be able to love her. But he couldn't wager her future against the slim chance that he might *not* be his father's son.

Chapter 16

The next day it rained hard all day. Confined to the inn, Anne and Cynthia caught up on their correspondence, forwarded to them from Cynthia's estate.

"Lady Ashfield is quite tetchy," Anne reported. "She wants to know if I have heard from my guardian and when I will be coming to her. I think I shall tell her Morrissey's last letter was lost in the Irish Sea."

"She has no idea we are in Wiltshire, then?"

"Her sources of gossip are not as good as I thought. Maybe I should drop her a hint. I could write to her from here instead of sending the letter for your steward to forward to London."

"Keep still, will you." Cynthia looked up from the sketch she was making of Anne, in the absence of any Roman artifacts. She pronounced herself relieved to have a subject who was both alive and modern. "I think it's time to leave here. We can go back to my house and with luck no one will ever learn that you have been Lord Lithgow's maid of all work."

"And wed Lord Algernon?"

"You are stronger than you think. You can summon the fortitude to resist your guardian without having to ruin your reputation."

Anne thought Cynthia might be correct. She felt a different person from the timid young woman who doubted her ability to ignore the wishes of her elders. The old Anne would never have ignored her guardian's order to stay at Lady Ashfield's house. If this was what association with Marcus Lithgow had done to her, she couldn't regret it.

"I want to stay longer. I've almost reached the furnace."

"You're quite mad. It's December, for goodness' sake. Very likely it will start snowing."

"Give me a little more time. If I don't find the furnace soon, I'll stop and we'll leave."

"Praise God! No more housework!"

"You don't mind polishing furniture, you said so."

"True, I don't. And I've enjoyed drawing those funny little things. But you do realize your next task is going to be cleaning the fireplaces. Have you ever watched a servant doing that? It's a filthy business."

"Scouring iron grates isn't an appealing prospect," she agreed, "but I haven't minded the other work too much. It's quite a lovely house."

"I prefer a modern place with more light. And servants. And no ghosts."

"You have no romance, Cynthia. I thought I was the staid and practical one."

Cynthia arched her brows. "Romance? Could your passion for a very dilapidated manor be connected to its owner?"

"I'm not going to marry Lithgow."

"That's not an answer to the question."

Anne had no answer. She didn't want to talk about the way her head jerked toward the door at the sound of a footstep, the thrill when Marcus appeared, the disappointment when someone else came in. Nor could she bring herself to consult Cynthia about the belt buckle. Better not to know, she decided, and hid the thing behind a row of books.

"I've rarely enjoyed myself more," she said instead. "The villa, you know." *And its owner.* "While I agree on the necessity of servants, and I have resolved to treat mine with more gratitude in the future, I also find a certain freedom in not having people around me at every turn." *Except Marcus.* "And my days are my own, with no duties or expectations imposed by others."

Except an hour and a half a day that was no burden. She actually looked forward to playing servant, found a perverse pleasure in being ordered around; it had turned into a game.

"I'm even getting used to the spiders." Not really, but she enjoyed being rescued from them.

Cynthia said nothing but her look spoke volumes.

"Marcus Lithgow is an unprincipled fortune hunter," Anne said.

"I'm not so sure," Cynthia said. "If I based my opinion only on what I've seen I wouldn't think so."

"Remember what I overheard."

"Perhaps he has changed."

It frightened Anne how much she wished Cynthia was correct.

The rain continued all the next day, a relentless downpour sometimes mixed with lumps of sleet. Anne finished reading the books she'd brought with her and even the equable Cynthia grew irritable. Anne could not in good conscience keep her at Hinton much longer. They agreed to leave for Hampshire, to spend Christmas with Caro and Castleton, in good time for the holiday.

The third day dawned brighter and after breakfast they donned their warmest clothes and headed out into the village. Though not much of a place—they'd long since explored the churchyard and exhausted the possibilities of the few shops—anything was better than the four walls of the inn. By the time they reached the bottom of the street the meager charm of Hinton had palled and the road across the brook beckoned. "I'm going to the manor," Anne announced.

"Betty says it will start raining again by afternoon."

A glance at swelling gray clouds told Anne that Cynthia's weather prophet, she of the presciently curling hair, was likely right.

"I'll walk to the villa. I won't go up to the house."

"You naughty thing. Are you going to cheat

Lithgow by conducting a little excavation without paying first?"

"Certainly not. I'll just look around. I need the exercise. Will you come with me?"

"No thank you. My boots and skirts will get muddy. I'll content myself with the draper's."

It was less than a mile down the lane to the swollen brook. The bridge creaked alarmingly but Anne barely noticed. Across the field at the villa stood a man in a topcoat.

Marcus. She was going to see him today after all.

As she hurried over, with a pang of disappointment she recognized Mr. Bentley, crouching to examine the area on which she'd expended so much effort.

"Miss Brotherton." He stood to greet her. "I didn't expect to find you here today. I see you are made of sterner stuff than most young ladies."

"I needed air."

Bentley looked down at the columns of the exposed hypocaust. "You've made progress. I congratulate you. Have you done it alone?"

"Lord Lithgow helps me on occasion, when not occupied elsewhere."

"And have you found much of interest?"

"Oh yes! Quite a trove of artifacts in this part of the villa. It's why I haven't yet reached the furnace. Assuming you and Mr. Hooke are correct about its location." The area in question was still covered with grass. "I've made myself proceed methodically, much as I long to disinter it."

"A pleasure prolonged is a pleasure doubled."

"I hope so! I'm ready to start on it as soon as the weather improves. Then I must stop for the winter."

"All best wishes for success, Miss Brotherton. If I don't see you again, may I say how much I have enjoyed our brief acquaintance? I must leave now if I'm to get home dry."

"I won't linger myself. Good-bye, Mr. Bentley."

Although last time he'd come over the hills, he headed for the bridge. Anne supposed he'd left a horse or carriage in the village but hardly cared. She walked slowly around the perimeter of the building, memorizing the outline of the various walls, taking mental notes for future work. She needed to measure them so that she could draw an accurate plan. Lifting the canvas, she checked that the precious terrace had survived the storm without damage and said an affectionate good morning to Frederick. There was so much to do, so much to discover. A whole second building filled with who knew what wonders.

Above all, the furnace was a siren call. She would just start the process of removing the sod, softened by the rain.

It was easier than she thought and soon it became clear that Mr. Hooke had in fact uncovered this area before. On her knees, scraping away at the edge, she discovered brickwork a few inches below the surface. In the glow of satisfaction that accompanied a new discovery, she worked away, scarcely noticing the darkening sky. Water on the back of her neck stopped her for a moment. Just another few inches. She was wet already and would be soaked by the time she walked home, so why worry?

Pieces of sod piled up behind her as the uncovered brickwork grew. She set aside the trowel to grasp a large dock whose roots had penetrated the bricks. The plant proved a tough adversary. As she squatted to gain purchase, her heels slipped in the mud and she crashed forward through crumbling bricks into a deep hollow.

She'd found the furnace.

Her first reaction was fascination at the dimensions of the brick-lined circular chamber, at least four feet in diameter and even deeper. She could barely see out standing on tiptoes. Beneath her feet she could feel debris but it was too dark to know what kind. She must tread lightly in case she break anything. She removed her soiled gloves to run her fingers over the walls, which seemed to be in a remarkable state of preservation. This was an important find and she imagined the report she would write for a journal, complete with detailed measurements and drawings. She hoped the rain, now coming down hard, wouldn't damage it. The piece of canvas used to protect the tools would make a temporary cover.

Then it occurred to her. She was stuck in a deep hole with no obvious exit.

With a nasty qualm in her stomach, she assessed the situation. She was neither tall nor strong enough to pull herself up by her arms, unless she could climb at least halfway up the walls. Exploring them by touch, on one side she found a narrow ledge of protruding bricks a couple of feet from the floor. With a crouch to lend momentum, she stepped up onto it, grabbed the jagged top of the wall, and sprang. The bricks crumbled under her hands and she fell back hard with something sharp sticking into her bottom. All she'd managed to do was widen the opening for the driving rain.

Time for a new approach. She thought of all she knew about the construction of a furnace. There had to be a door for the stoking of fuel. It didn't take her long to find the place where the wall gave way to earth in an area about two feet square. She would fit through it, if she could dig her way out that way. Too much to hope that the trowel had managed to fall in with her. It hadn't. Back onto the ledge to grope for the tool, which remained maddeningly inches beyond her grasp.

The earth deep down was dry and packed as though it had been baked. All she got for what felt like hours of labor were broken nails and sore digits. Then she jammed her forefinger into a shard, tasted blood and dirt when she sucked on it and felt a flap of broken skin on her tongue. She slumped down, put her head on her knees, and started to cry as icy water poured down her neck and penetrated her collar.

What in heaven's name was she to do?

Stupid! Cynthia would think she'd gone up to the house and send the carriage. Then Marcus would come down and find her. She just had to wait. Unable to read the tiny hands on her watch, she had no idea of the time. Surely she wouldn't have to wait long.

Minutes passed, then hours as she grew colder

and wetter. Her voice was hoarse from calling out in the vain hope that someone would hear her.

Oh God, she prayed. *Don't let me die here.*

The roof repairs to Burt's cottage had survived two days of hard rain but Marcus wasn't nearly as sanguine about the dam, which could burst at any time and flood the meadows. He despaired of paying for improvements to the drainage. This damnable storm, which matched the state of his spirits, might destroy all hope of keeping Hinton Manor. Uncle Josiah had given him one more chance and he'd failed. Having rejected the course his father would have taken, he couldn't succeed at respectability. The irony failed to entertain him. The only thing left was Lewis's mysterious treasure.

Back home, he went into the study, intending to look over the estate books, hoping to detect a glimmer of light where his knowledgeable attorney had failed. But the room had been taken over by Anne. The neat rows of miscellaneous antiquities labeled in her hand threatened his resolution to let her go. He flipped open a notebook, her catalogue of finds. The last entry made him smile. *Metal object, possibly a bronze belt buckle, formed of a cylinder and two spheres.* He would have enjoyed giving her a practical lesson in its true identity, but it was not to be.

The drawing room wasn't any better. Anne had swept this floor, washed the window glass, de-cobwebbed the mantelpiece. There wasn't a spider left in the place. Finally he retreated to the kitchen, where Travis was ironing his shirts and neckcloths. Heaven forbid that he shouldn't look his best.

As he assembled the ingredients of a hearty ham and vegetable soup and set it on the fire, he half listened to Travis's sonorous complaints about the difficulties of drying laundry and the absence of his cohort Maldon. Mostly the latter. Marcus knew how he felt. He refrained from telling the valet that Miss Brotherton's maid would soon be gone forever, along with her mistress. They could mourn together as they left Hinton and resumed a life of aimless wandering.

"Where's Jasper?" he asked. "He's usually here by now, looking hungry."

"He drove the gig into the village this morning for supplies."

"He must have decided to stay with his brother there. Likely warmer than the stable cottage."

Travis frowned. "Jasper hates his brother."

"He hates everyone."

It was raining harder than ever. If the dam broke, the flood could sweep away the bridge and anything else in its path. Jasper might have been coming home just at that moment.

Marcus gave the pot a stir. It smelled good. Practice had improved his cooking, one reason Jasper never missed a meal. "He's a tough old bird. He can look after himself." But Jasper was also old and bent from a lifetime of hard labor. "I'm going out to look for him," he announced.

"You'll be soaked," Travis protested.

"It can't be helped. He could drown in this mess."

Bundled in his still damp topcoat and guided by a sturdy storm lantern, he headed down the drive, battling wind and rain of biblical force. As he'd feared, the brook had risen to a raging torrent, doubling its width and destroying the bridge. He slogged downstream, straining his eyes in the dying twilight. Of Jasper, gig, and horse there was no sign. He could only pray the old cuss had stayed with his relations in the village.

Why the villa even entered his mind he would never quite know. The Romans knew enough to build away from the danger of flooding, but he thought of Frederick and how upset Anne would be if he was damaged. He wanted to be sure the lion was covered. Postponing his return to the welcoming warmth of his house, he diverted his steps to check on the fruits of her labor. This he could do for her.

By the light of the lantern he surveyed the site through the teeming rain. The canvas was in place, as far as he could tell, and held down by pools of water. When the faint cry penetrated the gale and the roaring of the brook he thought it a trick of the wind.

"Hello there!" he called, feeling a little foolish. No one sane would be out in this weather. He was mad himself.

"Help!" Was that a human word, or a stray cat caught in the ruins? "Help!"

Surely she wouldn't. He was desperately afraid that she would.

"Anyone there?"

"Here. Help me." Then some words he couldn't comprehend.

"Keep talking," he yelled.

He stumbled over an exposed wall, trying to follow the voice that swirled around in the wind. Where was she? In the rapidly falling darkness, his light illuminated only small areas at a time. Why did the Romans have to build such large houses? Swallowing panic, he forced himself to stop, listen, and think over the howling of the storm and his own beating heart. Once he narrowed down the sound to the vicinity of the hypocaust, he wondered if she'd fallen in and hurt herself. Walking slowly along the edge of the pit he could see nothing. "Where are you?"

"In the furnace."

Where before there'd been grass and weeds, a jagged hole lay dark and ominous. Mud squelched over his boots as the ground gave way underfoot. He fell to his knees and crawled forward, holding the lantern over the hole. Anne's upturned face glowed ghostlike a foot down. "Marcus?"

"It's all right. I'll get you out. Give me your hand." Instead she disappeared from view and no longer replied to his calls.

Forcing himself to think clearly, he dismissed the idea of going in after her. Too much danger of them both being stuck. "Anne," he called, praying she hadn't fainted. "Stay awake. Can you stand up and reach me again?"

"Can't." She was slumped on her behind against the wall of her prison. Water already covered the floor. He needed to get her out fast before she froze to death.

"Try very hard to stand up. Hold up your arms and I'll pull you out."

Lying on his stomach, he ignored the mud and rocks piercing his clothing as the rain battered him from above. "Come on, Anne. You can do it."

She was only a shadow in the dark chamber as his senses strained to follow her movements.

"I can't move." Her voice was barely detectable.

"Anne," he said sternly. "Get up at once."

His sharp order got through where gentle coaxing failed. He heard her shift and rise. A white hand appeared for a moment, then slipped out of the grasp of his sodden gloves. He stripped them off using his teeth. "Both hands, darling. Now." This time he caught them, slender and icy cold. "That's my girl. Keep your arms high. Now I'm going to slide down to your elbows."

He had to push aside the folds of her water-logged cloak before he had her in a firm grip and started to work his way backward to pull her out. She managed to contribute to the effort by stepping up onto something. Once he had her half out, balanced precariously on the edge of the hole, he knelt up and half tugged, half rolled her out by the waist. There was no time to ponder his aching muscles. He needed to get her home and dry promptly.

Alas, the struggle to escape had knocked over the lantern, although he'd wedged it next to a rock. Thus began a nightmare journey through the impenetrable dark of the storm, across rough fields rendered lethal by the rain. Sometimes she walked a few steps but mostly he half carried, half dragged her. Unable to speak, she shivered uncontrollably, and he feared for her health and even her life. He could only guess how long she'd been imprisoned but he knew when it had started to rain. She'd been out in the wet in falling temperatures for four or five hours. The last part of the journey, when the terrain was smoother, he scooped her into his arms and made the best possible speed until he staggered through the back door of the manor and into the kitchen.

His valet jumped up, eyebrows flying. "Quick, Travis. Fetch blankets and towels, immediately."

Anne stood passive and barely conscious. Marcus wanted to warm her in his arms but their clothing was soaked through. Everything must come off before he could get her dry. So he stripped her from bonnet to boots and was fighting the wet laces of her stays when Travis returned.

"My lord!"

"This is no time for prudery."

"I cannot remain in the room with an undressed lady. Nor should you. Think of her maidenly modesty."

"Better immodest than dead. If it offends you, turn your back. And fill the bathtub with hot water."

A knife made quick work of the laces. Stays and shift fell to the floor and she stood naked, unable even to move her arms to protect her small pointed breasts or private area. Marcus enveloped her in a blanket, every inch of her wet and ice cold and shivering, and guided her to the chair next to the fire, where she sat, eyes closed.

"Talk to her, sir," Travis said. "That's what you did for me when you saved me. It kept me going when all I wanted to do was sleep and would have died in the snow."

"I'm going to get you into a bath. That'll warm you up." He kept talking as he and Travis carried the cans of hot water to the metal tub beside the stove. "Then we'll get you into a warm bed."

"Sleep," she said.

"You can't sleep yet. You have to get warm first. Then everything will be well."

God, he hoped so.

He was still talking soothing nonsense as he lifted her into the hot bath and scooped water over her exposed shoulders and back. Anne crossed her arms over her breasts, for warmth he fancied, not shyness. She was beyond embarrassment or even thought.

"Travis," he barked at his valet, who was unhappily trying to look away. "Go and stoke the fire in my bedchamber and take the warming pan."

Once Anne's cold limbs started to respond to the water, he turned his attention to her hair. Most of the pins had fallen out but her braids were so tight they were almost dry inside. He fingered her hair loose and rubbed it with a towel. This was not the circumstance under which he'd hoped to learn that her locks reached almost to her waist. Finally, he lifted her out, tenderly dried her off, and carried her upstairs.

Since the fire in his room was kept banked all day, Travis already had it blazing. Still, it would take hours to dispel the chill when cold air blasted through the ill-fitting windows. Marcus pulled one of his shirts over Anne's head, slid her between the warmed sheets, and heaped her with blankets. She hadn't opened her eyes in an age but continued to shiver. She lay on her back, dark hair spread over the pillow, utterly still. He'd never seen a more beautiful sight than her face, as pale as ivory, nor one that filled him with greater despair.

"Anne," he whispered. "Can you hear me?" If only her eyes would open and give life to the frozen countenance.

"Cynthia? Maldon?" The voice was a low, husky rasp.

He stroked her forehead. "It's me, Marcus. You're safe now."

Her head moved from side to side. "Grandfather? Felix?"

Who the devil was Felix? Oh yes. Her dead betrothed.

"No," he said urgently. "It's Marcus."

She didn't seem overly hot but he feared the onset of fever. It was going to be a long night.

"Marcus?" she murmured.

He hadn't known how tense he was until he felt his muscles relax. "Yes, Marcus. I have you safe. Now sleep.

Leaning over her still, pale body, so frail and lifeless, he realized he still wore his wet clothes. After changing into a dry shirt and breeches, he slipped into bed beside her and gathered her close, her body firm and slender in his arms, willing his heat into her shivering form.

She was his now and he didn't have to let her go. He wished it was the best thing for her.

Chapter 17

Anne didn't think she'd ever be warm again. Sometimes she woke up and thought she was still buried at the villa, despairing of rescue and certain she would die. She tried to call for help but her throat was raw. Soothing words assured her that she was no longer trapped in the hell of icy water. "You're safe, sweetheart," the voice said. "You're warm now and I'll look after you, darling." No one had ever called her sweetheart or darling. How lovely. She settled into the embrace of the warm body that had somehow got into her bed. She asked no questions, aloud or to herself, merely reveled in the heat penetrating her frozen bones.

When she woke it was still night. A lamp glowed on a table revealing a room she'd never seen before. Her memory of what happened between her endless hours of captivity and this warm, pleasant awakening was indistinct. She knew only that Marcus had found her. An urgent physical call made her slip gingerly down from the high bed. Glad to find her legs in working order, she tottered across the cold floor and found a chamber pot behind a screen. In the dim light she took in masculine clothing hanging on a row of pegs, a pair of tall boots, and a guitar propped up in one corner. A washstand held a pair of hairbrushes, a razor, and other masculine accoutrements. She must be in Marcus's own bedchamber. Aware of legs shockingly exposed from the knee down, she hurried back into bed and sat back against the pillows. Good Lord, she was wearing a man's shirt and nothing else. How she got into it, not to mention out of her own garments, she had no idea. Someone had removed every stitch, down to her stays and shift. Her cheeks burned with shame mixed with an odd excitement.

The door handle rattled and she pulled the covers up to her neck.

Marcus came in.

"You're awake. How are you?" His eyes were dark with weariness, his hair damp.

"I'm quite well, thank you. Have you been out again, in the middle of the night?"

He drew the curtains. "It's just past noon. And still raining."

"Gracious! How long have I been asleep?"

"The best part of a day. It was late afternoon when I found you." He came over to the bed and felt her forehead. "You don't have a fever. Amazing after that soaking."

"I rarely get so much as a sniffle."

She was alone with a man in a bedroom. His bedroom. Surprisingly she felt no great embarrassment, perhaps because he regarded her with concern rather than desire. She must look a mess. As she raised her arms to push her unruly hair back from her face, the shirt she wore gaped open.

"Is this your shirt?" she blurted out, hastily covering her bosom.

"Your clothes were soaked."

"Thank you. Thank you for coming to find me."

"I suppose there's no point asking you what you were doing at the villa, down a hole, in the worst rainstorm I've ever seen."

"The hole was an accident. I just wanted to clear away the top before I went home and I slipped in the mud and fell through."

"That was a stupid thing to do," he said with a frown. "It was only by chance that I found you."

"I thought Cynthia would send the carriage for me once it started to rain. I don't know why she didn't."

"The brook flooded and swept away the bridge. We're trapped at the manor until the waters go down."

"Cynthia will be frantic."

"I spoke to Jasper this morning. Not much of a conversation with us yelling at each other across a torrent, but I managed to tell him to assure Lady Windermere that you are here and safe."

She ought to be upset but now that she knew Cynthia wouldn't worry unduly, except about the impropriety of her staying at the manor alone with Marcus, she felt quite content. Her stomach growled. "I'm starving."

He grinned, more carefree than he'd been since

he entered the room, and wonderfully handsome. She twitched her shoulders in response to an involuntary tingle lower down her body.

"I'm happy to hear it. I'll bring you some dinner."

Ten minutes later he returned with a tray bearing bread and butter and a bowl of soup. She filled her spoon and blew on it.

"It was hot when it left the kitchen but I think the journey through the cold house makes caution unnecessary."

"I'm a cautious person." He shot a look of disbelief. "Delicious," she said, tucking in. "Did Travis make this?"

"Remember, valets don't cook. I did. One of my favorite recipes."

She giggled. "Really?"

"Not really. I just throw things in a pot and hope they come out well."

"I've never known a man who cooked."

"You've never known a man like me." There was an undercurrent of wariness in his words.

"True. Meeting you has been an education." She wasn't sure what she meant. A few weeks earlier she'd have said he'd confirmed her distrust of the motives of men's intentions toward her. But she'd also learned to fight for what she wanted, not merely to let life happen to her.

He sat on the edge of the bed, careful not to tip over the tray of food laid across her legs. Not long ago she'd have been dead of shock at having a man in her room, sitting on her bed. Now it seemed natural. Besides it was his bed. And she rather thought she'd shared it with him, though her memories of the night were hazy. He clearly had something to say and he seemed troubled.

"I'm sorry, Anne. I didn't mean this to happen."

"It's not your fault. I was foolish to be out in the rain, but in my defense I really didn't mean to fall down a hole."

"Not that, though I beg you to be more sensible in the future. I mean our situation. You've spent a night under my roof with no chaperone but my valet. Your reputation will be hopelessly compromised. That's what I didn't intend."

"Really," she said with a little edge, "I would think it suited your purposes perfectly. Wasn't your goal all along to persuade or trap me into marriage?"

"To my shame, yes. I wondered if you'd guessed. I suppose that's what those visits to the more fascinating byways of London were about."

"Oh yes. And my dreadful behavior. I'm not really such a haughty wretch. I quite enjoyed the deception, which you thoroughly deserved."

"You did it far too well and had *me* fooled."

"I did do well, didn't I? There was one time I thought you were going to throw me out of the carriage window."

"You tempted me. I almost decided you weren't worth the trouble until you came down to Hinton and played into my hands."

"Is that what I did?" She couldn't help a little smile at how wrong he was.

He appeared not to share her humor. "No self-respecting fortune hunter could resist such an opportunity. Forcing you to act as a servant was risky, but I wanted a little revenge and I knew I could maneuver you into a position where you had to accept me. Then I learned the spoiled heiress wasn't really you and I couldn't continue to use you and ruin your life. And now look at us. You're trapped here, there's bound to be a scandal, and I can't see any way out other than our marriage. I'm so sorry." She found his remorse convincing but not terribly flattering. While renouncing his plan to wed an heiress for her fortune was creditable, she supposed, she'd be more pleased if he actually wanted to marry her, for other reasons. "I promise you, Anne. I'll do my best to be a good husband."

"Is this a proposal?"

"I suppose it is."

She pursed her lips.

"You deserve better than this, Anne. You ought to have a man of birth and honor on his knees before you, someone begging to prove he's worthy of you, someone who loves you. Someone much better than me."

Marcus seemed so upset she decided to stop teasing. "Marcus, stop." She rested her hand on his clenched fist. "You don't have to marry me, and I don't have to marry you."

"If only that were true. But you're ruined."

"You don't understand, do you? I came here to cause a scandal, perhaps not quite such a large one, but it'll suffice. You were pursuing me for your ends and I was doing the same."

"You're right. I don't understand."

"I'm the most desirable match in all England. Dozens of gentlemen, hundreds even, want to marry me. It's nothing to do with me personally, of course. Merely because of the property that comes with me. Nothing I do can make me unmarriageable. Ask Lady Ashfield."

"That old witch!"

"She knows society. And she assures me that no matter how plain or dull I am, or how scandalous, someone will marry me."

"Any man would be lucky to win you."

She brushed aside the compliment. "Be that as it may, I'm not sure I want to marry any of them. Especially not Lord Algernon Tiverton."

"Tiverton! I should think not. I was at Oxford with him."

"I don't suppose he was any better back then."

"You couldn't possibly want to wed such a self-satisfied bore."

"Exactly. Since he's my guardian's choice I had to render myself unacceptable to him and you were the perfect man to do it. My association with you will get him out of the way and I hope any others of his ilk. I've decided I'd just as soon not be married at all. But if I change my mind someone will have me."

"But . . ." Marcus stared at her, quite flummoxed by the revelation. "What . . ." Then he smiled, his biggest, most devastating grin, his eyes alight with mirth. "My dear Anne, I salute you. You played me perfectly and I didn't think I could be played. You should be proud of yourself. I'm proud of you."

"Thank you, Lord Lithgow."

"Call me Marcus. I hate the title."

"Why?"

"Because it means nothing. It's an obscure peerage that came to me through a cousin of my father's so distant I had no idea of his existence. It brings me no property, not even a seat in the House of Lords. It has nothing to do with me."

She could appreciate his point since she'd often felt the same about her wealth. "Why use it then?"

"I'm a rogue and I'll take advantage of anything that might give me entrée to those who can be of use to me."

She touched the back of his hand, feeling the elegant bone structure under the rough masculine skin. "I don't believe you're as bad as you say."

"Whatever can have given you that idea? I've proven quite the opposite."

"You saved my life yesterday."

"Perhaps."

"Why did you come to the villa in the middle of a storm?"

He averted his eyes. "I was making sure Frederick was covered up and safe."

"That was a very sweet thing to do."

Abruptly he stood up and strode across the room. "Here," he said, handing her a hairbrush.

"Do I look so untidy?"

"It'll give you something to do."

"I'd rather get up."

"Absolutely not. You must stay in bed, at least until tomorrow. Besides, your clothes are still wet."

"At least give me a book."

He returned to the dressing table and almost threw a volume at her. "I must go. I have to see about getting that bridge repaired."

Anne shook her head in puzzlement as the door slammed behind him. What had got into him? He hadn't seemed upset by the revelation of her ruse. Apparently he really didn't want to marry her, which was good. It proved he wasn't a completely mercenary scoundrel. But it would have been more flattering if he'd shown an iota of regret. She found his failure to press his suit unaccountably depressing.

She leafed through the battered volume of Hoyle on *The Game of Whist*. Though interested in the fact that the calculation of odds in card play was such a precise business, she'd never been one for arithmetic and soon grew bored. Which left her hair.

Maldon, who had been her mother's lady's maid and stayed on as personal attendant to the orphaned infant, had always brushed her hair. Her mother had lived in an era of huge coiffures, and her maid missed them. Anne hated having her hair about her face, and the difference of opinion was a source of discord between them. The tight plaits were a compromise because Maldon became mutinous when Anne took a fancy to sport a fashionable crop, like Caro. Not that Maldon was opposed to fashion, quite the opposite, except in this one matter. She longed to wield curling papers and hot irons. But her grumpy loyalty to Anne was absolute, despite the latter's stubborn resistance to coiffed excess.

By the time she'd worked out all the tangles, Anne regretted not being firmer in the matter of the crop. Applying the same determination with which she uncovered a new section of Roman wall, she worked away until she could run her fingers through the almost waist-length locks without a single snag. Curious to see the result of her labor, she got out of bed to the dressing mirror and saw a new Anne Brotherton. Dark hair formed a cloudy halo around her head and shoulders, emphasizing the pale face and making her eyes seem bigger than usual. Clad only in Marcus's shirt, she looked wild. The prim heiress, neatly dressed to the point of dowdiness, had been replaced by an exotic, wicked creature, a seductress.

That was silly. She wasn't the type to drive men mad with desire. Still, she wondered what Marcus would think of her like this. Nothing, probably. When they first met he'd appeared to admire her, but that had been a ruse. Since she came to Hinton, he'd shown no sign of being attracted to her. The almost-kiss at the villa had been part of his deception. Rather than stay in her company now, he'd preferred to go out in the rain and look at a bridge, which certainly couldn't be repaired until the weather and waters calmed down.

She wasn't staying all alone in this dull room. To hell with Marcus. Thinking the oath gave her a little thrill of naughtiness. A quick inspection of the wardrobe and chest of drawers having revealed no cache of feminine attire, her eyes settled on a pair of unmentionables. Why not?

The intimacy of wearing *his* clothing against her bare skin gave her a frisson of excitement. The long shirt protected her privates from contact with the soft leather breeches. Holding them up was a problem until she found and worked out how to attach a pair of braces. His stockings sagged on her slimmer calves but they'd have to do. Intimidated by a drawer full of wide, perfectly starched and ironed neckcloths, she settled for going bare-throated. Even buttoned, the too-big shirt revealed her neck and collarbones. The ensemble felt more comfortable than a heavy gown. Men had all the luck. With a happy swagger she made her way downstairs to the kitchen.

Travis was ironing linens at the kitchen table. He looked up and goggled at her, Adam's apple aquiver, bushy eyebrows shooting toward the ceiling. "Miss Brotherton," he said, in accents of great shock.

"Good afternoon, Travis. I understand my clothes are still wet so I borrowed some of His Lordship's gear."

"Indeed, madam. Your gown—a very fine-quality kerseymere, may I say—was soaked through with mud." He then proceeded to tell her, in exhaustive detail, the measures he was taking to restore it. "I apologize for not having it ready for you," he concluded.

"Don't apologize. I'm comfortable as I am."

"May I offer you some tea, madam?" He avoided looking at her, the indecency of her attire evidently offending his sense of propriety. "I'll bring it up to the study."

"I'll stay here. I've never spent time in a kitchen and it's warm and cozy and smells good. I'm thirsty but I don't feel like tea."

"I'm afraid it will have to be water. The only other thing we have is beer and you wouldn't want to drink that."

"Yes I would. At least, I've never tasted it but I should like to."

She sipped from the tankard provided by an obviously reluctant Travis. Bitter but pleasingly yeasty. As she drank, she watched Travis apply the irons, heated on the metal stovetop, to a couple of shirts. "You're very skilled, Travis."

"Thank you, madam. I take pride in turning out my gentleman without a wrinkle."

"Have you been with Lord Lithgow long?"

"A few months, since he saved my life."

This was a story Anne had to hear. "Please tell me what happened."

"My master, an Italian marchese, was crossing the Alps and I naturally followed in the luggage coach. Being early in the spring, the roads were slippery. As we descended from the pass we went off the road and fell down the mountain. The driver and horses were killed, as was madama's maid."

She took a gulp of beer. "That's terrible. How did you escape?"

"I am a nervous traveler and the narrow mountain roads had me in a state of constant fear of such an event. I'm not sure how I had the presence of mind, but when I first felt the carriage lurch, I opened the passenger door and threw myself out of the falling vehicle. By the hand of Providence I landed on a rocky outcrop. From what I gathered later, my employer had no notion what to do, except comfort the marchesa, a lady much given to the vapors. I have no doubt that had His Lordship not appeared on the scene I should have died there."

"Oh Travis! He did the very thing for me last night."

"Quite so. At considerable personal risk, he climbed down the precipice to my precarious perch. I'm no climber at the best of times and I was both bruised and frightened. Yet he helped me climb up a rope, with constant words of encouragement to keep me from succumbing to my terror. I resigned my employment with the marchese on the spot, despite the impropriety of quitting my post without due notice. I continued the journey with Lord Lithgow and have been in his service ever since."

"And is he a satisfactory employer?"

"I wish he would allow me to curl his hair, otherwise I have no complaints. His reputation in the world is not of the best but in my opinion is undeserved. Those who speak ill of him are not aware of his struggles in life, nor of the real generosity and heroism of his character."

Heroic, indeed, Anne thought with a quickening heart and a buzz in her head. It was so easy for those who had never known trouble to pass judgment. Herself included. Why had she become so angry when she learned Marcus was a fortune hunter? She was acquainted with fortune hunters by the score and regarded them with nothing but resigned tolerance. She even expected to marry one of them at some point in the future. She'd blamed Marcus for this unexceptional sin because she'd wanted more from him. Back in the night garden of Windermere House she'd fancied herself in love and wanted him to love her back.

She wasn't sure if she felt the same now. She knew him better and her feelings were deeper and more complicated. That he was good at heart, she believed. But his bad reputation was not undeserved. He'd done something that put him beyond Caro's forgiveness, most likely tried to steal something. It would be easy to fall deeply in love with Marcus, but she wasn't sure she could ever trust him. Until she decided, she must guard her heart.

That did not mean, however, that she could not enjoy his company. Until the bridge was repaired she had no choice.

Chapter 18

How the hell was he going to stand it, having Anne lying in his bed with her long hair gloriously about her like the most abandoned courtesan? When she'd leaned forward to touch his hand, giving him a shadowy glimpse of small but shapely breasts, it had taken every ounce of restraint to walk away. Anxiety about her health told him to stay and wait on her, make sure she kept warm and didn't develop a fever. But he couldn't do it. For he suffered a powerful desire to jump into bed with her and formally complete her ruin. He'd bolted out of the room and out of the house into the continuing rain, which provided the cold bath he badly needed.

When had Anne Brotherton become a siren? And a wicked one too. Her bold ploy to use him for her own ends excited him. Still, compared to him she was a novice in the art of deception and she still needed to be protected from his baser side. Especially now that one of his baser desires had been fully awakened.

An hour later he was chilled to the bone and certain he could resist Helen of Troy, or Venus herself if she paraded naked before him.

"Travis," he called from the back passage as he stripped off gloves, coat, and boots. "Start filling the bathtub." He'd already unbuttoned his waist-coat when he burst into the kitchen to discover Travis had company.

Anne lounged in a kitchen chair with her feet up on another. My God, her legs were endless. He'd seen her naked, of course, but at the time he'd been more concerned with keeping her alive than assessing her assets. Clad in his best breeches, those assets were displayed to stunning effect. He might as well have stayed warm and dry because the lust-depressing effect of an hour in the rain vanished in an instant.

She looked up at his entrance with a smile. "My lord, er . . . Marcus."

Then she hiccupped.

"Have you been drinking beer?"

"It's delicious. Wonderful. Why have you been keeping it a secret?" She shook her glorious mane of hair, reddish glints varying the dark brown in the light of the table lamp. "It's very mean of you, Marcus. Cruel of all men to keep it to themselves. I feel as delicious as the beer. Give me some more." She held out her tankard with an all-too-familiar imperious gesture, this one surely genuine if pot-valiant.

"How many have you had?"

"Two. Maybe three. Travis, how many times have you filled this?"

"Twice, madam."

"How could you, Travis?" Marcus accused.

"I am a servant, my lord. When requested, I serve."

"When it suits your purpose."

"If you'll excuse me, sir, my purpose now is to take your clean shirts upstairs."

"Wait . . ." But Travis, the least servile damn servant in the history of the world, turned deaf and disappeared, leaving Marcus alone with a tipsy goddess.

He fetched a glass of water. "Drink this," he ordered.

"I want beer."

"Too bad." Although it might be better to let her drink herself into a stupor and remove the source of temptation. "I'm going to make us some dinner."

Anne watched him with interest as he assembled ingredients. "Can I do anything?"

"Have you ever chopped vegetables?"

"No, but I can try."

"In your present state I'm not trusting you with a knife. You can make pastry."

She listened attentively as he explained the method and started to work butter into flour with her fingers while he sliced up potatoes and carrots to add to the beef stew that had been cooking over a slow fire. "This is fun," she said, sending a cloud of flour into her face and all over the table.

"Careful there. The idea is to keep it in the bowl."

"Tyrant. How did you learn to cook?"

"I picked it up along the way." He didn't want to talk about his father. "My mother showed me how to roll out the pastry for jam tarts when I was no more than a tot."

"You're lucky. My mother died before she could teach me."

Marcus doubted that the lady in question, the daughter of a marquess married to an earl's heir, even knew how. Making tarts was a task for children in cottages, not mansions. Which, now he thought about it, was a pity.

"Am I making jam tarts now?"

"I was thinking of apple dumplings, but maybe we should fill the gap in your education. Raspberry or plum?"

Continuing to crumble the dough, Anne creased her face in grave thought. "I can't decide. Would it be very greedy to have some of each?"

If he needed further convincing that the Miss Brotherton who'd cozened him into ordering an expensive dinner was a sham, this did it. "Certainly not."

"Thank you. Is this ready?"

As he bent over the bowl, her hair tickled his face. "Good enough." He hastily stepped back. "Now add a little water and form the paste into a ball."

She was tentative, adding too little liquid so that the dough kept falling into crumbles. Finally he had to reenter her dangerous proximity to demonstrate and her nearness drove him mad. There was something perversely exciting about recognizing his own scent on her shirt, his soap haunting her skin. To get away from her he lingered in the pantry, taking longer than was needed to locate the rolling pin and tart molds.

She set to work rolling out the dough with more enthusiasm than finesse. The motion made her breasts press their linen covering. Turning aside didn't help. His brain possessed perfect recall: small, beautifully shaped, curved below to send tight pink nipples tilted upward. His mouth watered; he could *feel* the stiff peaks under his tongue.

"How's this?"

To avoid the occasion of temptation he walked around to peer over her shoulder. His breeches were too big on her so the fine doeskin bunched up over her rear. It didn't matter. The firm, surprisingly curvaceous bottom, bared for bathing, flashed across his mind. With a particularly strenuous forward pass of the rolling pin she arched back into his groin. God's breath! He'd led the life of a reprobate, but did he deserve such torment?

"Are you all right?"

"Fine."

"I thought I heard you groan."

"An expression of admiration for your remarkable . . . pastry."

She spun around. "Are you teasing me?"

"I would never."

"Hm. What now?"

"Cut out circles to fit the molds. Careful with that knife." He hovered over her in case she cut herself, but she seemed to have sobered up and he was able to retreat to a safe distance. "Now put a spoonful of jam in each."

She applied the preserve with an exaggerated concentration that made him smile. He saw himself kneeling on a chair in the kitchen at the cottage, doing the same thing under his mother's gentle direction. And he saw Anne taking the mother's role in this kitchen, teaching her children to make jam tarts. That vision was hastily dismissed. For those children would be his too, and it was never going to happen.

"There," she said. "We have four of each kind and one left over. I'm going to try mixing the raspberry and plum."

"I see you are an *artiste de cuisine*."

The tarts were a success, especially the mixed jam one, divided in three as the culmination of the meal.

"The finest pastry I've ever tasted, madam," Travis said. "Now may I take the liberty of suggesting that it is time for you to retire to the drawing room? I lit the fire earlier and it should be warm by now."

"This is hardly a formal meal," Marcus said. "Are you expecting me to linger over my brandy and nuts? I have news for you. We have none."

"I was also going to suggest, my lord, that you accompany Miss Brotherton. I will clear the table and wash the dishes. In due course I will bring a tea tray."

Marcus narrowed his eyes at the unusually helpful valet. He could be trying to impress Anne, or to throw her and Marcus together. If the latter, he ought to resist. During dinner Anne had seemed to grow more beautiful by the minute. Being alone with her was dangerous. And alluring. He let himself be persuaded and resolved to keep his hands to himself.

"It's a lovely room," Anne said once they reached the drawing room.

"Thanks to your hard work." By the subdued light of a pair of candelabra and the blazing log fire, the peeling plasterwork and any shortcomings of housewifery were unnoticeable. Without curtains the tall windows revealed a vista of unrelieved black, with the pounding rain a soothing counterpoint to the warmth and light within. Marcus moved a small table and a pair of chairs over to the hearth. "Let's play cards."

"I won't be much of an opponent."

"What games do you know?"

"I used to play piquet with my grandfather. I'm not very good at it." She eyed him with suspicion. "I won't play for money against you."

"We'll play for love." Damn. He shouldn't have said that.

"Good. Because you'll beat me to flinders."

"I think you may be surprised."

She was right. She wasn't very good and it didn't matter at all. Despite unwise discards and failing to save the right guards, with such spectacular cards the merest novice couldn't fail to win. Not that he played his dismal cards with great skill given the distractions on offer: her slender, unpracticed hands fumbling a little as she sorted her cards; the way she bit her lower lip as she pondered her choices; a funny little sound in her throat when she won a hand.

"I capotted you," she crowed when she brought the rubber to a triumphant conclusion by taking every trick. "I don't think I've ever done that."

"Congratulations."

She looked up sharply. "Did you let me win?"

"No. You did it on your own."

"I hope you don't mind me saying this, but I find it surprising that you have made your living as a gamester. Though perhaps the luck did fall my way."

"My dear Anne, the luck was completely with you, or rather against me. Otherwise you wouldn't have a chance."

"There's no need to boast."

"Let me show you something." He pulled a coin from his pocket. "Heads or tails?"

"Heads."

He tossed the coin and caught it on the back of his hand. "Heads it is," he revealed. "Again."

"Heads."

"Heads it is. Again."

A dozen times she called heads, a dozen times she won. "This is unusual, isn't it?"

"It's against the mathematics of probability. I haven't been able to win at any game since I left Italy. I'm in the middle of the longest, most spectacular run of ill luck a man has ever suffered."

"No wonder you wanted to catch an heiress. You were desperate."

"I wouldn't have to be desperate to pursue you." As he spoke he gathered up the scattered cards. "The Camber fortune," he said with calculated callousness, "is far beyond the possible winnings of the most successful gamester."

"I see." He'd hurt her and it was better that way. "You told me you wanted to give up gaming and find a different profession."

"The truth, just not the whole truth."

The fire crackled and silence fell heavily between them while she scrawled aimlessly on the score sheet. He should send her to bed to dwell on that truth. And he? He would stay downstairs and get as drunk as was possible on nothing but small ale. By God, he wished there was brandy in the house.

When finally she looked up, though, she appeared more alert than upset. "I'm curious," she said, sweeping her glorious hair back with both hands. "Couldn't you cheat? You must know how."

He couldn't blame her for the unflattering assessment of his character. "I decided a long time ago that I would always play straight. My father was a cheat and it got him into constant trouble. I prefer a peaceful life and a whole skin. As they say, honesty is the best policy."

Her brow creased as she digested his statement. "I've always thought that an odd proverb. Surely honesty is a matter of morality, not policy."

"That's easy to say when you've never wanted for anything. I haven't had that luxury. I don't object to cheating, or for that matter lying and stealing, if it suits my aims. And if I won't get caught. It happens that fair play is my choice, my policy. Morality is not an issue." Saying these things made his heart plummet but it was no more than the truth and Anne, at least, he owed honesty.

"I do not believe morality is a luxury of the rich."

"Nor is dishonesty confined to the poor. You haven't been entirely honest in your dealings with me."

"I am truly sorry that I made you spend so much money. I know now that you could not afford it and I see how much you need it for the Hinton estate."

He hated to hear her sounding like a guilty child when her sin had been so slight. "Don't blame yourself. It was no more than I deserved. My point is that no one is ever entirely honest. However, I am probably the greatest scoundrel you've ever met, or ever will."

She stood up and walked around the table. In his clothes she was more desirable than any raving beauty in a fashionable gown designed to entice. That was it, then. Instead of leaving the room at once, she stood over him and he made himself meet her eye, expecting condemnation. As she regarded him gravely, her cheeks grew pink, and her lovely mouth twisted into an odd smile.

"Marcus," she said, so close that her heat and scent teased him. She leaned in, and her breath was warm on his face. "Will you kiss me?"

Anne waited, dizzy with longing as she had been all evening. When he explained his shocking moral code she heard and understood the words, but her body seemed divorced from her brain and was crying out for Marcus. Dismissing his past and any thought of the future, she summoned her courage and demanded what she wanted.

He sat with his feet planted to the floor, folded his arms, and frowned. "Not a good idea, Anne. You don't know what you're doing."

"You told me before, if I wanted a kiss I should ask for one. I'm asking." She dared to reach for him, caressing his cheek with a trembling hand, his chin a little rough beneath her palm.

"Why do you have to remember every little thing I said?" he bit out. "I say some damn stupid things."

She snatched back her hand. "You don't want to kiss me."

"Hell and damnation, Anne! You stand over me in my clothes showing off the longest, loveliest legs ever owned by a woman. Your breasts peep out of my shirt and I can't take my eyes off them because I want to see them and touch them when you're not freezing to death. As for your hair, I want to wind it round my naked chest and discover if it's as soft and silken as it looks. And yes, I want to kiss you. Do you think I'm made of stone?" Her mouth fell open. Never had she heard anything so alarming or so wonderful. "So, my dear, unless you're ready to risk getting a lot more than a simple kiss, you'd better sit down. Better still, get out of the room."

She wavered, poised for flight, then stiffened her resolve. Marcus wasn't lying. This might be her only chance in her whole life to discover what it was like to kiss a man who found her truly desirable.

Her breeches made her brave. "I want to kiss you, Marcus, and that's what I'm going to do."

Giving him no chance to object, she grasped his shoulders and swooped in. She'd only once felt his lips on hers but the sensation was instantly familiar. Heart pounding, she reveled in an experience unlike any other. She closed her eyes and sank into the touch of warm flesh beneath hers, until she realized something was wrong. The awkwardness of pressing her attentions on a man who remained utterly still sapped her confidence. Still she persevered, yearning for shared pleasure, encouraged by an acceleration in his breath. In bold desperation she parted her lips and ventured to dart her tongue out to trace the seam of his mouth.

His response almost made her lose her balance. But he caught her, pulled her down onto his lap. Muttering a profanity, he took possession. The kiss became hot and wet as his breath filled her mouth. The stroke of his tongue induced a blissful humming in the tender flesh within, eliciting a gasp from her, a momentary retreat on his part.

"You asked for it," he muttered, his soft growl tickling her lips. "Last chance to stop."

Refusing the offer of escape, Anne took his head in her hands and pulled him back to her. After that there was no more quarter requested or given on either side.

She wondered hazily how people willingly

gave this up once they'd discovered it. She could become addicted to sharing space and air with a man. She'd thought a kiss was a finite thing but this one had no end. It continued without cessation, growing only deeper and hotter. Accustomed as she was to the cool politesse of her well-guarded life, the raw intimacy threatened to explode her brain. Carnal. The word floated through her mind. An experience of the body, the flesh.

Her thin shirt was no barrier to the heat of his hands caressing her back, her shoulders, the tender privacy of her ribs and belly. Her breasts ached for attention too, and he seemed to know it. An incoherent groan of protest arose from her throat when he traced them through soft linen, just for a moment. Then melted into a purr of happiness as he slipped through the opening at the neck of her shirt and cupped them, skin to skin. She arched into him, wanting more and receiving it.

Still they kissed, his particular taste flooding her senses in accompaniment to the magic of his touch. Then he stopped.

"Don't stop!"

"Hush. You'll like this."

He slipped the leather braces from her shoulders and pulled the loose shirt down, exposing her halfway to the waist. Dazed, she peered down. Surely her nipples weren't usually so pink or so pointed.

"Do you remember me telling you about wild strawberries?"

He was talking about *food*? *Now*?

He drew her backward in the cradle of his arm and took one of the stiff peaks into his mouth, licking and sucking and sending a line of sensation straight down her torso and into the secret area beneath her breeches. As her pelvis gave a little buck he laughed softly. "In a while."

She had lost the power of mobility and the will to reclaim it. She let him do what he would and yearned only for what he'd do next, where he'd take her, wherever that might be. His clever hands seemed to find every sensitive spot of skin: the nape, the shoulder blades, the curve of her waist. Who knew that her navel longed to be touched? He did.

He could do anything to her, anything at all, and she would welcome it. She yearned for it and surrendered joyfully to thralldom.

His mouth took hers again and the kissing was too good to protest, even as her swollen breasts regretted its loss. As his taste flooded her senses and their tongues tangled, a fever arose in her, a desperate, aching heat. His hand slid lower, crept beneath the loose waist of her breeches.

Oh Lord oh Lord oh Lord! He was going to touch her there. He wouldn't, surely, but please God let him. She wanted it. *Needed* it. A small, sane voice in her head told her she was on the road to ruin and a louder shriek said she didn't care. She closed her eyes tight to exclude the murmurings of discretion and envisioned Marcus's long finger penetrating the forbidden place. As wish turned to fact she shrieked, thrust furiously, and tumbled off his lap.

"Ow!"

"Sorry." He sounded strained. "One of the perils of attempting seduction on a plain chair. Given the dilapidated state of this house and its furnishings, we should count ourselves lucky it didn't break."

On hands and knees she looked around the room, eager to continue. "Where would be best?"

"A more capacious chair, bed, a sofa, or a soft carpet on the floor," he said, reaching down and caressing her head through her wild cloud of hair. She nuzzled into his touch.

"The sofa here is quite comfortable," she offered.

Abruptly he withdrew his hand. "No. It's just as well I dropped you before things went any further. Are you hurt?"

"No, I'm not hurt. You want to stop?" she asked incredulously.

"I have to stop. *We* have to stop. I apologize for getting carried away."

She prepared to argue but as the sensual spell faded, she reluctantly admitted he was right.

She shifted to a sitting position on the floor, hugging her bended knees. She wanted him, liked him, was perhaps even in love with him. If she gave herself to him fully she'd have to marry him. An alluring idea, but contrary to inculcated notions of duty to her position and her own common sense. Once she'd considered wedding Marcus, when she only suspected him of being a rogue.

Now she knew he was, and she feared he was irredeemable.

Not wholly irredeemable, surely. He could have had her tonight, probably still could. If he set his mind to it, she doubted she'd resist. Yet he refused to take advantage. She glanced up to find him still seated, gazing down at her, his fine cheekbones flushed, green eyes troubled. Then she noticed something else, visual evidence of the hardness she'd scarcely noticed under her bottom when her senses had been otherwise occupied.

"I think I understand now what Milton meant when he wrote of 'carnal desire inflaming,'" she said.

"I never read him."

"Are you all right?"

"Anne. Please go to bed."

"Where?"

"Take my room. And no, I will not be joining you. I'll find somewhere else to sleep."

She stood up, sad the evening had come to an end. It was the most enjoyable she'd ever spent and one she'd remember when she returned to her proper Brotherton life. "Thank you, Marcus."

"You have nothing to thank me for."

"Yes," she said. "I do. For many things."

"What—" He cut off his question and shook his head. "Good night, Anne."

Chapter 19

They ate breakfast together in the kitchen while Travis labored away at the never-ending laundry.

"Why are you still wearing breeches?" Marcus asked. "Your gown is dry."

Anne swallowed a mouthful of ham and put down her knife and fork. "I like these clothes. They're much easier to move in. I have the rest of my life to wear long skirts. Or perhaps I'll become an eccentric and ride around Camber astride, shocking the neighbors."

She seemed remarkably cheerful this morning. Apparently she hadn't spent the night tossing with thwarted lust. Of course she'd had the bed, while he had reason to know that the comfort of the drawing room sofa was overrated. He finally managed to drift off to sleep, only to be woken by the frigid atmosphere and a strange silence. The fire had died to embers and the rain turned to snow.

"What are we going to do today?"

"You stay here and keep warm while I check on

my tenants and look into the prospects for getting the bridge repaired."

"Is there no other way out of the estate?"

"Two or three miles downstream there's another bridge, which may not have survived the dam burst. There's also a path over the downs, but since Jasper has the gig it'll be a long slog to get back to Hinton that way. We have enough food for a few days so I'm not inclined to try it unless things get desperate."

"That's right. Mr. Bentley came that way. Can I come with you to see your people?"

His people. He'd never had people, but now he supposed he did and he was responsible for them.

"Better not. While we can't hide the fact that you are stranded in my house, let's keep the gossip to a minimum by not having you jaunt around in my company dressed like that. I intend to put it around that you are prostrate with shock from the storm, and from the appalling fact of being forced to remain in my disreputable company."

She grinned. "Tell everyone I'm suffering a prolonged attack of the vapors." She took a healthy bite of toast. "What shall I do while you're gone?"

Marcus played his cards close to his chest, literally and figuratively. Reserve was a necessity of his profession that he carried over to the rest of his life. Contrary to every instinct, he trusted Anne.

"There is something. I've been searching the house."

"I noticed. What for?"

"I don't know. For something that may not even exist."

Anne listened intently as he described his father's letter. "What was in the trunk we found in the attic?"

"Nothing of importance," he said. "I'd dismiss the whole affair as nonsense, except that someone searched the house before I arrived here."

"The ghost," Anne said at once, clever lady.

"I suspected Jasper of playing the ghost to scare away the other servants but I don't see him searching the house so thoroughly. It's more likely that someone else knew what my father left here."

"Who would he have told?"

"I don't know. My father was not given to confidences. Every word he spoke was intended to deceive."

"You're not at all like him."

Marcus searched for sarcasm in the offhand statement and detected sincerity. He decided not to argue with the deluded girl.

Anne fell silent. "He entrusted this thing to Mr. Hooke, you say," she said after prolonged thought.

"Without telling him what it was."

"So it's either disguised, or it has a significance that a stranger wouldn't recognize."

"Which gets us nowhere."

"So let's think of it from Mr. Hooke's point of view. Where would he hide an apparently worthless treasure? Remember the hidden cupboard in the drawing room? Perhaps there are others like that."

"If you would like to devote some time today looking for them, I'd be eternally in your debt."

"It'll give me something to do."

"I'll tell you where I've already looked."

"No, don't. A fresh pair of eyes may see something you missed."

Marcus left the house whistling. Maybe there was something to the notion that a problem shared was a problem halved. He returned in a dark mood. Only the news that she'd stumbled over a cache of pure gold could relieve the gloom induced by the state of his property.

He'd scarcely had time to discard his topcoat and pour himself a reviving midday beer when Anne joined him in the kitchen. "I've been in the attic bedrooms. Goodness, your uncle kept a lot of rubbish." She broke off, tilting her head. "What is it? Bad news?"

"Half the fields on the estate are flooded, and repairing the dam is a major undertaking. Some of the tenants have lost livestock too."

"I'm sorry, Marcus. Perhaps it won't be so bad once the weather improves."

"If it ever does. This is England." He hadn't yearned for Italian sunshine for weeks, but he might as well since it looked like his only option was to sell Hinton for a pittance and leave the country. With his luck and the activities of the French army he'd end up in Russia.

"Are your tenants safe?"

"No one was hurt, but the Burts' roof couldn't handle the torrent and the chimney leaked badly. Even if we repair it, all their coal was soaked, along with much of what they own."

"You should have brought them to the manor."

"I offered, but they have animals to care for and prefer to be at home, doing their best to arrange things before it rains again. Or snows hard. I came home to collect food and coal for them, then I'll go back and help with the roof." He slumped into a chair and ran his hands through his hair. "Oh Lord, Anne. You should have seen them. Trying so hard to keep up their spirits in an uninhabitable house. The other cottages are at least dry, but not otherwise much better."

"They sound like good people, prepared to wait and make the best of things until you can make improvements."

"I don't know what I'm doing. It's a joke that I should even think of running an estate. I'm only used to looking out for myself."

"You took care of me."

He shook off the comfort of her hand on his shoulder. He was being whiny and self-indulgent but somehow, now he'd started to confide in her, he couldn't stop. He had to tell her what was on his mind. "You don't understand. I don't have the means and no prospect of gaining them. Quarter day is coming and I don't see how I can collect even a fraction of the rents with the land unusable. My accounts will be empty."

"I wish I could help. I've never found it so frustrating that I have no control over my own fortune."

"That's not what I asked. I shouldn't burden you with my troubles."

"I know you didn't ask and it's no burden to listen to a friend. Do you remember, once you offered me friendship?"

"I didn't mean it. I was trying to make you fall in love with me."

Only the low hiss of the kettle disturbed an atmosphere that had, in a single second, turned thick and charged with uncertainty. Whatever lay between them wasn't friendship. Or it was, but something more as well. Once again, marriage tantalized him. The arguments against it hadn't altered, but rather grown stronger. For his newly awakened conscience—if that was the source of his bizarre scruples—told him he had nothing to offer. He couldn't even consider wooing her unless he had something to bring to the table.

"Mean it now." She wore her determined look, the one that boded ill for fortune hunters and recalcitrant lumps of antiquity-laden earth. "Be my friend and I shall be yours. And the first thing I'm going to do is come with you to help your people. I found extra blankets and some of your uncle's clothes."

"I thought we'd agreed you should stay here."

"You can't carry everything by yourself, and no, I'm not wearing my gown. Your uncle's topcoat will cover me to the ankles."

Marcus pushed a wheelbarrow over a track whose ruts contained a lethal mixture of water, ice, and slush, while Anne carried the basket of food. The state of the Burts' cottage appalled her. It didn't need much knowledge to see that the structure had been in poor condition before the deluge. Now it had been degraded to a hovel. The principal room, serving as kitchen, dining room, and sitting room, was strewn with the family's meager possessions. Holes in the wooden floor exposed the dirt beneath; a scratched dresser displayed a pathetic collection of battered pots and cracked crockery; such furnishings that could be seen through clothes and blankets spread out to dry were ancient and comfortless. Barely warmer inside than out, the house smelled damp. A rhythmic plop of water leaking from the roof into a bucket completed the depressing picture. Mr. and Mrs. Burt appeared on the edge of desperation.

"This is Miss Brotherton," Marcus announced. "She was trapped by the flood and is staying at the manor."

They looked at her without much interest, too absorbed by their own problems to sniff out a potential scandal. The youngsters, two boys and a girl with dirty faces, shivered in their shabby garments.

"I'm sorry for your troubles," Anne said. "His Lordship has brought food and coal."

"Much obliged, my lord." Mr. Burt tipped his cap and his wife showed signs of animation.

"Let's bring in the things from the barrow," Marcus said, "then we'll take a look at the roof and chimney. Do you think it's safe to light a fire?"

"I reckon it is," Burt replied. "At the top of the ladder I could reach where the flashing had come loose and fixed it back in place. It should hold till I can get up there with cement. The roof's another matter. There's an ice blockage needs to be cleared before we can find the leak."

"We'd better get up there, then." The steep slate roof had glistened with ice as they approached. Climbing on it seemed perilous.

Anne hovered near the door, anxious not to get in the way. "Is there anything I can do to help?" she asked Mrs. Burt as the men and the eldest boy went out.

"Thank you, miss," the woman replied with precarious dignity, "but there's not much to be done till we get the fire going and start getting things dried out. I'm sorry to receive you with the house like this. I can't even offer you a cup of tea." She appeared on the verge of tears.

Wishing she hadn't come, Anne cast about for something to say. Meaningless remarks about the weather were hardly appropriate for this woman beset by the elements. She felt overwhelmed in the face of such distress and genuine need. At Camber the land steward would see to everything. But at Camber things would not have been allowed to decline so. Her tenants would have ridden out the storm, warm and dry. "Thank you, but I don't need anything," she said. "Where shall I put this?" Her hostess's patent inability to make a decision amid the chaos dissolved Anne's hesitation. She placed the heavy basket in a safe corner.

"What's in there?" asked the smallest child, a boy of perhaps five or six years old.

"Hush, Johnny," said his mother. "Don't bother the lady."

"It's no bother. All sorts of good things to eat. Why don't you wait and find out when your mother unpacks it. It'll be a surprise. Perhaps she'll let you help."

"I helped clean the wet coals out of the fire-place," he said.

"That's excellent. What a good boy."

"And I spread the blankets out to dry," boasted his sister.

"Fancy that. What's your name?"

"Anne."

"Good gracious! That's mine too. What a coincidence!"

"Mam!" young Anne called. "Dad!" she added as the male party came in with the coal. "This lady's called Anne too. She says it's a con-si-dence."

"I'm not surprised. All the prettiest girls are named Anne," Marcus said.

Her new young friend would never be a beauty by any standards. The girl raised her eyes warily, both pleased and skeptical. Anne knew exactly how she felt. The Lithgow charm was in full working condition. A tiny shy smile stretched to a huge grin, revealing crooked teeth in her long, sallow face. Marcus turned to Anne and gave her a little wink that disordered her insides.

Full working condition indeed.

"You've done wonders since I called this morning, Mrs. Burt," he said. "We'll have the roof sound in no time."

"Thank you, my lord."

"Don't thank me. Burt's the expert. I'll just hold the hammer and hand him nails."

"We're glad to get help from the manor, Your Lordship."

"Why don't you see to that fire?" Marcus said gently. "He'll be ready for something hot when he's finished."

Simple words, but they dispersed Mrs. Burt's paralysis. "Things are going to be better in the future," she said.

"That's the spirit."

The atmosphere in the room grew warmer, less desperate. Marcus had the ability to set people at ease. Knowing how much he feared for the future of the estate, he couldn't be as cheerful as he sounded, but in this case deception was a virtue. The concern and reassurance on his handsome face made the Burts feel better. In Anne it provoked a warmer reaction. Gazing at Marcus made her dwell on kissing again, not suitable thoughts when calling on a family in distress. She dragged away her gaze and imitated his bracing tone. "You must be proud to have such helpful children, Mrs. Burt," she said.

"They're good little ones. Having them in the house for two days of rain has been hard, and I can't send them out to play because they'll catch their deaths in damp clothes. They're used to running around all day and they're getting fidgety."

"If you don't mind, I'll move these blankets from the settle. Anne and Johnny can sit down out of your way. I'll find something to entertain them."

The harassed mother accepted gratefully and commenced the tricky business of starting a fire with very little dry kindling. The men went outside, and indoor activities became punctuated by sounds of banging on the roof. Anne wrapped each of the small children in a dry blanket from the Hinton attic. They sat on either side of her, fixing her with huge, expectant eyes.

She had no idea how to entertain children.

She cleared her throat. "How old are you?"

"Five."

"Seven."

What now? She needed a question that couldn't be answered in monosyllables. Should she inquire about their schooling, or would it shame their mother if they had none?

"Do you like cats?" young Anne asked, apparently possessed of better social instincts than the heiress of Camber.

"I do. My cousin Caro has a cat named Tish. He's yellow."

"Ours is called Blackie."

"He's black," added Johnny.

"In that case, he has a very good name. I should be honored to make his acquaintance."

The little girl giggled. "He's gone hunting."

So much for that promising line of conversation.

"Why are you wearing breeches?" the boy asked. "Aren't you a lady?"

The front of her coat had fallen open, revealing her knees. Too late now. "My gown was wet."

"Were you out in the storm?"

"Not just out. I was trapped in a big hole in the ground until Lord Lithgow found me."

The children nodded, unsurprised that His Superb Lordship had come to the rescue. "He's

the bravest man in the world except my dad,"
Johnny said.

"Are you the lady who's been digging?" the girl
asked. "Dad says Mr. Hooke used to do it a long
time ago. It's a house from the olden days."

"A villa, built by the Romans nearly two thousand years ago. A Roman house is called a villa."

"Tell us a story about these Romans," Johnny
begged.

"Well, I don't know anything about the specific
people who lived here. We can only find clues
about how they lived by finding things that were
buried when they left."

"Treasures? Are they made of gold?" His eyes
gleamed.

"I haven't found anything like that. Mostly
broken bits of pots and metal." And the occasional
belt buckle.

Little Anne was unimpressed. "It sounds dull."

Wracking her brain for a tale with a bit more
dramatic potential, Anne came up with the tale
of Horatius, who saved Rome from the advancing
Etruscans by holding the bridge over the Tiber
while the outnumbered Roman army escaped. It
was a big success. Apart from dodging impossible
questions about weaponry from Johnny, she managed to hold them enthralled. "And then," she
concluded, "once they'd torn down the bridge so
the Etruscans couldn't cross, Horatius jumped in
the river and swam home."

"Why couldn't the 'Truscans jump in the river
and swim across too?" Her namesake might not
be pretty but she was sharp.

"That's a very good question, Anne. It was because their armor was too heavy."

"Didn't Horatius have armor too?"

She'd wondered the same thing herself. An explanation of how historical accounts differed as to whether Horatius survived the river would, she felt, spoil the story.

Little Johnny had the answer. "Horatius was stronger than all the 'Truscans," he said scornfully. "Otherwise he wouldn't have been able to fight so many. 'Course he could swim wearing armor."

Apparently it took the male mind to appreciate a good war story.

A huge crash outside and a shouted oath made her leap up, heart in her mouth. Marcus! He wasn't used to this kind of work. Supposing he'd fallen off the slippery roof and broken a bone? Or worse? She reached the door just ahead of Mrs. Burt and both women burst out, regardless of the chill.

Anne thrust aside the other woman and fell to her knees beside Marcus, who lay flat on his back with his eyes closed, horribly still. "Oh God." Her eyes blurred and her hand shook as she stroked his forehead. "Marcus, wake up!"

He opened his eyes, and something inside her that had sunk to the pit of her stomach rushed upward to her heart.

"Are you injured? Where?"

"Only my pride. What a damn fool thing to do, falling off the ladder. Knocked poor Joe down too. I've had a nice little rest and now I must get back to work."

The elder Burt boy was also on the ground, being fussed over by his mother. Mr. Burt peered anxiously from his perch on the roof. "Are you all right, my lord? My fault. My foot slipped and knocked the top of the ladder."

Marcus clambered gingerly to his feet. "No harm done, except a slight pain in a place I'd better not mention. How are you, Joe?"

The boy was fine too. The alarm over, the women went back inside, delivering dire injunctions to the roofing party to be more careful. "I don't like this, miss," Mrs. Burt said. "I was that worried that Burt or Joe was hurt. And His Lordship too."

Anne felt a little guilty that she hadn't given much thought to the possible injury of Burt or his son. What would happen to this family if the father was killed, or even seriously injured? How would they survive? Seeing Marcus stretched out was the most terrifying sight in all her experience. Supposing he'd died?

Johnny tugged at her sleeve. "Tell us more about the Romans, miss."

A couple of stories later Anne had little voice left and fewer ideas. The men returned and pronounced the roof airtight. Hungry eyes surveyed the food basket. It was time to leave the Burts to their own devices.

She clutched Marcus's arm as they stumbled home in the fading twilight, relishing his warm *living* body.

"I feel small in the face of such hardship," she said.

"Don't. Mrs. Burt was grateful to you for distracting the children. You have a talent for it."

She'd enjoyed the youngsters, she realized. They were much easier to amuse than adults. When she thought of motherhood at all, it was in terms of duty, the provision of another heir, preferably male, for her heritage. Marcus would be a good father. The direction of her thoughts scared and thrilled her.

"At least you were doing something practical," she said.

"It's my responsibility. I don't imagine any of your tenants live like that."

"The Camber lands have always been well managed. You inherited a neglected estate and you're doing your best. And you did not order the weather."

She sensed his muscles stiffen and the chasm widen between them. He must surely resent her abundant fortune when he had so little, especially now she knew how poor his options were.

"You know," she said, tightening her grip on his arm lest he slip away. "I have no control over my estates. Nothing can be done without the consent of Morrissey and the other trustees. Did you know that I cannot wed without their permission?"

"You are almost of age."

"In February, but it doesn't matter. If I marry with Morrissey's approval my husband will take over. If not, the trustees remain in charge."

"I'm not surprised. Heiresses to great fortunes are usually well protected."

It was too dark to see his face, not that his expression would tell her anything. From his curt tone of voice she guessed he'd favor her with that bland look that disguised every thought and emotion. She opened her mouth to ask this rogue, this fortune hunter, what he meant by pursuing her if he knew it might get him nothing. He might tell her he didn't care for her fortune, that he wanted her without it. If he said that she would surely die of joy because she was in love with him. She loved Marcus Lithgow.

She didn't ask the question because she knew he'd tell her the truth and if it wasn't the right answer she couldn't bear it. She preferred to revel in a state of hopeful ignorance, at least for a while.

Chapter 20

Another evening of tea in the drawing room. It would have been wiser for him to send Anne to bed after dinner and to go for a long walk or take a cold bath. His resistance was low.

They took their places in front of the fire in a silence fraught with unspoken thoughts and repressed desires. She hooked one calf over her knee in a masculine pose that displayed the long limbs and slender thighs and drew attention to the buttoned fall of the breeches. The area looked wrong on a woman, without male equipment to disturb the line. The line of his own breeches was becoming more disturbed by the second.

She regarded him with a less guarded expression than he'd ever seen her wear, as though something had shifted in her view of him. He still couldn't read her face with any certainty, but he both yearned to know and dreaded what her new softness might mean.

"Do you play chess?" she asked. Perhaps she also sought a distraction.

"Are you already tired of destroying me at cards?"

"There's no luck in chess. We'd be equals."

Her care for his self-esteem touched him. "It's not my best game. I've never studied it because there's little money in it. But the principle of seeing several moves in advance is similar to a number of card games."

She went over to the tallboy between the windows. "You'll probably beat me then. There's a set in the bottom drawer." Her kneeling to retrieve it gave him a splendid view of her bottom beneath its soft leather covering. He doubted he was going to be much good at looking ahead tonight. On the chessboard, that was. He gritted his teeth and lined up the pieces. Damn it, why did she insist on helping? Her hands brushed against his and contact wasn't a good idea.

Happily, his competitive instincts kicked in. Even severe unresolved lust wasn't enough to spoil his ingrained habit of playing to win. Or so he thought, until she played him into a corner and forced him to resign in a couple of dozen moves.

"Has your brain gone the way of your luck?" she asked sweetly. "That was too easy."

That was a terrible thought. "Line them up."

He kept his eyes off his opponent and his mind on the board, the only sounds the clock ticking and the hissing coals punctuated by the thud of chessmen moved from square to square.

"Check."

He brought in a bishop to foil the attack. "Check," he said a few moves later, forcing her to sacrifice a rook. A hard-fought game eventually ended in a draw.

"You held back on me, Anne. You're an excellent player. At least as good as I." She looked happily smug. "Your grandfather made a better job of teaching you the game than he did piquet."

"Grandfather didn't play. Felix taught me. He studied the game."

The image of her intended husband as a callow idiot wavered. "I never got the impression he was an intellectual sort."

"Felix was very clever. He was brilliant at Cambridge and always said he'd like to have been a scholar or a barrister if he hadn't been heir to the earldom."

Marcus didn't like it. He didn't like it one bit. "But he never kissed you."

"No, such a shame. I think you should kiss me now to make up for it."

"Are you managing me, Anne Brotherton?"

Her eyes widened with utterly false innocence. "Don't you want to kiss me?"

"Want has nothing to do with it," he ground out.

"Please, Marcus."

He was only so strong. Reaching across the table, sending chessmen flying, he snatched her onto his lap and seized her lips. There was neither finesse nor restraint on either side, merely a crazed mutual union of tongues and teeth and saliva. She gave as good as she got, and any doubts he'd harbored that Anne Brotherton was a passionate woman were dispelled forever. Digging her fingers into his skull she demanded ever more, emitting little groans of pleasure that had his cock swelling to the point of pain. His head buzzed and he knew he was losing control. This couldn't go on, so, once again, he put her aside, inelegantly pushing her to her feet.

"Why?" She was panting.

"Sit down."

She responded to his sharp command and retreated behind the table. He took a deep breath.

"Do you know what happens between a man and a woman?"

"Of course. Caro told me."

"And did she explain what happens to a man when he's inflamed?"

"With carnal desire, you mean."

"Exactly. There comes a certain point when he no longer has the slightest inclination to control himself, and I'm perilously close. My cock is *painfully* inflamed so unless you intend for me to relieve you of your virginity you should keep your distance." This was plain speaking but he wasn't up to euphemism. If his crudeness scared her away, so much the better. Indeed, her eyes widened in shock, then she pursed her lips and wriggled in her seat. "Keep still. You're not helping."

"I think I might be a bit inflamed myself."

He hadn't thought himself capable of mirth in his present state of agony but that made him smile. Damn, she was sweet. And desirable beyond measure. "Tell me about Felix and his brilliant academic career." That should kill his cockstand stone dead.

"I'd rather talk about you. Tell me about your education. You know Latin and Greek. Where did you go to school?"

An account of his checkered academic history ought to kill her desire too. "When I was eleven I entered Mr. Pinkley's Academy. Until then, my education had been . . . intermittent. Every now and then my father would hire a tutor, most likely pretending to be a responsible father in order to impress a lady he was trying to cheat."

"But he sent you to school in the end?"

"He left the country and Mr. Hooke—Uncle Josiah—enrolled me."

"What was it like?"

"A small and very strict establishment filled with very unpleasant boys." So they'd seemed—and acted—but from the perspective of adulthood they'd done no worse than defend their territory from an outsider. "I started by teaching them various games of chance, which they enjoyed until I relieved them of their pocket money. Then they tried to fight me, but I learned self-defense in a hard school and not even a boy twice my size gave me much trouble. Once they discovered they couldn't bully me, they left me alone."

"Did you have any friends?"

"Not one. They called me the foreigner and avoided my company."

"How horrid."

"It was for the best," he said, twisting his mouth. "I had nothing to do but study and it turned out I was good at it. Any semblance of a classical education I retain I owe to Mr. Pinkley and his pupils."

"Then you went to Oxford."

"I even won a scholarship. I lasted there less than a year."

"Oh, I know what happened next. Caro told me the story often. The four of you were sent down for breaking into the Bodleian Library."

"Who knew that we were violating a sacred oath? I thought it was a prank."

"Whose idea was it?"

"Robert's, of course. He was always the leader. That was the end of my formal education. We all took off for Paris together, saw the fall of the Bastille and the Revolution in action. The others came home but I've spent most of the ensuing years abroad, living on my wits and my skills as a gamester."

"I cannot imagine living anywhere but England. My French is terrible."

"Sweetheart, Europe is full of countries. They don't all speak French."

"How many languages can you speak?"

"I can get by in French, German, Italian, and Spanish. I know enough Russian, Polish, and Portuguese to play cards, order dinner, and make love."

"Have you made love to a lot of women?"

"Hundreds." He exaggerated. Although he was hardly a model of purity, he'd been too busy for prolonged affairs.

"It must be hard to know so many languages. Don't you get muddled?"

"I have a facility. I had trouble learning Swedish so left after three weeks." He didn't add that he'd run afoul of a nobleman whose wife he'd relieved of her virtue and a large sum of money. There was a limit to how much he could bear to blacken his character in Anne's eyes.

"Do you miss your life? Do you long to be on your travels again?"

He shook his head slowly as he realized the question was moot. It appeared increasingly unlikely that he could keep the estate, so Europe it would be, and he'd better pray his luck turned or he'd die of starvation. "I expect I'll be in Italy by spring. Or maybe Portugal. Very hospitable people, the Portuguese."

"I think it's a shame," Anne said, "that you met Robert Townsend. If you'd stayed at Oxford you would have done great things."

He tasted the notion with a sinking heart. It was an article of faith that his friendships at Oxford had been the best things that ever happened to him. "Robert was my best friend."

"That's as may be," she replied. "I know we're not supposed to speak ill of the dead but from what Caro told me, and now you, he was nothing but trouble."

"My uncle disowned me after Oxford," he said softly, speaking mostly to himself.

"Yet he left you Hinton."

He imagined living at Hinton, leading a useful life as a landlord, improving the estate. He envisioned a wife and children. This wife and their children. His own family. A pain in his heart made him wonder if he was dying.

"Yes. He gave me another chance. Too bad there isn't a chance in hell I can make it good."

Travis insisted on giving up his room next to Marcus's, and Anne insisted Marcus take his own. She huddled under the blankets and thought about Marcus in his large bed, just the other side of the wall. Without recalling everything about the night of her rescue, she retained an impression of his body enclosing hers, keeping her warm and safe. Her flesh shivered at the memory, but not with cold. She wore another of his shirts to bed. She now recognized the aching feeling below her belly. She wanted his hands on her skin, not his linen.

After half an hour or so, she left her bed and the room and opened the door to his, driven by wishes that overcame doubt and reason. Was she foolish to offer herself to him? Probably. Rejecting every precept of her upbringing, she surged forward to take what she wanted. Darkness, leavened only by the glow from the fireplace, lent her courage. She tiptoed up to the shadowy mound of bedclothes, assessing his breathing. Unaccustomed to sharing a room, she couldn't be sure if he was asleep. Closing her eyes, she lingered for a moment, not from fear but to enjoy the intimacy of sharing this little dark corner of the world with the man she loved, and the anticipation of uncharted joys.

As she slid under the covers his heat welcomed

her and his scent enveloped her senses. She reached for him, tentatively exploring the firm contours of his arm and shoulder, the texture of skin beneath the scanty hair on his chest. Desire pooled below.

His muscles tensed under her fingers. "Anne?" He wasn't asleep now.

"Were you expecting someone else?" she asked with a nervous laugh.

"I wasn't expecting anyone. Were you cold in your room?"

"Perhaps."

"If you came in because you were cold, I am sorry," he said, as though suffering strangulation, "but you'll have to leave."

"What if I wasn't cold?"

"Then you have precisely five seconds to change your mind or it'll be too late. Think about it."

She let her heart and her body do the thinking. "One . . . two . . . three . . . four . . . five," she counted. "Too late. I wasn't cold. I want you, Marcus." There, she'd said it.

He muttered something that sounded like an oath, a whisper of resignation as though tried beyond all bearing. A final stab of uncertainty melted into relief when he rolled over and gathered her in, so they lay on their sides, face to face. Thank God. She'd been waiting for this, wanting this, forever. It was like being home in a strange place, setting out on the most thrilling adventure without a single qualm.

"Anne." He drew out the syllable so that her plain name became a lyric of a beautiful song. His hands stroked her head. "My Anne." The use of the possessive thrilled her to the core. Then he took her mouth in a deep kiss that lasted an age. Nothing had ever been so delicious or so right. With every nerve and instinct she owned she knew she was in the right place doing the right thing. The universe shrank to two joined mouths.

Just as she began to want more, he read her mind. His hands—how she loved his hands—pushed up her shirt, caressed her ribs, and found the breasts that longed for him. She arched forward, demanding more, and meeting the hard evidence of his desire.

How he managed to remove her garment she couldn't be sure. They must have stopped kissing but the separation was mercifully brief and within seconds they were skin to skin between the sheets, a tangle of linen and hands seeking each other's touch. Being under cover in the pitch dark dispelled any inhibitions. She discovered how different and how wonderful the male body was, hard and a little rough. She traced the central ridge of his back, pressed the ticklish center of her palms against his hips and around to the taut hills of his buttocks.

Her breasts felt huge under his fingers and her nipples glowed like burning candle flames when he pinched them, not enough to hurt, merely sending sharp spirals shooting down her torso.

He picked up on her pleasure. "You like that? You'll like this more." It was even better this time. Who would have thought the graze of teeth would feel so good?

Her eyes shut tight and she floated in a starry sky, lost to terra firma. Her head fell back, and her body, so she lay supine with her legs parted in mindless invitation.

His hand covered the entrance to her sex. It was too much and not nearly enough. She'd never known anything better or felt such urgency for something more. She was filled with joy and maddeningly empty.

More. Whether she said it aloud or not, Marcus understood. Clever fingers soothed the slippery cradle and it felt right, not embarrassing, for him to penetrate the most private part of her body. He found the little knob of flesh that she'd occasionally shamefully explored. Finally she was certain of its purpose. His male member, grown hard and hot, knocked against her thigh.

"Aren't you going to . . . ?" Eager for his ultimate possession, she hadn't the words to complete the question.

"Hush," he murmured against her breast. "You'll enjoy it more this way."

A languorous lick of her nipple calmed her and she sank back trustfully, letting him lead the way with a rhythmic stroke that concentrated all her nerves, her entire existence, into one little spot until she felt herself let go and her limbs collapsed into a lyrical, boneless state of total relaxation.

"Goodness," she said when she emerged from her ecstatic haze. His arms were about her, one leg entwined with hers, his lips on her temple.

"That was beautiful," he said, and took her mouth in a shallow, tender kiss, a long mingling of breaths. "You're beautiful. I'll try not to hurt you too much."

"Will it hurt?" She found it hard to believe and wanted desperately to find out.

"Only the first time, so I'm told."

"I don't mind. I want to belong to you. I love you." She'd never have dared say it in the light.

His breath caught sharply. She was glad she couldn't see his face, in case it showed discomfort, or worse still cold triumph that he'd finally conquered her. She relished her submission, her final surrender. Later she might regret it but now she wished to make him happy, even if only by the selfless giving of her body to his pleasure. It was a novel idea and one that stirred a new excitement in her.

"Please, Marcus. Take me."

It did hurt a little. Not a sharp pain so much as a relentless stretching of her never breached passage, followed by a glow of satisfaction as he slid all the way in.

"All right?" he asked.

"Perfect."

"Liar," he said with a little laugh, and started to move.

The sensation was too odd to take her out of herself again. Instead she concentrated on him and his reactions: the bunching of muscles beneath her hands, the quickening of his breath, the increasing pace of his thrusts. When instinct told her to wind her legs around him she felt the connection deepen. Raising herself to meet his forward drives drew growls of approval. His obvious satisfaction when she clenched her inner muscles more than made up for her own lingering discomfort, which gradually faded, leaving only a lovely intimacy. "I love you," she told him again, and was rewarded with an unruly kiss. That he was carefree, uncontrolled, lost in his own gratification, brought her fierce satisfaction. When he sped up and raised his head for an incoherent shout, nothing had ever brought her greater joy. She felt a warm gush inside her, the loosening of tension, and a delicious weight as she sensed him drift to earth and lay his head on her breast.

Wide-eyed in the darkness, she stroked his hair, heard his breathing calm, sensed his chest rising and falling against her skin and his perspiration cooling in the chilly air. She drew up the disordered blankets and tucked them over his shoulders. She would swear he was smiling.

Chapter 21

Marcus smiled into Anne's collarbone, her skin silk beneath his cheek. He wished he could stay silent and replete, entwined with her like a pair of wintering creatures, forgetting the world outside. But he'd done what he swore he would not and the piper needed to be paid. It would be easier for him if he were the one who would be doing the paying.

Reluctantly he withdrew from his happy berth, sliding onto his side and keeping Anne soft and warm in his arms. She'd told him she loved him. Twice. It made him feel ten feet tall and the world's worst villain. And painfully, ludicrously hopeful.

"Anne," he said, loving the sound of her name, drawing out the syllable to a semibreve. "How do you feel?" He'd tried to be considerate, introduce her to love the way a virgin required, not that he had any experience in the matter, unless he counted his own initiation at the hands of an Oxford barmaid. That had not been gentle, though he'd enjoyed it in a terrified kind of way.

"Wonderful. You're wonderful." Her unshadowed trust made his heart thud. It would be so easy just to declare love and leave it at that. It wouldn't be an utter lie but neither would it be the whole story. He owed her the truth.

"No, Anne, I am not. I'm a villain to have taken you like this."

"I think it was my idea."

"I should have resisted you."

"You find me irresistible?" She sounded adorably pleased with herself.

"Completely. I can refuse you nothing."

"How powerful I am. I wonder what I should ask for."

He procrastinated by finding a breast and conjuring up the vision communicated by his slow, questing hand. He couldn't wait to see her in the light. "You like that, don't you?"

"Yes."

"And this?" He'd noticed that her rib cage was particularly susceptible.

"Oh . . . yes."

He kept his strokes long and languorous, intended to soothe rather than arouse. She stretched like a cat in the sun, her breath deepening as unconsciousness approached. Dropping a shallow kiss on her lips, he found them smiling as she drifted into sleep.

He shouldn't have waited. An offer of marriage was essential, he was quite clear about that. Even an unprincipled adventurer knew that one did not bed a virgin without offering to do the right thing. Except in his case it was the wrong thing.

He still believed—knew—that she was better off without him.

Better off? Without him she was the wealthiest woman in England; with him she had nothing. Perhaps she would be wise enough to turn him down. She said she loved him, but it wasn't as though love and marriage always went together. She could enjoy a romantic interlude with a rogue, then return to her real life and marry some idiot like Lord Algernon Tiverton. The thought was extraordinarily painful.

Yet when he eased out of a dreamless state, a surge of optimism made him light of limb and heart. After a long drought he'd satisfied his desires, and something more. The reason for what felt perilously like happiness stretched out in an abandoned sleep, her breath tickling his chest. He stroked her head, fingering the lustrous hair. She pressed into his touch with an incoherent murmur but didn't awake. Apparently no longer able to sleep late, he reluctantly ignored the throb of morning lust. She must be sore and needed her rest. He dropped a kiss on her forehead and slid to the floor.

He cracked open the curtains so that he could relish the sight of Anne in his bed, her pale face in lovely repose amid masses of dark hair. His chest tightened and an involuntary smile tugged at his lips. How rare not to be using them to coax, cozen, or deceive. Before restraint melted he turned to the window to find chill sunlight gleaming on the icy fields beyond the unkempt garden. He threw on some clothes without the help of Travis. Not that he had ever needed a valet, but Travis was meticulous about presenting himself for service. Marcus suspected the man had already been there and tactfully withdrawn. Without dispelling his good mood, the fact brought him down to earth. Shoals lay ahead, especially for Anne.

He'd never cared much for the strictures of polite society, one of the advantages of living outside it. She'd blithely claimed not to mind being "ruined," but it took a certain fortitude not to care what people thought of one. She wasn't used to it. While she claimed indifference to the position her birth brought her, if she agreed to marry him the scorn of aristocratic ladies, not to mention the wrath of her guardian and the loss of her fortune, would be harder to bear than she thought.

If she accepted him, selling Hinton for what he could get and resuming his wandering was no longer in the cards. He had to turn the estate around, and his best hope was to find whatever it was that his ghostly intruder was seeking, whether it came from his father or not.

In the kitchen he found the enticing scent of fresh bread and Travis, in conversation with Mrs. Burt.

"Good morning, my lord," she said. "Thought I'd better come and milk the cow."

"Thank you." It hadn't occurred to him, though he'd checked on the small farmyard since the storm, making sure the livestock had food. "Was it—er—she all right?"

"After three days without milking she should have been glad to see me but she didn't show it. Tried to knock over the pail."

"I'm happy she didn't. We need milk. And do I see you've brought bread?" He bent over the large round loaf on the table and inhaled. "Still warm! You are a true heroine."

Mrs. Burt looked much less harassed than she had the previous day. "It was no trouble to make extra. Burt and I reckoned you'd be tired of stale and we weren't sure if your man was a baker."

"Not as far as I know. Do you know how to make bread, Travis?"

"It has never been one of my duties, my lord."

"How's the roof holding up, Mrs. Burt?"

"Very well, thanks to you, my lord. And I've almost got the house back in order. If it would suit, I'd be glad to come and work up at the manor for an hour or two a day. My sister's two girls in the next village are looking for places. I'll take the liberty of mentioning it in case you were looking for maids."

It was good news that the local embargo on employment at Hinton was about to be lifted. Servants required wages but maidservants didn't make much. "By all means. Send them up to see me as soon as the bridge is repaired."

"Burt said to tell you he'll take the horse around the long way to the village later today and I'm to tell him anything you'll need."

"I'll make a list, but most important is timber and labor for the bridge. Do you suppose the other tenants would help?"

"They'll be wanting to get out too."

"Has this happened before, the estate being cut off by the river?"

"Burt's grandfather heard of a time, in the time of old King Charles." Country memories were long. "Squire's lady drowned when her horse went through rotten planks. Horse was killed too."

"It looked as though it hadn't been replaced since then. My uncle was guilty of negligence."

Mrs. Burt was too respectful to agree. "Mr. Hooke got a little funny. Didn't like anyone telling him his business, and he didn't care to tell them either. Very closemouthed gentleman. Kept his secrets."

"Secrets, eh?" He betrayed nothing but idle curiosity. "What kind of secrets? A skeleton in the cellar? Or buried treasure perhaps."

"Only *treasure* round these parts was that Roman rubbish."

"I understood he gave that up some years back and the place was left to molder until Miss Brotherton resumed the excavation."

"A few times I saw him up on the hill and thought he might be starting that tomfoolery again."

Marcus tucked away the thought for further examination. The Roman villa offered plenty of hiding places.

He walked down to the river, which remained in spate. In his judgment, not that he knew anything about the matter, it would still be a day or two before work could commence on a new crossing. A stone bridge that would withstand the elements would be more practical. And costly. Calls on his other tenants confirmed their willingness to help, also their willingness to suggest a variety of expensive improvements to their land and dwellings.

He came home by way of the villa, on the chance he'd see something. For the first time he appreciated the size of the site. He paced out the main building and guessed it to be about eighty feet wide and forty deep. In addition there was a smaller attached building, which Anne called the kitchen, and the partially uncovered second villa that might well be twice the size. Completing the search could take months, even if it wasn't winter and he wasn't hampered by the finicky digging methods of his bride-to-be. There'd be hell to pay if he tore in with a team of laborers wielding shovels.

He peered into Anne's recent prison, keeping his distance from the crumbling edge. There wasn't much to be seen except a layer of ice, encasing anything that might be on the floor. Once the thaw set in he'd take another look.

Glancing back, he spotted a man in the middle distance, walking briskly toward the downs. One of the tenants, perhaps, but something in his garments and stance suggested a gentleman. Marcus had a feeling he knew him, though, Bufton aside, he'd met none of the local gentry. Strange that. Could be that fellow Anne had mentioned. A curiosity about the mysterious Mr. Bentley stirred in his gut.

"**A**re you awake? I've brought you breakfast."

Anne undulated back into the pillows and blushed. In fact she felt pink all over and exceedingly well. The sight of Marcus, framed by the open curtains, made her smile inside. This was much better than being brought her morning chocolate by Maldon.

"Good morning, my lord."

"Strictly you should say good afternoon. It's a little past midday."

"No wonder I'm hungry."

"I bring fresh bread and butter, courtesy of Mrs. Burt. And Travis has contributed a nice cup of tea, his words not mine."

Beneath his cheerfulness she saw wariness. She'd come to his bed last night without any commitment on his part, or mention of marriage. He knew that wedding her did not necessarily bring wealth. Her heart told her, contrary to her experience and his own testimony, that Marcus was a gentleman. Her brain half expected him to bolt. A nasty weight in the pit of her stomach was listening to her head.

He'd moved a small table next to the bed to hold the tray. He'd used the best china, a pretty blue and white Chelsea service kept in a pantry cabinet. A spray of dried honesty in a blue vase completed the appealing arrangement.

"Pretty," she said, touching the translucent ivory disks.

"I would have brought you roses, but Hinton unaccountably lacks a hothouse. This is the best

I could find in my poor excuse for a garden." He lifted her chin and dropped a light kiss on her lips.

She nestled her cheek into his palm. "Your hands are cold."

"That's because I've been out and about this morning, visiting tenants, checking on Frederick, picking dead flowers. I even almost milked a cow."

"Almost?"

"Luckily Mrs. Burt got to her first. I'm afraid cold hands are a hazard of life as a farmer. Could you get used to it?"

"Will I have to learn to milk cows?" she asked, tamping down a rising exhilaration.

"If you marry me, I promise not to make you."

"Is that a proposal?"

"Will you do me the honor of accepting my hand in marriage?"

How sweet of him to observe the formalities. "I am honored by your offer and yes, Marcus, I would be proud to be your wife." Spoiling the solemnity of the moment, she shoved back the blankets, just managing not to knock over any china, and flung her arms about his neck. His arms came about her but the embrace was perfunctory and all too brief.

This was not how it was supposed to go. Felix's formal offer, long awaited, had been unexciting but comfortable. She had expected the same— with less comfort—from whichever suitable man Morrissey chose for her. But from a highly unsuitable man with whom she was madly in love, she would have liked more . . . rapture. To be enfolded, passionately kissed, seduced. To hear words of love.

Instead he handed her a cup of tea.

"Drink it while it's hot," he said. Then he cut buttered bread into tidy strips and handed them to her one by one, as though she was a small child and he her nurse.

"I'm surprised you're not dipping it in milk," she said peevishly.

"Would you like that?"

"No I would not. I am neither a child nor an invalid and I do not need to be fed pap."

"Two days ago you nearly died."

"And yesterday I strode around in breeches. Clearly I have recovered." She gave him what she was fairly sure was a seductive smile. "And if you're in any further doubt about the state of my health, may I remind you that last night I did not behave like a child and you didn't treat me like one."

The smile wasn't working. "No. I owe you an apology. I am sorry for it." He sounded strained and not at all seduced.

"I am not. It's true that it's not quite proper to do *that* before we are wed but no one need know. And now we are betrothed so what does it matter?"

Tossing a finger of bread onto the plate, he stood up. "We shouldn't be betrothed," he burst out. "I shouldn't have offered and you shouldn't have accepted me. Luckily it's not too late to draw back. As you say, no one will know." Standing by the fire, he gesticulated wildly. "As far as the world knows you were trapped here by the flood. Your reputation will be a little tarnished, but so great an heiress will always be forgiven. You told me yourself." She'd never heard Marcus speak so desperately, with so little calculation. He wanted her to withdraw her acceptance and make their engagement the shortest on record.

She sank back against her pillows, searching for warmth.

"You're cold," he said. Crossing the room, he found a quilted cotton banyan and placed it around her shoulders in a caring gesture that failed to comfort.

She shrank away from him. "I understand. You only offered for me because you are a gentleman. Now you want me to withdraw, also because you are a gentleman and cannot do so yourself."

"I don't know what it will take to convince you that I am no gentleman."

She blinked back tears and struggled to remain composed. Last night she'd flung herself at him, both her body and her affections. If this was the end of it she would retain her dignity. Never mind that she wanted to howl because Marcus didn't want her without her fortune and if he didn't, no man would.

Sitting up straight and folding her hands on her lap, she prepared her speech. "If you don't wish to marry me, I withdraw my acceptance. Let me assure you that I have no desire to wed a man who doesn't truly want me. It would have been kinder not to mention the subject at all. You let me make a fool of myself."

She would not cry.

Marcus wanted to tear his hair out. Despite her disheveled presence in his bed, Anne appeared like the prim, collected young lady he'd first met. Only a telltale dampness in the corners of her eyes betrayed how much he'd upset her. Of course she was upset! He'd made a thorough muck of the encounter. He allowed himself to touch her rigidly clasped hands.

"My darling—" The endearment slipped out unawares. "If you marry me you'll lose everything. How can I ask you to give up so much? Your guardian will never accept me as a suitable match for you."

"No, he probably won't and I don't care. But perhaps you do. From what you said earlier I gathered you knew about the situation. If you won't take me without my fortune I understand."

Her desperate bravado twisted his gut. "With or without your wealth, any man would be lucky to win you. And I especially. Because for what it's worth I care for you. Very much."

"Then I don't see the difficulty." Her voice wavered. "Do you think you could kiss me again? You make me so happy."

This was not a request he had the strength to deny. He climbed up beside her and gathered her in, slender in his arms with a fragility that belied her inner strength. She was tough and clever, Miss Anne Brotherton, soon to be Lady Lithgow if she didn't come to her senses. And so very sweet. That he had apparently won the love and hand of such a woman made his head reel.

I love you, Anne. But he wouldn't say it aloud because he didn't trust that it was true. What did he know of love? *I love you.* He tasted the words that he knew she wished to hear, but above all he owed her honesty.

The unspoken words melted into their shared breath as though there were no boundaries between feelings and deeds. Through a long kiss he let himself pretend everything would be fine. That this was the first in a lifetime of shared embraces between avowed lovers. That they set out on a long life together. That she was his very own.

But self-deception was a luxury he'd never been able to afford. He broke away, allowing himself only the pleasure of an arm about her shoulders, his fingers lightly caressing the joint beneath his draped banyan.

"Because I care for you," he said, resuming his argument as though the romantic interlude hadn't happened, "how can I ask you to give up one of England's greatest fortunes?"

Her arms encircled his torso and held him tight. "I hate my fortune. It has nothing to do with me and brings me no pleasure," she said with rising ferocity. "I don't want to be tied to the duty of my estate. I reject it. I want to live with you, the man I love, here at Hinton or wherever else we decide and I don't give a jot if we are poor."

"Thus speaks the woman who never lacked for anything. I promise you wouldn't enjoy it."

"I don't imagine my trustees, even Morrissey, would allow me to starve. They just wouldn't turn over the Camber estates to you." She raised her head from his chest to face him. "Would you mind too much?"

"What do you think? I pursued you for your wealth," he said brutally.

She tossed him a saucy grin. "Too bad. Now we're betrothed and I've decided I *won't* release you from your engagement."

"You never did tell me how you discovered I was an unrepentant fortune hunter. Or was it merely a good guess?"

"Not at all, you had me quite deceived."

"Glad I hadn't lost my touch." Incredibly, they were joking about his despicable behavior.

"I was halfway in love with you when I overheard you talking to the Duke of Denford over the garden wall at Windermere House."

Marcus cast his mind back, trying to remember a conversation that had been clouded with brandy and cigars. He and Julian had engaged in their usual competitive nonsense. "What were you doing outside late at night in the cold?" he asked severely.

"Thinking about you."

"Oh dear. What did I say?"

"You said I would soon be begging for your attentions."

"What an ass."

"And you called me a spoiled heiress."

"I didn't even believe that, not when I first knew you. I suppose you decided to show me how such a woman would behave. With great skill, I may add."

"I was angry, more angry with myself than with you, I think. Caro warned me, Lady Ashfield warned me. Everyone warned me against you but I thought I knew better."

"I won't argue with their assessment."

"And now I'm angry with you again," she continued, "because you *should* argue with me. I know you are a better man than you believe, yet you wallow in your unworthiness. You can change your ways. You already have. The selfish man I first knew wouldn't have gone to so much trouble for the Burts."

"I'm trying, Anne. I am. But I can never be the man you deserve."

She pulled out of his arms and knelt on the bed in front of him. It was cold without her. The way she flung back her hair spoke to her frustration. "Why are you so sure of that?" she said. "Why shouldn't we be happy?"

He rested his elbows on his knees, his head down to evade her fierce interrogative gaze. "My father was a fortune hunter too. My mother didn't have one tenth of your wealth, but it was early in his career so it must have seemed enough. He ran through her money, betrayed her with other women, and made her miserable. After she died— and he may as well have killed her—he took me away with him and taught me all he knew." His mother's letters haunted him, as did the memory of her last days.

He raised his head to look her dead in the eye. "That's who I am, Anne. Right now I want to live with you and our children, grow old with you and be buried in the same grave. But it won't last. I'm just like him."

Through an age of silence, he awaited his fate. She knelt before him utterly still; the tension in her body matched that of her face, pale and serious in a cloud of hair. She was going to throw him over and it was for the best. For her. Damn it, why hadn't he pulled out early to prevent the risk of pregnancy? Selfish bastard that he was, he hadn't even taken that elementary means to protect her.

"When your father offered for your mother, how did he regard her? Did he want to live with her forever and share a grave?"

"Hah! Lewis Lithgow? He never had a romantic idea in his entire wretched life. His only use for love was as a weakness in others for him to exploit."

"If you mean what you just said, then I'd say there's a big difference between you and your father."

Anne had never seen a condemned prisoner reprieved but she wasn't entirely without imagination. Her knees gave way and she slumped back onto her heels at the transformation of Marcus's expression from raw misery to hope.

"You don't have to be like your father." She pressed her advantage. "Be yourself. Do what you want and what you think is right."

"I wish they were the same thing."

"They are."

"What makes you so sure, Anne Brotherton?"

"My grandfather always said I was a wise little thing." She gave a wry little smile. "Of course, he usually said it after I'd given in to him on some matter."

"Are you going to tell me I'm wise?" She'd missed the mischief in his voice.

"Not until I'm sure you've given in."

"I have, I have. I surrender to the greater wisdom of Anne Brotherton."

"That will be Lady Lithgow, thank you very much." Happiness rose in a bubble of mirth. Marcus hadn't said he loved her, but she suspected he did. In a way his failure to avow his love convinced her of his sincerity. With the old Marcus the lie would have slipped from his tongue as easily as a false compliment. Deep in her heart she knew that he cared for her and that was more important than three little spoken words. She launched herself at him, grasping his shoulders, and somehow fell in a twisted heap with him sprawled on top. Shared laughter turned to kisses that turned from celebratory to heated.

"Don't do that." She turned her head sideways and batted at hands that attempted to remove her shirt. "It's daylight."

"You have a lot to learn, oh wise one."

Anne felt they ought to be continuing the serious conversation about their future. On the other hand his touch felt awfully good. What she now knew to be desire came roaring back. But he wanted to take off her only garment. During the day. And see her body. He'd seemed to like it in the dark but she knew she wasn't exactly the ideal of feminine beauty. No sinuous curves or bountiful breasts.

"I want to see all of you," he said firmly, and before she could protest he'd rolled her off him and whipped off her shirt. Panicked, she sat with her knees bent, arms crossed over her bosom. Her face must be the color of boiled lobster. While Marcus, the wretch, was fully covered even to his tall boots. Heat surged in her core and she found it perversely thrilling to be stripped naked before him.

His intent gaze held no trace of disappointment. "You're so beautiful," he murmured hoarsely. "I want to see your legs."

"My legs?" He thought she had lovely legs. She extended the limbs that she'd never given much thought to, flexed one at the knee to show off, until she realized what she exposed by the movement and snapped them together. "Do they live up to expectations?"

He shifted back to kneel at her feet. "Exquisite. Longer than the Via Appia. I'm going to start at the feet and kiss every inch, all the way up."

That sounded delectable and extremely naughty when she considered what lay at the end of the journey. Excited and alarmed, she pressed her thighs together, and the glow inside her intensified.

It turned out to be quite impossible to keep them clenched when she was being kissed, licked, and nibbled from the tips of her toes on up. She learned that the backs of her knees were particularly sensitive, drawing happy little moans when subjected to wet tongued kisses.

"Stop!"

"Truly?" Thankfully the question was rhetorical and her objection ignored. As he moved north, her heart wavered between longing and apprehension. Surely he'd stop before he got *there*.

No. No he didn't stop. He actually put his mouth over the entrance to her most private place, breathing heat and making her writhe with embarrassed bliss. His tongue followed and he was consuming her with powerful strokes, raising her desire to a raging fever. Leaning back against the pillows she watched him, genuflecting before her like a worshipper at a shrine. A shrine of which she was the presiding goddess.

It didn't seem right.

"Marcus." He continued his ministrations, licking and sucking and driving her wild even as she wanted him to stop. She wanted him to continue but she also wanted something more, or something different. "Marcus! Stop!"

He looked up, his eyes reflecting her own pleasure. "It gets even better."

"I'm not doing anything."

"This is all for you. Just let me love you."

"I want to love you too. I feel as though . . ." She struggled to express her feelings. "I feel like you are serving me."

"What's wrong with that? I want to make you happy."

"It doesn't seem fair. It doesn't seem . . . equal."

He wasn't upset, more thoughtful, pondering what she'd said. "It pleases me to please me."

"And it would please me to please you."

"You please me by letting me please you."

Untangling the exchange took a moment. "I see what you mean. I just don't like"—she hesitated and fell back on her original thought—"I don't like to see you serving me."

"Would you prefer me to plow in and take my pleasure without regard for yours? If that's what a gentleman does, I thank God I am no gentleman."

Anne shivered. Taken. Seized and taken without regard for her own needs. Already sensitive from Marcus's attentions, her private place throbbed, wet and hot. "I think I might enjoy that," she whispered.

"Your request has been duly noted. Now lie back and let me pleasure you." He smiled broadly. "It will be my pleasure."

So she ceased complaining and let herself enjoy something that half an hour earlier she would have found unimaginable. His straight hair, coarser than hers, brushing her thighs; his faintly bristled chin rubbing the cleft of her bottom; that relentless tongue demanding her response, offering no quarter. She was torn between wanting him to stop, because she couldn't bear the gratification that bordered on pain, and aching for the ecstasy that lay the other side of a steep hill, if only she could climb it. Firm hands grasped the hips that twisted with longing, forced her to be still and suffer and revel in what was done to her. Squeezing her eyes shut, she released her anxiety and trusted him to take her on the final ascent, then stroke her over the top into shattered bliss.

As her shudders subsided, he laid his head on her stomach. With trembling fingers, she touched his hair, caressed his cheek. She was going to marry Marcus Lithgow and he'd just licked her between the legs. Both facts were slightly incredible and wholly delightful.

"Marcus," she said, craving the greater intimacy of complete union. "Will you take me now?"

"With the greatest of pleasure."

She sat back to watch him strip off his clothing and learned two things. Firstly, that she'd won herself as fine a specimen of male beauty as any statue. And secondly, that the male organ, or cock, when excited was long and hard and often depicted in artifacts by the Romans.

"You knew what that belt buckle was," she said. "And the pendant in that London shop. I am mortified."

"Would you have preferred it if I'd said something at the time? Either time?"

"I have to admit I would not. I had no idea studying the Romans would be indecent."

"You never know what new vistas education will open."

She didn't like the look on his face. Or she liked it very much. "Vistas?" She could hardly get the word out. The vista he presented, kneeling before her, sucked away her breath and revived a sharper desire. The play of skin and muscles across his chest was perfection itself, marred only by a small jagged scar in his side. One day she'd ask how he'd acquire it. For now she had no wish to hear the exaggerated tale of villainy he'd doubtless feed her. No longer interested in Marcus's disreputable past, she cared only for their better future and glorious present.

His hands grasped her ankles and tugged. Before she knew it she lay flat on her back with her legs over his shoulders. She'd never felt so vulnerable when he folded her like a sheet of paper, her knees framing her breasts and her opening utterly exposed to his eyes and the swift, sure entrance of his male member.

With the new posture there was no trace of discomfort, only a marvelous fullness deep inside and mounting pleasure with each firm thrust. Best of all, in daylight she could see Marcus's face, focused, intent, muscles straining. Their eyes held as they found a rhythm and she understood why the carnal act was one of union, of the bodies and the emotions. Love consumed her mind and body until there seemed no divide between the two. Once again she ascended to the peak of bliss, easily this time, as though strolling up a shallow rise on a gentle spring day, and fell over the edge in a smooth glide. Quivers of delight shot through her veins. As her sinews slackened she murmured his name and her love and watched his dear face grow wild and uncontrolled as he drove his way to his own finish.

This time, however, before she felt the exploding warmth within, he pulled out at the last moment with his final shout, and lay panting between her legs.

"Why?" she asked, stroking his damp forehead.

"To prevent getting you with child. It's what I should have done last night."

"Does it matter? We're to be married, after all. With or without consent I can wed whomever I want after my birthday in February."

"Better to be careful," he said. "We can't be sure what will happen."

A puff of chill wind ruffled her joy.

Chapter 22

Anne was full of plans for the villa once spring arrived. Her grand scheme involved scaffolding, a protective roof, and a team of laborers trained by her to dig with due care. Marcus loved to see her so excited and had no objection to anything she wanted to do. Except for the expense. Though his bride-to-be believed herself a lady of simple tastes, she was unaccustomed to consider cost when anything took her fancy. She was equally full of ideas for the manor house: new curtains, more comfortable chairs, repaired plasterwork, improvements to the kitchen and other domestic offices. "Travis and Maldon will be much happier with a new laundry. And of course a laundry maid," she remarked when once again she'd discovered Travis doing his endless ironing on the kitchen table. "I daresay a cook wouldn't allow him to work in here."

In truth her expectations were modest. She had no craving for jewels, a fashionable wardrobe, or fine carriages. But every time she said, "We must order that once the bridge is restored," whether a volume on antiquities or a stouter pair of boots, he inwardly flinched.

If she retained her pin money, their income would be sufficient for a quiet country life, conducted with economy. Fired with a new virtue, Marcus hoped to make the Hinton estate profitable. He *would* do so. But to be unable to provide his wife with the necessities of a genteel life was intolerable. His mother's last years still troubled him, though he was buoyed enough by Anne's confidence to put every effort into being a good husband.

The only way he would feel worthy of her, and safe from his own baser nature, was to accumulate a reasonable capital sum. Since he couldn't win it at the tables, the sole recourse remained Lewis's legacy. Convinced that the villa was the likely hiding place, he couldn't search there while the hard frost continued and the ground was frozen.

"Tell me everything you remember about your Mr. Bentley." For the second time they shook out every volume on the shelves of the study. "He's the best candidate I have for our mysterious ghost. He may be quite innocent but until I can get across the river I can't find out anything about him."

"You think he may have searched the house?"

"The servants were frightened off before I arrived. During that time someone made free of the place. Let's assume he found nothing."

"*We* certainly haven't. The good thing is by the time we're finished there won't be a speck of dust left in the place." She took a rag to an ancient estate ledger and replaced it on the shelf.

"If Bentley is our man, he may have decided next to try the villa but you had already taken possession of the ruins. He wouldn't be able to find what he wanted at night and couldn't risk being discovered in daylight."

"He seemed a respectable man." Her voice held a note of doubt.

"Perhaps he is. What is he like?"

"Like any country gentleman, I suppose. Though he did say he lived in London and didn't spend much time in Wiltshire. I had the impression he had also traveled abroad."

"Where he could have met my father."

Anne creased her brow. "I'm trying to remember our conversations. He knew your mother and he was well acquainted with Mr. Hooke. He knew all about the excavation. His memory was quite helpful."

"What does the fellow look like?"

"Quite handsome, I suppose." Damn villainous charmer, cozening Anne with antiquarian chatter. "But there's something about him I couldn't quite like. Almost as though he was trying to make up to me. I hate flirtatious men."

He flicked a smudge off her nose and kissed it. "Good. In that case you won't be tempted to flirt with anyone but me."

"If not for him, I wouldn't have known where to look for the hypocaust and furnace."

"And you wouldn't have nearly died."

"Never mind that." She waved her hand dismissively as her face lit up with excitement. "I've thought of something. Mr. Bentley definitely implied that Mr. Hooke never found the furnace chamber, but obviously he had. Perhaps Bentley was away from the county and didn't realize it had been uncovered—"

"Or maybe he knew it was a likely hiding place and wanted you to take off the top layer so he could get in without anyone noticing."

At the end of their second day together the weather turned. They found the villa enveloped in a warm winter mist and made straight for the furnace.

"Be careful!" Marcus said. "We don't want you tumbling in again."

His lady was not to be held back once her enthusiasm was aroused. She fell to her knees and peered over the crumbling edge of her recent prison. "I can't see much."

From his superior height he could tell the ice had melted, leaving a murky pool. "When you were trapped, did anything strike you as unusual?"

"Having never been in a Roman furnace before, everything was unexpected." She pursed her lips and thought. "There was quite a lot of loose stuff at the bottom. I assumed it was broken bricks and other debris. I was too busy trying to find a way out to give it much attention, except," she said wryly, "when I fell on my bottom and struck something sharp. There's a sort of ledge of bricks a couple of feet from the ground. I groped around it but I could have missed a part. Can you see if anything is sitting on it?"

"No. I'll have to go in." He walked around the edge, testing the ground, which seemed firmer now that it was dry. "I think this is where I lay to pull you out."

"I'll climb in again. We know you can get me out."

"It would be more sensible to fetch a ladder."

"I don't want to wait."

He didn't either, and he had no idea whether he owned a suitable ladder, or where it would be kept. "I'll go."

"Didn't we speak before about gentlemen having all the fun?"

He threw up his hands in surrender. "I hope I won't regret this."

Daylight made things easier. With his help, she dropped down to the ledge, and thence to the floor. "The cold water is soaking my boots."

"You insisted. Look quickly then."

"It's not very deep. Less than an inch." Even on his knees he couldn't see exactly what she was doing, and had to content himself with the sound of her fumbling on the floor, and listened to a running commentary on bits and pieces she lifted and discarded. "I don't think there's anything much down here. Now I'm going to look at the walls and ledge. Oh! How fascinating! I've found the flues that conducted heat into the hypocaust chamber."

"That's very interesting, but could you postpone your antiquarian speculations for the moment? More to the point, is there anything in them?"

"They're clogged with earth but one looks promising. Hold on, I'm going to stand on the ledge and see if I can get a closer look."

"Careful you don't damage any important historical evidence."

She tilted her head and stuck her tongue out at him. "Reach your hand in. I shall grab it for balance as I step up." She missed and the essay ended in an ominous crunch and a shriek as she once more ended up on her behind.

"Heavens! Now I am wet. Oh my goodness!"

"What?"

"The brick I stood on fell out and there's a hole behind it, a kind of niche. Marcus! I think I've found it. There's a small metal box in here and it doesn't look Roman to me."

Marcus had seen a lot of boxes lately, all of them containing revelations. His father's old letter, the story of his mother's marriage and death. Now that he'd found what he'd sought so long and arduously, he was afraid.

He wished he could enjoy another evening with Anne, playing chess, talking, making love. Then in the dead of night he'd slip out of her sleepy body, creep downstairs, and learn what shameful legacy his father had bequeathed him. Deep down he feared any gift of Lewis's providing would be a Trojan horse.

Anne sat across the desk in the study, regarding him with innocent anticipation. The moment could not be postponed. Suppressing a sigh, he pulled his set of picklocks from a drawer and set to work on the stout little strongbox that had refused to yield to more straightforward methods.

"How do you come to have such tools?" Anne asked in wonder. "I never saw such a thing."

"Just a little souvenir of my father's education."

The mechanism proved tricky and it took several tries before he felt the lock yield to his delicate pressure.

"Ooh!"

Every extended syllable of her exclamation was warranted. From a nest of crimson velvet two enormous gemstones blazed like cold fire.

"May I?" she asked.

He nodded, stunned into silence.

She held them up to the light. "I have never seen such huge diamonds. Oh my goodness, Marcus. They must be worth a fortune. If they are real you're rich."

The inevitable question of how his father had acquired them was thrust far into the deepest recesses of his mind. They were his and now he could marry Anne and restore Hinton.

I'll never set a foot wrong for the rest of my life, he bargained with the God he had resolutely ignored for most of his life. *This is the last time. Just don't let Anne find out.*

Anne was subjecting the jewels to the kind of attention she usually bestowed on artifacts of a more mundane kind. "I believe they are perfectly matched. I can see no difference at all. And how clever the setting is. They can be worn as either brooches or earrings. Look for yourself. The whole pendant is almost as long as the width of your hand."

He laid one in his palm, this miracle of crystal whose thousand facets threw tiny rainbows onto the walls and desk. Before his eyes they vanished to be replaced by a different vision. Dams, bridges, and drainage ditches. Solid cottages for prosperous tenants. Horses for work and for riding and to pull a carriage. Maids and footmen and plasterers and painters. Warm winter clothing and sensible boots for a country gentleman and his family.

"The workmanship looks quite old. What do you think?"

Her question pulled him out of his agreeable reverie. The diamond drops hung from elaborate pendants of chased gold, studded with large and lustrous pearls and smaller diamonds. "Perhaps Tudor," he said, "but more likely later. Seventeenth century, I think."

"Such fabulous ornaments must have been made for a queen. We have nothing so magnificent at Camber." His lovely girl was sometimes naïve but she was nobody's fool. "How did they come to be here? To whom do they belong?"

"They belong to me," he said firmly. "They were found on my land."

"Are you sure? Ought we not to look for the true owner?"

"They've been at Hinton for at least fifteen years, if my father hid them here. But that's mere supposition. They could have been hidden even longer ago by someone else. If they were acquired by underhanded means, it's far too late to find the truth now."

He spoke arrant nonsense. No one ever forgot gems like this. Disposing of them would have to be done carefully and he wouldn't achieve full value from the sale. But it would be enough. Instinct and his own worldly knowledge told him that he had very special merchandise on his hands.

He steeled himself to face her candid gaze without wavering. Though a man to whom reserve was a credo rather than a habit, he had to fight the urge to confide his suspicions about where Lewis Lithgow had obtained these beauties. If she heard that it would be all over and he would have no chance of keeping them and the money he needed so badly for their future together. He had become accustomed to confiding in Anne, and deceiving her now felt almost like dying. It was for her own good, he told himself.

People were always ready to believe what they wanted to believe. He knew Anne so well he could follow her unspoken thoughts. He felt her dismiss her doubts and accept the wonderful and convenient truth that he was now in possession of a fortune.

They were in possession. It was for both of them.

"Come here, love," he said, holding out his hand. "How shall we celebrate our good luck?"

She fell eagerly into his arms, melting against him. He reveled in the press of her body against his chest, the scent of soap and starch, the taste of her fervent kiss, which had grown skilled and knowing with practice, enticing him to pleasure.

"Let's go upstairs," he whispered.

"In daylight?" She only expressed shock to tease him now. Propriety had become a game she played, and not with any degree of diligence.

No longer could he imagine living without Anne. He'd do anything to keep her. Anything.

Chapter 23

It felt like the end of an idyll. Marcus was helping a team of workmen rebuild the bridge and Anne was wearing a gown. Later today, tomorrow at the latest, she would have to cross the river and return to a censorious world that would not approve of her chosen husband. She minded more for him than for herself, though dealing with Morrissey was never pleasant. Still, she was prepared to stand up to her guardian and salvage some kind of income. She honestly didn't care where their money came from, but it was important to Marcus that he should be able to provide for them himself. She respected the pride that made him think that way, understood it as part of his path to an honest life.

So she kept telling herself every time she dismissed the queasiness in her stomach at the thought of the diamonds. The gems were a blot on her happiness that she refused to allow to grow. She assuaged the niggles of her conscience by telling herself that they were safe for the moment and the issue would resolve itself, one way or another. While trapped at Hinton there was nothing to be done, and she doubted they could be disposed of in Wiltshire.

Since she was going to be the bride of a man of modest means she had better further her acquaintance with the arts of housewifery, so she collected her polish and rags from the broom cupboard. Next door in the laundry Travis was muttering about the damage she'd done to Marcus's best breeches. He'd greeted their return from the villa with horror, removed them from her room in the middle of the night, and left her gown in its place. Not by so much as a sideways look or a raised eyebrow had he indicated that he knew she and Marcus shared a bed.

During her weeks of servitude she'd swept and dusted the smaller parlor but otherwise spent little time there. With plastered walls instead of the paneling found in much of the house, it was both light and cozy. She would make it her own sitting room, leaving the bookroom to Marcus, who would doubtless be glad to see to estate business without being surrounded by Roman remains. There wasn't room for them in here either. One of the spare bedrooms would make an excellent museum, until their family grew too large. She hoped it would happen soon. If she was with child it would put an end to Morrissey's hopes of finding her a different husband.

As she applied her rag to the spiral legs of a pretty little table, she beguiled the time imagining herself in this very room, writing letters, speaking to the cook and housekeeper and nurse-maids, cataloguing her finds on days when it was too cold or wet to work outside. And then Marcus would come home and find her here, perhaps in the middle of the day when he wasn't expected.

When Anne dressed that morning she'd missed her men's attire, felt the loss of freedom when her legs were no longer free from the constraints of two petticoats and the heavy skirts of her woolen winter gown. The stays and high neck seemed almost choking after days in a man's shirt.

There was something about woman's garb that hadn't ever occurred to her before. Beneath the layers of kerseymere, flannel, and linen, she was bare. Accessible. Marcus had only to flip up her skirts and he could take her, without ceremony or the bother of undressing. Breeches, as she now knew, needed nothing more than a few loosened buttons and the male organ was ready for business.

She clenched her thighs together to trap the wet heat that gathered down below. She'd have to see about getting a comfortable divan for her parlor. Meanwhile, the carpet was in fair condition, its pink roses faded but with plenty of pile. Dizzy with longing, she enclosed the table leg in her fist, rubbing it up and down without troubling about the fiddly little crevices. Then she realized what she was doing and laughed. Who would ever have suspected that Anne Brotherton was capable of such lascivious thoughts?

The bridge wasn't finished but it now spanned the river and could carry a man, or a horse, or a man on a horse, but not a carriage. Marcus inspected the work, reluctant to let the world intrude on the island of Hinton Manor. Gritting his teeth, he set boots to wood and walked to the village.

He returned with a pile of mail and the news that Jasper would return soon, along with a couple of maidservants. He should be glad, he supposed, but he wouldn't have minded another day or week making free of the house with Anne. Servants could be devilishly in the way, except for Travis, who possessed preternatural tact. She wasn't going to be pleased with one particular piece of news. Or perhaps she would.

"Anne!" he called as he entered the hall and wiped his boots.

"In here."

A lovely sight awaited him in the small parlor. Anne on her hands and knees, her lovely bottom all the more enticing for its veil of dark blue cloth. Desire arose quickly and he wanted to fall on her without ceremony. Not the right way to treat a lady and his wife. Except she'd said something once, something about wanting to be taken without regard for her own satisfaction. Taken selfishly for his pleasure alone.

"Are you all right?' he asked.

"I dropped the button box." Buttons were scattered over the carpet. Buttons that had previously lived in a drawer in the drawing room and had no reason to have migrated to the parlor.

"I'd better help you pick them up."

Looking over her shoulder, she batted her eyelashes at him. "I'd be grateful."

She plucked a small pearl button that decorated the center of a carpet rose and placed it in the box, giving her bottom an almost imperceptible and entirely unnecessary wiggle as she did so. His hands accepted the unspoken invitation, kneading the voluptuous globes through thick material. They pressed back into his palms. It was the work of seconds to push up her skirts, leaving them naked to his eyes and the urgent demand of his cock. A little gasp was her only audible response, in time with further undulation of her glorious rear. With both hands he unbuttoned the fall of his breeches and released his aching organ.

Settling himself in place he leaned over to speak softly. "I'm going to plow into you without regard for your pleasure."

A further gasp told him he'd read her correctly. Without more ado he opened her with his fingers and surged in. She was hot and wet and completely ready.

"You're a wicked girl and deserve what you get," he said, and other words unsuitable to be addressed to a lady. Judging from the noisy groans that arose at each thrust, each lewd phrase, she didn't mind. She dropped onto her elbows, the better to accommodate his entrance. So he took her at her word and thought only of himself, of the unctuous grip on his cock as he worked her slick passage, slamming into her to the hilt of his shaft so his balls banged against her bottom.

"Don't dare move," he ordered, grasping her hips. Instantly obedient, the only movement was that of her inner muscles, driving him rapidly to his peak.

It was quick, it was messy, and it was probably the best single act of coitus he'd ever experienced. He didn't bother to try and make it last, just let himself be driven by his own lust until he came with a great shout, calling out her name a dozen times as he released into her. Amazingly, as his orgasm subsided he felt her own begin. Waves of satisfaction accompanied by the world's most beautiful words.

"I love you, Marcus! I love you."

He collapsed onto the carpet, taking her with him, turning so they panted face to face. He stroked her ecstatic face and covered it with frantic kisses. "Oh God, Anne! That was extraordinary. You are extraordinary. It was what you wanted, wasn't it? I didn't hurt you?"

Her smile dazzled him. "I planned it just like that and you knew. You were perfect."

"You're perfect and we are perfect together."

Then he kissed her, endlessly and so deeply that he felt he was taking her into his body and she him. If he died tomorrow, at least he had experienced greater happiness than anyone in history.

"I don't like this gown," he said idly, five minutes or an hour later. Anne lay on her back smiling while, resting on his elbow, he feasted his eyes on her and caressed her well-covered breasts. "I want to feel your skin."

"I think it's quite convenient. You didn't have

any trouble finding a different part of my body."

"I hope you possess many others with low bodices."

"One or two. But sometimes it might be fun to have you hunt for your pleasure."

"I am the luckiest man in the world."

"I'm glad you think so, Marcus. I never expected anyone would feel that about me."

His heart missed a beat. "If they don't that's because all men are idiots."

"Even you?"

"I'm a clever idiot."

They started kissing again and might have spent the rest of the day on the parlor carpet had his inconvenient conscience not intervened.

"I need to get back to the bridge. We need every pair of available hands."

"Must you? I don't want to leave here. I wish we could be cut off forever, on our own island."

He snatched one last kiss and stood, pulling her up with him. "I came back to bring you news, but you distracted me. Don't smile like that or it'll happen again. Lady Windermere is no longer at Hinton. She left you a letter."

"Cynthia has left?" She accepted the letter. "I hope nothing is wrong. What about Maldon?"

"Your maid is at the inn. She gave me your mail."

"Why didn't you bring her with you? Though I must say she would have been very much in the way for the last half hour."

"As I already knew, she does not care for long walks. However, Travis seems very anxious to see her. He's no walker himself, but he has braved the mud. I expect they'll find a cart to bring them part of the way."

"So we're completely alone in the house for the last time."

"Don't tempt me."

Leafing through his own letters, he selected one of particular interest. Anne interrupted him before he'd removed the seal.

"How odd! Cynthia had word that Windermere is on his way back to England. She has returned to London to meet him."

"I thought they were estranged."

"I'm not sure that is the exact word. She hasn't confided the whole story to me but she is very angry with him. Her flirtation with Denford was designed to . . . I don't know . . . annoy him."

"A dangerous game to play with a man like Julian Fortescue. I hope she knows what she's doing."

"I hope so too. When we left London she was already out of her depths. I wonder if I should go to her."

"Better leave them to sort it out for themselves. I've seen little of Windermere in recent years, and nothing at all since he came into his title. He was by far the most sensible of our group, never given to rash action. He cut off all contact after a big loss at the gaming tables." She looked up quickly with grave eyes. "No, he didn't lose to me. I never play high with my friends and I wasn't even in the country at the time."

"Yet you feel responsible." He was amazed at

her instinctive understanding and the comfort of her fleeting touch on his hand.

"I suppose I do. For Robert too, and his losses were far greater and more disastrous. I taught them how to play."

"Did you force them?"

"No. Everyone games."

"So you merely shared your skills with them?" He nodded. "If you hadn't, things might have been even worse. Larger fortunes have been lost gaming. You should have heard my grandfather on the subject of Charles James Fox. He cost Lord Holland hundreds of thousands of pounds. It isn't your fault they were fools."

"Thank you for your faith in me."

"Cynthia and I were both expected for Christmas at Castleton, but she writes that she will likely remain in London. Will you come with me?"

This was perilous terrain. "I won't be welcome."

"Caro is my closest relation and dearest friend. If only for my sake she will forgive you, and persuade the duke to do so. There's no reason the two of you cannot get past a childish quarrel. What happened anyway?"

Damn. Reentering the outside world reminded him of all the reasons he should have left Anne alone. They'd been living in a fool's paradise. "He blamed me for an injury to a horse during a visit to Castleton House with my father." That was the short version of an old tale that Marcus had always believed to be the truth. Castleton had given Caro a different account, one that did Lewis no credit at all. Marcus had his own reasons to postpone the full explanation.

"How old were you?"

"Eleven."

Anne cast her eyes upward and shook her head. "You will both have to get over it, and Caro and I will make sure of it."

Marcus had a tempting vision of being forgiven by Caro and tolerated by Castleton. Of Anne and Caro exerting their joint cousinly persuasion to force their husbands to reconcile. Pure fantasy. It would never happen.

Meanwhile, he had another matter to tackle. "My letter is from Sir William Hamilton. You may recall that I knew him well in Naples. He and Lady Hamilton have returned to England with Nelson and will be spending Christmas with William Beckford at Fonthill, scarcely fifteen miles away. I thought I'd ride over and pay my respects, to Beckford too. I was acquainted with him in Paris."

What he didn't mention was that Beckford's friends were the kind of people who would buy valuable jewelry of doubtful provenance. Perhaps Beckford himself, a collector of fabled wealth, would be interested.

"Lord Nelson! How I would like to meet him." Apparently Anne shared the nation's opinion of the celebrated admiral. She looked quite dazzled. "I don't want to stay here alone."

He muttered under his breath, cursing himself for mentioning Nelson.

"I've also read about the abbey Mr. Beckford is building at Fonthill."

"I didn't think you had a taste for the gothic."

"It's the tallest tower in England. Couldn't I come with you? Please?"

He wanted to please her as much as he wanted to go. There was another advantage to them appearing together. "If you come with me the world will soon know. We had better announce our intention to marry."

"I haven't the least objection." She smiled and offered her hand.

"I wouldn't take you if I thought his party would be disreputable, but I must warn you that Beckford is frowned upon by the *ton*."

"Excellent. Morrissey will stop plaguing me and Lord Algernon Tiverton will scurry back to Derbyshire as fast as his horses can run."

Chapter 24

In reply to Marcus's letter came an invitation to spend the night at Fonthill House and attend the apogee of the entertainment, a dinner at the uninhabited but almost finished abbey. Sir William Hamilton's wife agreed to act as Anne's nominal chaperone.

Lady Hamilton proved a neglectful duenna. Heavily pregnant, all her attentions were fixed on Lord Nelson. From veiled remarks by other guests, Anne gathered that the admiral, rather than her elderly husband, was the father of the child.

With an hour before she needed to change for the evening's festivities, Marcus having disappeared with some of the gentlemen, Anne found her way to the library. Mr. Beckford's collection of books was as magnificent as the rest of his holdings and she barely knew where to start. She wandered along the walls, dazzled by the leather and gold bindings and reading the spines for something to take her fancy.

Lost in a wall of recent historical works, she was about to look for the librarian for directions to the antiquities section, when a title caught her eye. A thick quarto lay on a table, among other volumes waiting to be put away. She had tried to set aside the uneasiness that arose whenever she thought of Marcus's treasure, but the coincidence of finding this volume pricked her conscience. *A Treatise on Diamonds and Pearls.*

It didn't take long to confirm that the twin pendants were indeed exceptional stones, both in size and in cut. The second half of the work went from generalities to the history of famous gems. Despite the somewhat crude execution of the engraved illustrations, there was no mistaking the identity of a pair of pendants known as the Stuart Twins. They hadn't been owned by a queen, but their provenance was indeed royal. They had been a gift of King Charles II to his mistress Mary Swinburne.

As she stared aghast at the page, her sudden chill had nothing to do with the temperature of the well-heated room. She didn't need to read further. Charles's son by Mary Swinburne was the first Duke of Castleton. The source of Marcus's future wealth was the rightful property of Caro's husband.

It was easy to guess what had happened. Marcus's rogue of a father had stolen the jewels during that long-ago visit to Castleton when Marcus and the present duke had quarreled over a horse.

Did Marcus know? He'd had nothing to do

with the original theft, which happened when he was eleven years old, of that she was certain. She believed he had no idea what he had searched for at Hinton, but he was too canny not to have made the connection.

She prayed she was wrong.

There were other oddities about the affair. Piecing together scraps of information, she was fairly sure Lewis had left England shortly after the theft, having consigned the gems in their strongbox—and his son—to the care of Josiah Hooke. Why had Castleton's father not pursued Lewis Lithgow? Did he not know the identity of the thief? Was there the faintest chance that Lewis Lithgow had somehow acquired the diamonds by legitimate means?

In that case there was no reason for him to have abandoned them. And however much Anne's mind explored the possibilities of the tale, probing for excuses like water seeking a crack in a pitcher, one horrible truth could no longer be ignored. Marcus intended to sell stolen jewels. And to her great shame she had condoned it. This was the result of consorting with a scoundrel.

Worst of all, she loved the scoundrel with all her heart.

She looked up to discover the librarian standing beside her table.

"Have you found what you needed, ma'am?" he asked.

"Yes, thank you."

"An interesting volume. Curious that you are

the second person today to consult it. Lord Lithgow was reading it, not an hour ago."

If Marcus hadn't known before, he did now. The only question was what he would do with the knowledge.

Chapter 25

Draped in a pall of anxiety, Anne rode to Mr. Beckford's abbey with three strangers who were too busy gaping to make conversation. As they passed through a gothic arched gate in the vast wall surrounding the abbey woods, the incredible edifice loomed above them in the twilight. Never a follower of the fashion for horrid novels, she couldn't help being affected by the sight, which matched the tenor of her own spirits. There had been no chance to speak to Marcus before their departure. The fleet of vehicles drew up before a door of gargantuan proportions that struck her as both absurd and awe-inspiring. With the same mixed feelings she joined the procession, led by Nelson and Lady Hamilton, between a double line of uniformed soldiers, into a lofty hall and thence to a vast saloon, one of the longest rooms Anne had ever seen. The party took their places at a table that filled almost the whole length, and they were treated to the oddest meal served on silver platters.

"The food has been prepared according to the custom of the Middle Ages," explained one of her neighbors. Anne picked at some unidentified meat and hoped it wasn't a big cat or a bear.

A continuing chorus of astonishment and praise swirled around her at the splendor of the chamber, the lavish service, the profusion of candles illuminating the shadowy vaulted ceiling, and the size of the Christmas fire of cedar and pine cones in the massive hearth. The conflicting sensory stimuli made her dizzy even while her mind wandered from the feast. She couldn't see Marcus among the dozens seated, but not for a moment was she unaware of his presence.

The interminable meal over, the party retired to a chamber like the nave of a cathedral, well over one hundred feet in length. In keeping with the architecture, the place was filled with papist treasures, including a shrine to St. Anthony and a bishop's throne at one end. An invisible orchestra played medieval music and, in case the guests hadn't sufficiently gorged themselves, tables were laden with gold baskets of confectionery and jugs of spiced wine.

At a gentle touch on her arm, she turned to find Marcus grinning at her, setting her pulse racing in a way that had nothing to do with the spectacle.

"Did you ever see such a thing?"

"Never imagined it either," she replied, smiling back in spite of herself. "I don't know whether to laugh or cry."

"Beckford must have spent a fortune on this evening alone. The cost of the whole folly is beyond calculation."

The folly of a host who could well afford to buy a pair of extraordinary diamonds.

Guests milled about. No one could see his hands slither down her arms to take hers in a possessive clasp. His breath warmed her ear. "I miss you, Anne."

She missed him too. Since Maldon's return they hadn't been together, for her maid shared her room, both at Hinton and now at Fonthill. They might never make love again, and she wasn't sure she could bear it.

"Slip away with me," he whispered, devil that he was. "Lady Hamilton is about to enact Agrippina inciting the Romans to avenge the death of Germanicus. All eyes will be on her and we can be alone."

She needed to speak with him, and some corner of the vast abbey might be their best chance at privacy.

Another oversized gothic chamber was deserted save for a footman or two carrying more gilt chargers of food. Behind a hundred yards of red velvet drapery they discovered an alcove whose purpose wasn't at all clear. Given the extravagance of the abbey's illuminations there was no need to question the pair of lighted candles in chased silver sconces. Marcus's proximity overwhelmed her. With her eyes closed she inhaled the human scent beneath the particular soap she knew so well. Light breathing overlaid the distant sound of an ancient carol.

"I miss your hair," he whispered, his palms feathering over Maldon's braided confection. "I miss your cheeks, your nose, your chin, the little pulse here." He kissed each named spot, ending in the niche between her neck and jaw, and lingered there, not moving. He consumed her, inhaled her essence as though it were the breath of life. As never before, she felt his love.

Marcus loved her, as he'd loved no one else in his lonely life. She was humbled and her doubts receded. They did not vanish but she put them away in a box deep inside her as her love for him flowed back. For this short time, in their red velvet haven, she gave herself up to her love for a man whom no one had truly loved for so many years. The only thing she knew was that she needed to give herself to him, to merge their souls. Grasping his shoulders she offered her body without shame, trembling with love as his hand dropped to her skirts.

Take me. Let me take you. No words were spoken, or needed to be. In a rustle of raised skirts and petticoats she was exposed, naked, free of the conventions that her layers of clothing represented. But as she offered herself as a sacrifice to his passion, she felt no inequity in the exchange. He was giving as much as taking. Their minds and bodies were in perfect balance and harmony.

Backed against the wall, she relished the smooth, cold stone on her back and shoulder blades, scarcely protected by her silk gown. His hands dug into her hips as he lifted her to him and she embraced him with all four limbs as she answered his entering thrust. The coupling seemed significant in its clumsiness, the lack of courtly form or comfort stripping away the artificiality of the human dance. His entry drove away the world, leaving only the two of them in a union that was perfect in its simplicity. She allowed herself only to feel because it was a luxury that could not last. She reached her peak almost as he did and fancied they soared off into an endless dark space where only they dwelt, liberated from earthly concerns.

Her feet slipped to the floor but they remained entwined in each other's arms, exchanging clumsy panting kisses, over and over again because they couldn't bear to separate and have it end.

He pulled away first, not far, just loosening the bonds of his arms enough to look at her.

His thumb caressed her cheekbone. "You're crying, Anne." His voice was hoarse. "Did I hurt you?"

"Of course not."

"Then why?"

"I feel . . ." She couldn't complete the thought.

"I know," he said with a heartbreaking smile. "I feel too."

She laid her head against his waistcoat. She wanted to stay like this, bathing in an ocean of love. But she could no longer remain silent and pretend there wasn't anything wrong.

"What happened at Castleton?" she asked. "Tell me the whole story."

The tension in his chest, a barely perceptible intake of breath, lasted only a second. "I told you about the horse that was injured when Thomas, the young marquess as he then was, attempted to jump a hedge beyond the power of his mount." He spoke lightly, as though he wasn't sure why she had raised the subject now but he might as well cater to her whim. "He told his father it was my fault. What I didn't tell you was that the duke ordered us to leave as a result."

"Is that really what happened?"

He stroked her back in a soothing motion. "Caro says not. Castleton told her we decamped in the night having stolen a miniature painting. I find the story ridiculous. My father would never have left for such paltry gain."

"Would he have left for a pair of diamond pendants?"

This time the breath was deeper. He pushed her back by the shoulders and faced her, all lightness and pretense vanished. "You know, don't you?" She nodded. "Did you guess?"

"Not who owned the diamonds, until I read about the Stuart Twins in the library this afternoon. In the same book you consulted earlier. Marcus, you have to give them back to Castleton."

Time trickled to a halt as she awaited an answer. His features settled into his gaming face, devoid of expression, giving away no secrets. The faint flicker of the candles revealed his watchful stillness. The vulnerability and innate honor she'd grown to love were hidden behind a mask of calculation. She prayed they weren't buried deep. Misgivings that they'd ever existed brought a lump to her throat.

No, she was sure those qualities had been real. What she doubted was their power to overcome the less benign influences that had ruled most of his life. She left him to his silent deliberation in hope and cold dread.

"Without the diamonds I shall have to sell Hinton," he said. "I will never have enough to improve the land and do the right thing for the tenants. Unless I do that the estate won't provide enough income for me, let alone for a wife. For you."

"We can manage with my pin money."

He waved aside her objection. "The snuff of a candle. You haven't a notion what it's like to live hand to mouth, to perch in poor lodging one step ahead of the poorhouse. I couldn't ask it of you."

"And if I persuaded Morrissey to let me have more?"

"I don't want to live off your money, Anne. I've discovered an inconvenient pride. With any other woman it wouldn't matter, but because I love you I want to come to you with some honor."

"Can you exchange one kind of honor for another?" she asked softly.

"Castleton doesn't need the diamonds and I've never known Caro to care about jewels. They've been missing for fifteen years and Castleton doubtless believes them long lost. His father was duke then."

She stared at him, waiting to see who would win the argument Marcus waged with himself.

"Let me do this, Anne. Let me have this one thing. I swear to you that after this I'll lead a life as blameless as a parson." She continued to say nothing. "I've found a buyer for them. Someone who will give me enough to do everything we need. No one will ever know."

She stood on her toes to give him a last kiss, making it fast lest she prove herself weak again. In the end she didn't find it hard to walk away. Painful, yes, so painful that her chest ached and her head was clogged with tears. But not for a moment was she tempted to stay. Drawing aside the heavy, bloodred velvet, she looked back.

"You will know, Marcus," she said. "You will always know."

Chapter 26

Marcus raged against fate.

He tossed on the fine mattress of his luxurious Fonthill bedchamber, cursing the chance that had led Anne to that one particular volume among all the thousands in Beckford's library. It was the final bitter proof that luck had deserted him. He had come to count on his father's "legacy" when he should have known that anything from that source would be tainted.

Fortune hunter or thief? Those were his choices now. Or there was the alternative of abandoning his love, his land, and his home and taking to the road again, wandering Europe forever, scraping a living from whatever fools he could lure to the tables.

He could have left Fonthill with a handsome bank draft in his pocket, Anne at his side, their future secure. He'd been nervous about arriving at Castleton for Christmas, but he'd counted on charm, groveling, and Caro's ancient affection to earn her forgiveness, and Caro's charm and persuasive powers to bring the Duke of Castleton to a similar, if less enthusiastic, state of acceptance.

Presenting Castleton with his lost family heirloom would doubtless help with the latter goal. It stuck in his gorge to give up his only chance at independent fortune. Yet he knew he had to, or lose Anne forever.

Somewhere in the house a clock struck five. Soon it would be dawn. Monks all over Europe were rising to recite the office of Prime. Perhaps he should turn papist and enter a monastery, a real one, not Beckford's fantastic folly that lay two miles away. A lifetime of prayer and atonement held a certain appeal in this darkest hour.

He remembered one Christmas at Conduit Street with Caro and Robert Townsend, soon after their marriage. With customary excess, Caro had dragged them out to Richmond Park in the middle of the night to gather illicit greenery, with which she festooned the house with more exuberance than art. Since they were suffering one of their periodic servant shortages, the Townsends' Christmas feast had come from a bake shop, but none of the young guests crammed into the small house had cared as long as the wine flowed, which *chez* Townsend always did. It was the happiest Noel he'd ever spent except for faint memories of quieter celebrations with his mother.

This one could have been even better because of Anne's presence. While Caro had turned respectable on becoming a duchess, she couldn't have changed that much. The food and decorations would be better prepared and the wine consumed with less abandon. Not even a ducal mansion and its very correct owner could douse Caro's warmth. He pictured her excitement at being reunited with her dearest cousin, Anne's joy in Caro's company. He would be introduced as a future member of the family and, after an interval for charming, groveling etc., accepted as such. Caro would be his cousin twice, through Anne and through Castleton. He would make the acquaintance of Castleton's sisters, who had been born after his sole disastrous visit to the ducal seat. He and Anne would dance at a ball and exchange stolen kisses under the mistletoe. Under the eyes of their relations they would complete their courtship and plan a wedding with a benign innocence outside his experience.

A viscount with his own estate, even if a small one, was a suitable if not brilliant match for the heiress of Camber. Morrissey might not relent, but Anne need not be entirely excluded from civilized society. And he, Marcus Lithgow, rogue and outcast, would, for the first time in his life, be included too. Part of his own loving family—himself and Anne—and of a wider kin by blood and marriage. Perhaps even the greater fellowship of the reputable world.

All this could have been his had Anne not read that damnable book. She would never have known.

You will know, Marcus. You will always know.

Those had been her parting words. Not *I will know* but *you*.

He, Marcus, would know. His vision of what

might have been dissolved into mist. It was a chi-mera, an illusion. He understood what Anne had been telling him. One could not be truly at home among honest people unless one was honest one-self. Selling the diamonds would make him per-petually a scoundrel and unworthy.

Chapter 27

Approaching Castleton, a mansion, of a similar age to Hinton but many times bigger, Anne contrasted them unfavorably. Marcus's house was so delightfully pretty and cozy compared to this vast barracks. Gray skies and her own black mood did not help her first impression of Caro's new home.

Happily the welcome inside belied the exterior. She'd hardly had time to take in the display of greenery trimmed in an excess of red ribbons, the dozens of candles that banished any hint of gloom, when Caro danced down the staircase, red curls bouncing furiously.

"My darling Annabella!" her cousin cried, wrapping her in a fond embrace. "We were worried you had been held up by highwaymen, were we not, Thomas?"

The duke, who had followed his wife at a more stately pace, shook her hand. "That was Caro's theory. I thought a broken wheel a more likely accident." Anne had never seen her erstwhile suitor so open and unguarded. He actually winked at her. Predictably, life with Caro had shaken Lord Stuffy out of him. "Welcome to Castleton, my dear Anne. Your presence makes Christmas complete."

"But where have you come from, my dearest? Cynthia wrote that you had been staying in Wiltshire with—"

"Caro," the duke interrupted with a warning glance at the servants. "Why don't you take Anne to her room. She'll wish to rest and change before dinner. My mother and sisters are dining with us," he added, "but you have more than an hour before they arrive." He and Caro exchanged a significant look and Anne prepared to be interrogated.

Luckily she'd had a journey of several hours to decide what to say.

Caro gave her about five minutes to wash her hands and face, then led her firmly to her own charming sitting room. "Let Maldon unpack. I know you won't need much time to dress, unless you have changed even more than I suspect."

"Oh, look! It's Tish." Anne bent over to stroke Caro's cat, who was stretched out on the carpet looking large. "He's plumper. Has your husband been feeding him from the table?"

"He always becomes fat in the winter, spending less time outside. Wait! You're distracting me. Leave him alone and sit down. I want to know precisely what you were doing with Marcus Lithgow after I warned you to have nothing to do with him. You've become very sly, you and Cynthia, writing to me that you were at her house when all the time you were in Wiltshire at an estate that

Marcus has somehow got hold of. Did he win it at cards?"

"An inheritance from a great-uncle. It includes the site of an important Roman settlement. I've been digging it up."

Caro leaned in from her unquiet perch beside her on the settee and examined her suspiciously. "I don't understand you, Anne. You're behaving like me, or rather like me before I became a reformed character. I understand about the lure of Rome, but you never do anything that isn't correct. What does your guardian think of this adventure?"

Anne merely raised her brow. "Did you ever encounter Lord Algernon Tiverton?"

The story of her attempt to taint her reputation to dispose of a tedious suitor was guaranteed to appeal to Caro. She laughed heartily at Anne's account of making Marcus take her around London. "You clever, wicked thing. But why put yourself in his hands at his own estate? I can tell you, when Thomas heard he was furious. If you hadn't arrived today he was ready to drive to Wiltshire himself and kill Marcus."

Anne had made up her mind not to reveal why the duke had even greater reason to do his old enemy bodily harm. Considerable restraint had been required not to creep through the corridors of Fonthill and shake him. She wanted to rage and argue until he bowed to her will, or seduce him into acquiescence. She fancied she could do either. But poor Marcus had got himself into a muddle over the question of honor. Believing with all her heart that he possessed a core of decency, she knew that he needed to believe it himself, and act on it.

She didn't want him to bow to her will. If he couldn't do the right thing for the right reason, their future together was doomed.

"You're looking very fierce," Caro said. Anne looked down at her lap and discovered her fists clenched. "Now tell me everything that happened and don't leave a single thing out."

Total disclosure was impossible. Her version of events omitted any mention of lost treasure, love-making, or betrothal. "So you see," she concluded calmly, "he saved my life and then I was stranded at his estate for days."

Caro's response was anything but serene. "You've ruined yourself," she shrieked.

"Really Caro, you're the last person I'd expect to get upset about this. Castleton has made you quite priggish."

"Luckily I have made him less so. We discussed the matter already and agreed that we will back you to the hilt if any gossip leaks out. I expect it will, even if you were stuck on an island in the middle of nowhere. You don't need to marry him."

"It's possible that Marcus will come here," Anne said, trying to sound careless when in fact she counted on it, dreaded his nonappearance. If by tomorrow he hadn't followed her to Castleton she would reveal the truth about the diamonds and try to persuade Castleton not to prosecute him. Tempting as it was to let Marcus keep them, and attempt to lead a happy and useful life at

Hinton with the money he badly needed, it wasn't an option. *She would know.*

She clenched her fists. Picking up the threads of her life without him was dreadful enough. If her actions led to his complete ruin she would never be able to forgive herself.

"Come here!" Caro took Anne's head between her hands to face her squarely. "You're in love with him, I can tell. Oh, Annabella! You're the last person I would expect to fall for a charming wastrel."

Anne squeezed her eyes to stop escaping tears. "You don't know him as I do. He's good at heart but he's never had a chance. I saw him at Hinton, trying to do what is right by his tenants. I saw how hard he worked."

"Working to impress and seduce you, as you were sensible enough to realize in London."

"I changed my mind. He changed."

"How can you be such a fool?"

"Am I a fool? He used to be a friend of yours."

"As Robert's best friend I was devoted to him for years. Then he tried to steal from me."

Anne winced. "He explained that," she said with as much certainty as she could muster. "As I understand, it was one of Robert's gaming debts. He is deeply sorry for it, but he was in grave straits and the matter wasn't black and white."

"He was vile to Thomas too. Thomas won't tolerate him."

"Even for me?" Anne asked in a small voice, praying that tolerance rather than prosecution would even be an option.

"I'm not sure he'd even do it for *me*. There's the

whole question of Marcus's father who also stole from *Thomas's* father. Not a paltry matter either. I can't tell you the whole story, but it makes any kind of alliance with a Lithgow absolutely out of the question."

"Marcus is not his father," Anne said, hoping she was right.

He must finally have slept or how else could he be awakened by Travis, with a swish of curtains and a cup of tea?

"Goddamn it, Travis, leave me alone. It's scarcely dawn."

"Long past, sir, and you need to get dressed and be on your way to Castleton."

Marcus's stomach roiled. "I'm not sure I'm going to Castleton." It depended on the result of his conversation with Anne.

"Of course you are, sir." Travis was at his most annoyingly brisk. "I've arranged for one of the Fonthill carriages to take you as far as Salisbury."

"*You* have arranged it? What about Miss Brotherton?"

"Miss Brotherton left an hour ago."

The roiling was replaced by sinking. "Left? Did she leave a note?"

"No, sir. Miss Maldon informed me of her plans. I have your shaving water hot and your bags packed. Are we going?"

"We most certainly are," he replied, thrusting the teacup back at Travis. He tossed away the covers and bounded out of bed. "What are we waiting for? Your researches don't happen to have revealed the time of the coaches from Salisbury to Basingstoke, I suppose."

"We will naturally hire a post chaise. It's the quickest way."

Marcus slapped his bare chest as though looking for his purse. "I don't think I have enough on hand to pay for one."

"Never mind that, sir. I have plenty."

Marcus stared at the man. "Travis, I don't even pay you. Now you're offering *me* money."

"The important thing is to get you there. You'll pay me back."

"I hope so. No, I will." His man's confidence made him unaccountably more cheerful. Now he had to restore Anne's faith.

Few guests were at large so early. Leaving messages for his host and the Hamiltons, Marcus and Travis set out for Salisbury. At the Red Lion they were told there'd be a half hour wait for a chaise so, possessing his soul in patience, Marcus settled in the empty coffee room and ordered breakfast. When he served the coffee, cold beef, bread, and butter, the host told him that a Mr. Bentley had arrived at the inn and was asking after him.

"Bentley, eh? Show him in." One mystery might be solved at last. The Stuart Twins were nestled deep in the left pocket of his greatcoat. The right contained his loaded pistol.

The voice exchanging words with the landlord in the passage made him shake his head. Anxiety must have affected his hearing.

The door opened fully to reveal a well-dressed

country gentleman. Last time Marcus had seen him, about three years ago, his hair had been longer with less gray, his garb that of an urban man of fashion. A year ago he was dead.

"My dear boy," said Lewis Lithgow, holding out his arms. "Aren't you going to embrace your father?"

His recent acquaintance with Anne Brotherton aside, very few things had ever surprised Marcus, let alone rendered him speechless. A good son would be thrilled at the resurrection of his parent. Marcus was not a good son.

"Lost your voice? You never were as glib of tongue as I. How often have I told you, never let yourself be at a loss for words. Except on purpose."

"How did you . . . never mind. I just wish I hadn't paid for your funeral."

"I hope it was a magnificent one as befit a viscount. Had I known the title had come to me, I might have stayed alive, despite the pressing problems that made my demise desirable. Regard it as my legacy to you, Marcus. Of course you have no right to it. Deception is, after all, the Lithgow stock in trade."

"I'm obliged to you for the education, Lewis." And the other poisonous legacy. Marcus was not, however, about to be the first to raise the subject of the diamonds. "Will you join me for some breakfast? Our reunion will have to be a short one. I am expected elsewhere."

"Did your heiress flee the coop? I hear she left Fonthill ahead of you. Fie, Marcus, I thought better of you. I'd have made a bid for Miss Brotherton myself but I didn't wish to poach on my son's territory."

"You astonish me." Marcus remembered that "Bentley" had tried to flirt with Anne.

"And you wrong me. I returned to England as the respectable David Bentley for only one reason: so that I could finally lay hands on the Stuart Twins. For years they've been my insurance and it was time to claim them. Enough time has passed for a discreet sale, and old Josiah's death left his house empty. I'd scared off the servants and almost finished searching when you turned up. Broke my heart not to be able to embrace my own dear son."

Marcus declined to indulge his father's theatrical nonsense, and Lewis, winning no greater reaction than a shrug, continued his tale. "I knew the gems would still be in their box. Josiah was too scrupulous to open it. When I didn't find it in the house, I remembered him telling me the furnace chamber at his villa had a fine hiding place for valuables. Miss Brotherton, splendid young woman that she is, did the heavy digging for me once I gave her a hint or two. I was keeping an eye on the place after the storm and saw you both leave with the box. Too bad you got there first."

Marcus permitted himself a humorless smile. "You shouldn't have been afraid to get your hands dirty."

"I am curious about one thing. You didn't find the diamonds by chance. How did you know to look for them?"

"You wrote to me, from Vienna in 1784."

"Ah, I remember! Very troublesome, those Russians. They had me quite worried for a while. Although I managed to shake them off, I never did get back to finish my business with the countess. She adored me."

During his boyhood Lewis would often return to their shabby lodgings to put up his feet and boast of his conquests while Marcus served him food and polished his boots. Now Marcus let him reminisce. As soon as the post chaise was announced he'd be on the road and Lewis would have run out of time for argument and bluster.

The latter sensed his lack of interest. "Enough with the polite chatter. Let's get down to business. It's only fair that since you have the heiress, I should have the diamonds. They are, after all, mine."

"As a matter of fact I believe they are the property of the Duke of Castleton."

"I earned them legitimately."

"Really? In that case why wait to sell them?"

"It was a matter of discretion, involving a lady."

"The only way you'd put yourself out to protect a lady's name was if it otherwise meant death."

"The late Duke of Castleton was an unreasonable man. He made it impossible for me to remain in England, or return while he lived. Hand them over and I'll trouble you no more. Don't worry that your bride will ever meet her unsuitable father-in-law."

Marcus folded his arms and couched his refusal in terms that Lewis would understand. "She won't have me if I don't return the lost Stuart Twins to her cousin's husband."

"My dear boy, why didn't you explain the problem? Nothing could be easier to arrange. You shall be held up by highwaymen on the road and lose the diamonds. We'll give you a black eye, or perhaps a trifling flesh wound in the arm, to lend veracity and make her sorry for you. The dear ladies do love to nurse us."

That was Lewis: ever ready with a shady scheme. Marcus shook his head in disgust, partly at his old self who would have embraced the notion with gusto. "Anne won't believe me. Besides, I need the money. If she weds without her guardian's permission she gets nothing."

"The lengths people go to protect the fortunes of heiresses is an affront to the honest adventurer."

"My mother was not so protected."

"No, but her fortune was small. I had small ideas in those days." He spoke with little thought, his eyes darting over Marcus's person, trying to guess if he carried the diamonds, and where. Lewis's blatant lack of respect or care for his late wife had Marcus's fists itching. He kept watch for sudden moves. Lewis in his turn noted a convulsive move of right hand toward the pocket containing the pistol.

"Aha," he said with satisfaction. "You haven't yet sold them. I assumed you went to Fonthill to find a buyer. I'd have done the same myself, except that both Beckford and Hamilton would recognize me, unlike the Wiltshire rustics who haven't seen me in fifteen years."

Marcus didn't bother to deny possession of the Twins. Lewis might have lost none of his cunning and Marcus had never equaled his father in ruthlessness. But he could best the older man in a fight and Lewis knew it.

"You are my son, Marcus. I'd be prepared to share the proceeds of the sale. What say you? Half and half. If you can't persuade the heiress's guardian, you'll have a nice little capital sum by grace of your father."

Hah! He'd be lucky to get ten percent by the time the negotiation was over. "Do you think you sired a fool?"

Lewis stared at him, trying to decide what Marcus's game was. "Now I understand!" he said. "You intend to parlay the return of the diamonds into Castleton's support for your marriage. I could help you with that. I recently learned something that he'd like me to keep to himself. I was saving it for a rainy day but I'll share it with my dear son. Against future considerations."

Aside from a natural curiosity about what Lewis could know to the discredit of the excessively proper duke, Marcus felt nothing but disgust. "I've done much to be ashamed of, but I never have and never will stoop to extortion."

The gray eyes that usually shone with spurious sincerity and humor grew cold, the only sign that Lewis was losing his temper. When angry he was vicious. "Show your father some respect. You think you're above me, do you? You still bleed when cut, your sweat still smells, and just because you're tupping an heiress doesn't mean you no longer need a privy."

"The only respect you'll get is when I refrain from giving you the beating you deserve. You will please speak of her as Miss Brotherton, if you speak of her at all."

"My God! You're serious. You're in love with the girl." Lewis laughed.

Of course he was. Of course he loved her. If there was one reason to be grateful for Lewis's resurrection it was this certainty. Anne had told him he wasn't like his father, and finally he believed it. Despite all the old devil's best efforts, Marcus was capable of love and decency. He was on his way to claim his beloved, and he couldn't wait to speak the words he had withheld out of fear and self-loathing.

He felt liberated from his parent as Lewis continued his vicious denunciation. "I was proud of you, Marcus, when I heard you'd gone after the richest prize in England and won her. But it turns out you're just a fool like ordinary people."

There wasn't any point arguing with a man who saw life only as a series of angles to be exploited. "I must be off," he said. "I have a carriage waiting. Nice seeing you, Lewis. An unexpected pleasure."

"Oh, Marcus!" Lewis shook his head in mock reproach. "Just because you're in love you think you're a reformed character. I know better. You and I are one of a kind, both by blood and through my careful teaching."

"You did your best and you may be right. But I also had my mother and Josiah Hooke. I don't know if we'll meet again, Lewis, but congratulations on not being dead."

Ready to counter any sudden move, Marcus stalked out of the coffee room and the inn, filling his lungs with clean air.

Soon afterward he and Travis rolled briskly east. As the miles passed, love and optimism fought fear of the task ahead of him. Longing to see Anne was fueled by an added anxiety. Lewis had given in too easily. The sooner Marcus reached Castleton the better.

Chapter 28

"**Y**ou're very quiet, Anne," Caro said when the party gathered in the drawing room after dinner.

"I'm enjoying the evening, Caro," Anne replied, not altogether truthfully. Throughout the meal she'd been on edge, wondering if Marcus would appear. Or whether he remained at Fonthill, concluding negotiations for the sale of the Castleton gems known as the Stuart Twins.

"Castleton is a beautiful house and I can see your touches everywhere." She pointed at a painting over the mantelpiece, a redheaded reclining woman, dressed in but a wisp of transparent fabric, her little boy at her feet. "That must be Venus and Cupid. Didn't you once own a Titian of the same subject? I thought you sold it."

"That is my Titian. We . . . recovered it." Catching Anne's eye, Caro mouthed a word at her. It looked like *Marcus*. Did she mean Marcus had stolen the Titian? It fit what Marcus had told her, back when she first met him, about trying to take Caro's cherished possession in payment of Robert

Townsend's gaming debt. The knowledge made her feel no better.

"She's lovely, isn't she?" The dowager duchess entered the conversation. "We never had many good pictures at Castleton. Thomas has begun to add to the collection and I'm happy to say he has better taste than his father."

Anne let the conversation wash over her, her concentration fixed on the door. She tried to prepare herself for bad news, stoically to accept the truth that she'd been gulled by an unworthy trickster. It hardly mattered. All she had to do was return to her former state as the great heiress of Camber and do her duty by finding herself a suitable husband. It might as well be Lord Algernon Tiverton, if he would still have her. At least her guardian and Lady Ashfield would be happy. And presumably Lord Algernon, though she found it hard to imagine him feeling or expressing joy, except possibly over the arrival of more Tivertons into the world. Or Brotherton-Tivertons.

She must not think of the never-to-be-born Brotherton-Lithgows because bursting into tears in the Duke of Castleton's drawing room was not the kind of thing Anne Brotherton-Tiverton did. Nevertheless, she wanted to stand up, perhaps on a table, and loudly proclaim her own wishes and desires: that she loved Marcus Lithgow and didn't care if he stole pictures, jewels, or anything else from them because he was the only thing in the world that made her happy. As she envisioned this shocking display, her attention wandered from the door and she missed his entrance.

"Mr. Marcus Lithgow," the butler announced.

It seemed like a month since she'd set eyes on him, when it was only last night that they had loved and parted in a secret corner of Fonthill Abbey. The sight of his strong, confident body and beloved face refreshed her. She would have run to him, taken his hands, kissed him even, in view of the Castletons and their servant. But she sensed a strain about him, a tension in his stance, a mixture of determination and fear on features that displayed not a hint of humor or easy charm. Finding her, he caught her eye and regarded her warily for a long moment, then addressed himself to his hosts.

"Caro, Castleton," he said, remaining motionless at the threshold of the great saloon. "I apologize. For arriving late and unannounced, and for other things."

In the course of his life Marcus had frequently entered places where no one wished him well and had stared down his enemies without betraying doubts of his survival. Never had he made a more difficult entrance than into the lions' den of Castleton House. His first priority was Anne. To his great joy and relief, her face reflected his own pleasure, her pale skin flushing. He deflected her approach. Before he could claim her—and he intended to do so with all triumph—he had work to do cleaning up some of the other messes of his life.

Castleton would like to knock him down and

throw him out of the house and would doubtless have done so had Caro not forestalled him.

"Marcus." She crossed the room ahead of her angry husband and offered her hand. Not the kiss on the cheek he would once have merited, but not a slap either.

"Duchess." He treated her to his best bow.

She smiled, a faded facsimile of her generous grin. "Don't be silly, Marcus." She addressed the oldest lady in the room. "Marcus and I have been friends for years, Margaret. Allow me to present Lord Lithgow. Unless"—she looked at him curiously—"your status has changed again. I notice you were announced without your title."

"I've decided to give it up. I only acquired it by accident and it means nothing to me." His father was alive and Marcus had resolved, as far as he was able, to live without deceit.

With properly duchesslike pomp, Caro presented him to the dowager duchess and her daughters. The latter, pretty and almost identical girls, looked only curious, but the dowager seemed appalled. Marcus had a faint recollection of her from years ago, a quiet, proud woman. Her looks had faded but her memories of the Lithgows evidently had not.

"Thank you for receiving me, Caro. I would like to have a word with you and Castleton in private." Better have Caro there and prevent bloodshed. Perhaps.

Anne stepped forward. "I will join you too."

"You sound too businesslike for after dinner," Caro said. "Later. My sisters-in-law are anxious to play whist and you are the very person to instruct them."

What was Caro up to? Something, for certain, but he couldn't see what, aside from postponing the moment when her husband tried to kill him. He wished he knew how much Anne had told her.

"Not tonight," the dowager said. "Sarah, Maria, it is time for us to leave."

Marcus possessed himself in patience as the family made their farewells and departed for the dower house. He prayed the older lady's obvious fear that association with him would taint her daughters wasn't a harbinger of the future. Even Caro seemed affected by the tense atmosphere. Hardly a word was said while Castleton escorted his mother and sisters to their carriage.

"Caro—" Anne said, as soon as the duke returned.

"Castleton—" Marcus began again, almost at the same time.

"Mr. David Bentley." The servant had returned and ushered in Lewis Lithgow, who sauntered in at his most confident. A part of the old Marcus admired the old man's gall, but only a part, a negligible grain. Mostly he felt nothing but disgust that he'd sprung from the loins of such a scoundrel.

"Your Graces." Lewis bowed with shameless bravado. "Miss Brotherton. You're looking as lovely as ever." Anne stared at him as though he were a snake. "And Marcus. I'm sorry to bring the duke news of a certain valuable property stolen from his family. It is presently, if I am not mistaken, residing in your pocket."

"You . . ." Anne's indignation warmed him. "Marcus did not steal it!"

"No, I did not." Marcus strode across the room and flung open his father's coat, patting his pockets and hips in search of a weapon.

"I'm quite unarmed, dear boy. Such distrust."

"That's because I don't trust you, Lewis." This time there were three gasps. "Castleton, Caro, Anne. Allow me to present Lewis, Viscount Lithgow. My father."

Lewis greeted the ladies with unruffled assurance. He'd always possessed an excellent leg, a graceful bow, and unlimited effrontery. "Recognize me do you now, Duke? You were only a boy when we last met. You've grown quite large."

Castleton, muscles turned to stone, fixed his eyes on Lewis. "What stolen property?"

"These," Marcus said. He pulled the diamonds, wrapped in velvet, from his pocket and thrust them at Castleton. "You would have had them in your hands in five minutes."

The duke unfolded the cloth and pulled out the dazzling gems. "You had them," he said quietly. Then looked at Lewis. "This is what you . . . took?" His muted reaction surprised Marcus, who would have expected Castleton to barrel in with both fists, hit one or other of the Lithgows, probably both, then call the magistrate. He had sustained a severe shock, that was clear, but his response was more complicated than the predictable righteous anger.

"Let's have a little talk about this," Lewis said. "I met up with my dear son this morning in Salisbury and we had a small falling out. A falling out among thieves, you might say. I generously offered to split the proceeds of the sale with him but he had his eye on a bigger fish. 'Thanks, Papa,' he said." Marcus had never called the old devil Papa in his life, and certainly not in the past ten years or so. " 'Thanks, but I have a better use for the Stuart Twins. I have a lovely heiress panting to wed me but she's just a mite distressed about me keeping stolen jewels from her dear cousin. I'm going to return them to the good duke in exchange for his support in winning over Miss Brotherton's guardians. For what, my dear papa, is half a pair of diamonds compared to the wealth of the Camber estate?' "

That was the genius of Lewis: to take a morsel of truth and twist it into a huge—and believable—lie. As far as Marcus could see, his only motive was spite against his son. He couldn't, surely, expect to walk away with the diamonds. Meanwhile, Caro was regarding Marcus with a look of betrayal as bad as when she'd found him with the Titian.

And Anne. She stared at him with her eyes huge and flat in a face as pale as vellum. He would like to think she trusted him, but what reason had he given her?

"You're a liar, Lewis. A liar as well as a thief." It was the best he could come up with and he wondered why he took the trouble. No one would believe him because, until this morning, he had been just as bad.

"Harsh words from my own flesh and blood."

At the mocking words his blood boiled and he made a vow. If Lewis's spite lost Marcus his chance at redemption, then he would add patricide to his long list of sins. His life would be over but at least the world would, once more, be rid of its most worthless citizen. "It's been a pleasure meeting you all, but I must be on my way. I'll just take those little darlings with me, if you don't mind, Castleton." Cool as a cucumber, Lewis held out his hand to the duke.

"I'm curious to hear why you think I should hand over my family property that you acquired from my mother." Marcus had seen Castleton pompous, he'd seen him dismissive, and he'd seen him angry. He'd never seen the duke look so grim. There was something more here and the dowager duchess was part of it.

Lewis smiled as genially as though accepting a cup of tea. "You wouldn't want those sweet sisters of yours to know who their father is, would you?"

Anne gasped at the revelation. Standing next to her, Caro covered her mouth with a hand and Marcus had the impression she wasn't surprised. Distressed, yes, but not shocked.

Lewis continued to address Castleton, whose large frame exuded coiled tension. "Lovely girls. I saw them getting into the carriage on my way in. It was all I could do not to introduce myself to my daughters."

"I'll kill you if you ever go near my sisters." The duke spoke softly but with deadly menace.

"I will too," Marcus said. For if Lewis told the truth—and a lot of things made sense if he did—they were his sisters too. The late duke had thrown the Lithgows out not because of a horse, or even a theft, but because Lewis had been up to his old tricks and seduced his host's wife. When discovered he'd cut and run, helping himself to the Stuart Twins and leaving the poor deluded lady with her own twins in exchange. Then, to escape the duke's ire, he'd left England, intending to return one day to retrieve the diamonds.

Far from cowed by the double threat, Lewis beamed at them. "It's such a pleasure for me to bring you two together now that you know what you have in common. It makes you almost brothers. But since I'm sure you'd prefer to celebrate your new kinship in private, I'll be on my way. Just as long as I have those pretty jewels there'll be no reason for me ever to mention the fact to a soul. Word of honor."

"Honor!" Castleton and Marcus spoke in unison.

"You can count on it. The honor of a successful thief. I've a mind to settle down with a nice little nest egg and live out my days in peace. I'll not trouble you again. Or I can walk out of here empty-handed and the whole world will be highly interested to know that the Ladies Maria and Sarah are no true Fitzcharleses." He stroked his chin. "Maybe I'd prefer that course. I'd enjoy getting to know them. I've always fancied a daughter or two, my son having been such a disappointment."

Castleton opened his large fist that had closed around the pendants and stared at them, actually considering Lewis's demand. Marcus could understand and respect his desire to protect his sisters. He would do anything if it were Anne in the same position. Giving up the jewels was nothing. He realized that now.

But Castleton didn't know Lewis as he did, didn't know that one could not, should not, take his word on anything.

Running through the options in his mind, he could see only one solution. Nausea fought grim determination. He was going to have to kill his own father.

The decision barely made, the door opened and the dowager duchess stood at the threshold. The exquisitely dressed lady with the air of deep reserve had vanished, to be replaced by a madwoman, her hair in disarray and a hectic flush on her pale powdered face. Convulsively she clutched the full skirts of her lavender silk gown.

"Mama, you shouldn't be here." Castleton stepped forward but his mother ignored him.

"Lewis." The single word was matched by an unmistakable agony in her faded blue eyes.

"Oh, Margaret," Lewis said in the simple, heartfelt tones that had gulled hundreds of women. "You're as lovely as ever. I always intended to return to you. You were my one true love. I'm here now."

"You stole the diamonds."

"When your husband discovered our trysts, I had to take a souvenir of the loveliest lady I ever met." He smiled. "I never knew I'd left you one in exchange. Two rather. What beautiful girls we made together, Margaret. You must be proud of them."

Marcus held his breath and he sensed the other spectators of the scene doing the same. From the corner of his eye he saw Caro and Anne, hand in hand, standing by the fire. Castleton appeared paralyzed as he watched his mother and her seducer.

"I'd like to meet our daughters, Margaret. Will you bring them in?" Lewis held out his hand.

"I sent them home. Stay away from them." A collective sigh, a ripple of air around the room, followed the duchess's words, spoken barely above a whisper.

"If that's the way you want it, Margaret," Lewis said gently, "I'm sorry. Advise your son to give me the diamonds and you'll never hear nor see me again."

She stared at him with wild eyes through an endless silence disturbed only by the crackle of the fire in the huge hearth. Then her right hand, hidden by her skirts, moved.

"Margaret, no!" Caro was the first to speak. Castleton's dismayed voice joined hers as the duchess raised her arm to reveal a pistol, pointed straight at Lewis's black heart.

"Now, Margaret," Lewis said, without betraying an ounce of concern. "You don't mean that. Put down the gun and let us talk like people who once loved each other."

The duchess swayed like a poplar. The small pistol seemed to weigh down her trembling hand and she raised the other to steady it. At any moment a flying bullet might hit anything or anybody in the room. Marcus edged back, ready to knock Anne and Caro to the ground if necessary.

"You never loved me," the duchess said, "and you will never hurt my children. I will not allow it."

Lewis fell as the pistol shot rang out. Marcus ran to him, sank to his knees, and heard his death rattle. Blood soaked his waistcoat. Straight through the heart. The duchess's aim was true.

He was half aware of events unfolding around him: the duchess collapsed in her son's arms and borne to a sofa; Caro comforting her mother-in-law; the duke sending worried servants away from the door with nonsense about a gun going off by accident.

Marcus knelt beside his father and looked at that handsome face for the last time. All he could think of was that he was glad he didn't resemble his sire in looks, had taken after his mother. He was glad that this time he could see the body, be certain that Lewis would never rise again. He was glad that his father was dead. He was also glad he hadn't had to kill him himself.

He felt a gentle touch on his shoulder. Anne knelt beside him, put her arms around him. He buried his head in her shoulder.

Chapter 29

Anne had sustained shock after shock: the discovery of Bentley's identity, his aspersions on his son's motives regarding the diamonds, and lastly Lithgow's amazing revelation about the dowager duchess. She'd thought herself numbed until the terrifying eruption of violence made her stomach churn. Only the grip of Caro's hand kept her from fainting.

Every conflicting thought aroused since the appearance of Lewis Lithgow paled beside Marcus's grief. She held him tightly and buried her face in his hair, feeling his chest heave and tears moisten her neck. His arms were iron bands about her waist and she welcomed the pain. When finally he raised his head she barely had time to see his glistening green eyes before he took her mouth in a desperate, searing kiss. Without thought for the future, or the living and dead in the room, she poured her love into the deepest kiss they'd ever shared. Knee to knee, bodies pressed close, arms fighting to draw each other closer, they devoured each other. There was no arousal in their embrace, only a profound desire for connection.

Neither had spoken since Lewis Lithgow had fallen dead. There was no need.

A touch drew her from their passionate communion.

"Anne." Caro's voice, Caro's hand on her shoulder.

They stood up, holding hands. She'd never seen Marcus's face so undefended, so unknowing. Then the dazed look faded, replaced by wariness. He would have withdrawn his hand but she didn't let him.

The scene beyond their circle of two came into focus: the dowager in a little gold framed chair, her slack mouth contradicting the stiffness of her posture; Caro wide-eyed with concern; her husband running a shaky hand through his hair. And the bloody corpse of Lewis Lithgow sprawled on the ebullient roses of the Wilton carpet.

"Lithgow." The duke broke a glacial silence. "My mother has killed your father. What do you want me to do?" Castleton would do the right thing, take the moral and legal path, no matter what the cost. His hands fell to his sides and his large figure dominated the room as he tensed, awaiting a blow he had no right to deflect.

Marcus glanced at the killer and then the victim. Slowly he shook his head and faced his old adversary the duke. Anne guessed that neither had yet grasped their new relationship resulting from Lewis's dramatic revelation. She waited to see what Marcus would do now he had the upper hand.

"My father died in Naples last year," he said, softly. "I have a certificate of burial from the authorities of the Kingdom of Naples and Sicily. I don't believe it is possible to murder a dead man."

Castleton's shoulders dropped. "We could pass him off as a chance caller and call it an accident." He glanced at his mother. "I'm not sure she is up to the task of lying and you understand why I don't wish any version of the truth to get out."

Marcus nodded slowly. "Lewis Lithgow is dead and David Bentley never existed. We'll have to do something with the body. If you have a place to hide it, I'll help."

Caro drew her husband aside and engaged him in a low-toned discussion, accompanied with a good many gestures on her part and some argument on his.

Anne squeezed her lover's hand. "I'm sorry." Her heart bled for his evident unhappiness.

"Why?"

"Because your father is dead."

"I'm not. He came back to cause trouble and he would never have left this family alone. He would have taken the diamonds and anything else he could get, year after year. My . . . Castleton's sisters would never have been safe from him. The only thing I care about is your forgiveness." He held both her hands to his chest and looked deep into her face. "I was on my way to return the diamonds to their owner without condition, I swear it. But if you believe what my father said about me, I understand."

Castleton interrupted them again. "Shall we go,

Lithgow? Caro has a plan to fool the servants into believing 'Bentley' has left the house. With a bit of luck no one will ever hear of him again."

Watching Marcus and Castleton drag the body of Lewis Lithgow through the garden door, she had the urge to call him back. To reassure him she couldn't live without him.

Dragging a body through a dark garden was a task that brought men together, even a pair with as much history of enmity as he and Castleton. Lewis had never been a small man and he'd gained weight in later life. They heaved and grunted across the lawn and through the shrubbery, and by the time they were out of earshot of the house and servants, the silent tension between them had palpably lessened.

"Only a couple of hundred yards now," Castleton said. They were making for the ruins of an old chantry, a remnant of the estate's monastic past. The place had a crypt that was kept locked because of its unsound roof. A perfect resting place for Lewis Lithgow, who had, Marcus recalled, converted to Rome at one point in pursuit of some long-forgotten chicanery.

By silent mutual agreement they stopped to rest, Castleton stamping his feet while Marcus huddled down into his collar.

"I suppose I should apologize." A sliver of moon illuminated Castleton's breath in the frosty air. Marcus could only imagine how he'd swallowed his pride.

"Don't. My father was a complete villain and the world is better without him."

"I fear he would never have left my mother and sisters alone. I was thinking about killing him myself."

"I was too." He'd never have expected to feel comradeship with Castleton. He hastened to set the duke's mind at rest on the topic that must be troubling him most. "You needn't fear that word of his revelation tonight will ever pass my lips. Your mother and sisters are safe."

"It's odd, what he said, about us having sisters in common."

"Did you have any idea?"

"I knew they were not my father's daughters, but not whose. Caro guessed. She wanted you to know them."

"Ah. Proposing that ridiculous game of whist."

"Typical Caro scheme. Even before we knew you'd found the diamonds, she was worried you might guess the truth. She thought if you liked them you wouldn't take it into your head to try anything that would put them at risk."

Marcus winced. Not long ago he would have accepted the poor expectations for his behavior with a cynical shrug. "I would never harm them." He hoped Castleton believed him.

"Shall we continue?"

While Castleton fumbled with the key to the chantry, Marcus pondered a past dominated by Lewis Lithgow. There was no ambivalence in his relief that it was over for good. Carrying the body down the narrow stairs to the crypt placed a full stop to the relationship, a culmination that he'd never sensed when he'd arrived in Naples to find his father "dead." It gave him a new appreciation for the ritual of the funeral. As the door of the tomb slammed shut he muttered a wordless silent prayer, for whom he wasn't sure, and turned with a lighter heart to face his future.

"I must say, Castleton, that the idea of having family connections appeals to me. I wish I could know your sisters better. Only as a friend."

"If you wed Anne, not that I approve, mind you, my sisters will be cousins of a kind."

"I will try to convince you that I am now a different man and I can make her happy, but first I have to convince her. I'm not sure she'll have me."

"That's not the way it looked to me, the way she was kissing you. Most improper." That was the old conventional Castleton. You'd never guess he'd just disposed of a body in what must surely be a criminal fashion.

"I'm not without hope, but she's a strongminded woman, not to be swayed by ordinary considerations."

"More like Caro than I thought, under that mild exterior."

"Mild? Clearly you don't know her at all."

"Perhaps not," the duke replied as they strode briskly toward the house. "As I constantly learn from Caro, people are not always the way they appear. Makes life difficult sometimes, but interesting."

"Since I have a new appreciation for honesty and candor, I'd like to explain about Caro's Titian."

There's no reason you should believe me, but I didn't intend to steal it. I followed a hunch about where Caro might have it hidden away, that's all. Then you and Caro caught me . . ."

"I was beginning to tolerate you, but just thinking about that day makes me want to hit you." Was that actually a hint of humor?

"I can be quite irritating when I set my mind to it, and on that occasion my mind was set on infuriating you."

"Let's not speak of it again. I am willing to pretend we never met before, to erase our past history and start again. I believe we are something like third cousins twice removed, and please don't ask me to explain how." To Marcus's gratified astonishment, Castleton offered his hand.

"It's an honor to make your acquaintance, Duke. I am madly in love with your wife's cousin and would vastly appreciate a positive word in the ear of Miss Brotherton's guardian."

Castleton loomed stern and forbidding. "Starting again is one thing, but you can't erase a lifetime of misconduct in a moment. If you think I'm going to ask Morrissey to hand over the Camber estates to you, you're much mistaken. Besides, I doubt I have that much influence."

"I don't want the Camber estates. I intend to put my own property in order. All I want is for Anne to be allowed sufficient income to afford a decent life. At the moment I can't even afford servants."

"I'll see what I can do, but be warned. I shall be keeping an eye on you."

"I'm glad."

"I'll only do it for Anne's sake, mind you." Castleton gave a brief crack of laughter. "She'd make a terrible housemaid!"

"You'd be surprised. She's a woman of many parts."

Chapter 30

Anne silently inspected the small sitting room, separated from Marcus by splendid furnishings and unanswered doubts. When he and Castleton returned from disposing of the body, all significant barriers to their marriage had been demolished. Yet her hands twisted together behind her back and she stood before the marble fireplace as lacking in confidence as the woman she'd been before she knew him. Darting glances showed a similar state of doubt clouding his beloved face.

"The drawing room at Hinton would fit into this room twice over, at least," he remarked finally. "Being here makes me realize what I asked you to give up."

She stopped pretending to be interested in the draping of the brocade curtains. "You know quite well that architectural proportions are not what lie between us."

He strode over to the hearth and stroked her hair gently, smoothed her frowning forehead with his thumb. She read hesitation and longing in his beautiful green eyes with no trace of reserve or deceit. "I love you, Anne. You're the only thing in the world I truly want. If I ever become a good man it's because you taught me how."

"No," she said. "You are a good man and you can be one without me. I love you, Marcus, but . . ." Her voice trailed off into a whisper.

"I broke your trust when I planned to sell the diamonds." He leaned forward until their foreheads touched. "Forgive me, Anne. I swear I came here with no other plan than to restore his property to Castleton."

"I know that." Love engulfed her and every instinct told her to trust him, to let herself grasp happiness with both hands. Yet deep-seated wells of reserve and caution reared their heads, as did her own shame. "What happened before is what troubles me. Not only that you were prepared to sell the diamonds, but that I lied to myself about it. I knew immediately that you couldn't be the rightful owner and I went along with it because I wished so badly for you to have the money you needed. Only when I learned that they belonged to someone I knew did I do the right thing."

His instant withdrawal left her chilled. "I see. You fear association with me will destroy your morals."

"No." That sounded horrible and priggish. "I'm sorry. I don't know what I mean."

Marcus took a few paces in obvious agitation, then returned to his spot in front of her. "The only thing I can do," he said, "is explain how I have changed. I should have known my association with *you* had affected me when I first saw the diamonds. I suspected they'd been stolen from Castleton because my father and I had just been there when we went to Hinton. A few months ago I would have felt no compunction about keeping them, but you were already penetrating the wall of my infamy. Like you, I ignored my scruples. I bargained with Providence, swearing this would be my last sin."

"Did you only change your mind because it meant losing me?" She wanted more.

"No, because of something you said. You said I would always know what I had done. Not you, but I. My newly awakened conscience cried out and I realized it would never leave me alone. That I could no longer be happy as a scoundrel." His voice fell to a hoarse whisper. "I want so badly to be happy. With you."

A surge of longing seized her brain. "How can I be sure? How can I know what is the right thing to do when all I want to do is believe you?" If he took her in his arms now she would surrender.

And Marcus, bless him, understood her doubt and declined to take advantage of it. "Let me offer the perspective of a gamester when it comes to assessing risk. You look at the known facts and the desired outcome and calculate the odds of achieving the latter with the cards you are dealt."

"You make it sound easy."

"With cards it is easy. It comes down to mathematics. The arithmetic of the heart is trickier."

Anne looked into that organ and couldn't make anything add up. Love had nothing to do with logic, only with faith. She closed her eyes and leaped off the cliff.

"Will you kiss me, Marcus?"

There was no more to be said. The world shrank to a tiny space occupied by two souls and their sighs and caresses.

Marcus was not pleased to see Travis. With Anne curled in his lap and the possibility of some seriously indiscreet behavior before they retired to their separate chambers, he was more than unusually irked by the intrusion of his valet.

"Ahem, my lord."

Anne scrambled off to sit next to him on the sofa, as primly as she could given that her braids had come down and her hair lay over her shoulders like a shining cloak. Maldon, who for some reason had accompanied Travis, looked pained.

"You may felicitate me, Travis. You too, Maldon. Miss Brotherton and I are to be wed."

"So I supposed. May I take the liberty of wishing you every happiness?"

"You may. We haven't set a date but we should all be returning to Hinton soon. I even intend to pay you wages."

Travis coughed and his bushy eyebrows shot up. "As to that, my lord. It is with great regret that I have come to tender my notice."

"And I too, miss," the usually silent Maldon piped up.

"Maldon!" Anne cried. "How can I do without you?"

"Miss Maldon and I feel that our talents will go to waste in Wiltshire. We have decided to seek new positions in London with people of fashion."

Marcus, who had spent many months trying to get rid of the man, was perversely bereft. "I saved your life, Travis! You can't leave me."

"I believe my debt has been paid in full and it is time for me to seek other challenges. Now that you are settled my work with you is done."

The next day Anne proposed a game of piquet.

Marcus picked up his hand. It was the best he'd seen in months. Against even a strong player the odds of losing were minuscule. He made his discards, expecting the worst, and discovered the best. Trouncing Anne's mediocre skills was child's play.

"My misfortunes at the tables," he said as he took the last trick, "began after Travis came into my service. I have occasionally wondered if the two events were connected, but I don't believe in that kind of superstition."

"Whatever the cause, your luck has returned," Anne said cheerfully, totting up her dismal score.

"No," he said, pulling her into his arms. "If I'd never lost my luck I would never have courted an heiress. That's what I call luck."

Epilogue

Anne looked up from her manuscript. With the second villa fully excavated, she'd turned to her account of the site for the *Journal of Antiquities* and Marcus had encouraged her to extend it into a full book. Combining scholarly precision with entertaining prose was a challenge she relished.

"How's the great opus?" he asked. After five years her husband's entry into a room still made her heart leap. He'd adopted the sober garb of the hardworking country gentleman, but she was thankful that he never lost the slightly raffish look of the scoundrel he no longer was. She accepted his light kiss, always a promise of even greater pleasure, and ran her hands through his hair, which he'd allowed to grow back to the longer style she loved.

"How was Salisbury?" she asked.

"Corn prices aren't what I would wish, but I did well enough."

"You mean you charmed those merchants at the Corn Exchange and fleeced them shamefully."

In five years he'd proven himself a brilliant estate manager and turned Hinton around so that her income could be used for luxuries, such as protective structures for Frederick, and the twin lion discovered in the second Roman building. Morrissey, persuaded by Castleton, had grudgingly granted her a fair allowance, though only a fraction of the revenues from her estates. The old martinet insisted that his first duty was to the integrity of the Brotherton fortune.

"Let me remind you that I am a well-respected member of the community."

Their three-year-old daughter, who had been playing quietly on the carpet, tugged on his leg.

"Up you get, Caro," he said. "Give Papa a kiss. What have you got there?" He removed the object from her little fist and turned to his wife. "Anne! You shouldn't let her play with such things. It's indecent!"

"Don't worry so much." Anne covered her sputter of laughter with her hand. "She has no idea what it is."

"And if I have any say in the matter she never will. You're going to stay with Papa forever, Caro, aren't you?"

With deep content, Anne gazed at the pair of them, and at their infant son, asleep in his cradle. Never once had she regretted the loss of her huge fortune and massive house; she had everything she wanted at Hinton with Marcus and their children. They even had servants, one of whom ushered in a visitor.

"Lord Morrissey!" Anne hadn't seen her guardian since he tried to argue her out of the marriage. Their only communication was a quarterly report on the condition of the Brotherton estates.

"Lady Lithgow. Lithgow," he said curtly. Morrissey was as stiff-necked as ever.

"Mrs. Lithgow. Marcus prefers not to go by his title."

Morrissey ignored her. Some things never changed. "If Lady Lithgow would excuse us, I'd like to speak to you alone."

"Anything you wish to say to me, you may say in front of my wife." Marcus forestalled Anne's objection. "And my children," he added when Morrissey glared at little Caro, doubtless appalled that she wasn't with her nurse.

"I suppose Lady Lithgow may stay. The matter somewhat involves her since it concerns her estates. You have a son, who by the terms of the settlement will eventually inherit them. I would be failing in my duty if I didn't ensure that he was brought up with the proper knowledge and awareness of his position. "

Anne didn't like this one bit. "What do you mean?"

"The heir to Camber cannot live in such mean surroundings. Young Chauncey merits a proper establishment and a superior education."

Her eyes flew to Marcus, who surreptitiously removed the Roman belt buckle from his daughter's hand and slipped it into his pocket. He settled the little girl more comfortably in his arms and quirked an eyebrow at Anne. He intended to let her do the talking.

"First of all, Lord Morrissey, our son's name is Charles. I saw no reason to inflict Brotherton tradition on him. Secondly, Hinton Manor is a beautiful house and our children are well cared for. I spend every afternoon with them to give them a good educational grounding. Charles is too young but Caro already knows several words of Latin."

A hastily repressed snort from Marcus drew a quelling look. *Phallus* was *not* one of the Latin words Caro knew.

"Thirdly," Anne concluded, "I will never allow you to take Charles away to the loneliness I suffered as a child."

"This feminine intemperance is why I prefer to do business with your husband," Morrissey said, turning to Marcus. "I made no secret of my objection to your marriage, Lithgow, but I hear good accounts of you now, from Castleton and others. I can no longer see any reason to withhold Anne's property. I am prepared to make arrangements to transfer the management of the estates to you."

"I think it is up to Anne whether she wishes me to have control of her affairs."

"Of course I do!" Anne said.

"That's settled, then," Morrissey said briskly. "There's another matter. Since Mr. Pitt's death the country is going to the dogs. The Earls of Camber have always represented firm government and common sense and are sorely missed. I have spoken to the king about having the earldom revived for you."

An hour later, Morrissey had taken his leave,

the children returned to the nursery, and Marcus remained in a state of shock.

"What do you think?" Anne asked.

"I'm glad you will enjoy everything you gave up by marrying me. If you don't want to move to Camber we can add a wing onto this house. I hope I shall prove a worthy steward of your fortune."

"Of course you will. You will revel in the challenge. But will you accept the earldom?"

"Do you wish to be Countess of Camber?"

She put her arms around his waist, feeling his agitated heart beneath her head. "Only if you are earl, and wish it. I'm not sure you will enjoy being Morrissey's protégé in the House of Lords."

"I never thought to be in Parliament," he said, stroking her hair. "And certainly not as a representative of firm government and common sense. Did I ever tell you how much I admired the principles of the French Revolution?"

"Well then! You shall surprise Morrissey and his cohorts, which will serve him right. I always knew you were capable of great things."

Author's Note

Archaeology was a science in its infancy in 1800. The word hadn't acquired its current meaning and referred to general antiquarian study. English gentlemen making the grand tour saw excavations of ancient sites and were inspired to do the same at home. Anne's villa is based on a 1786 journal account of discoveries in Northamptonshire by Hayman Rooke. Since I found very little in print about how the excavations were conducted, I figured Anne would have to invent her own method and I think she did quite well.

A list of Roman objects discovered in Wiltshire included a number of phallic pieces, including the belt buckle. The phallic pendant I found on the Internet and I offer no guarantees of its authenticity.

Nelson and Lady Hamilton really did spend Christmas with William Beckford, including a visit to the unfinished Fonthill Abbey. Beckford is one of the most fascinating characters of the era. Immensely rich, he became persona non grata in society because of a suspected homosexual affair.

Devoting himself to his building and art collections, he grew more and more reclusive. Nelson's reception was the only major entertainment ever held at the abbey.

I would like to thank the community of romance writers for the inspiration, education, and support that make it possible for me to grow as a writer and actually finish books. For *The Ruin of a Rogue* I owe particular thanks to Megan Mulry, Katharine Ashe, Janet Webb, Jill Tuennerman, and Kathleen Greer. Also, my agent Meredith Bernstein and my brand-new and very talented editor Tessa Woodward.

Miranda

Next month, don't miss these exciting new love stories only from Avon Books

Summer Is for Lovers by Jennifer McQuiston
Caroline Tolbertson has longed for David Cameron, a handsome Scotsman back in Brighton for the summer, since she was a girl. Though she will have to choose a husband soon, for now, she's free to pursue more passionate curiosities—that is, if David will agree to teach her. But will he be able to let her go when the time comes?

How to Tame a Wild Fireman by Jennifer Bernard
Firefighter Patrick "Psycho" Callahan never imagined a physician—sexy as she may be—could be hotter than the wildfire threatening his hometown of Loveless, Nevada. But as Dr. Lara Nelson gets to work patching up the firemen fighting the blaze, she'll be forced to reckon with a blue-eyed devil . . . and the embers of their decade-old attraction.

Destiny's Surrender by Beverly Jenkins
Andrew Yates is shocked when beautiful Wilhelmina "Billie" Wells arrives at his ranch with a toddler in her arms, claiming he's the father! Billie planned to leave their son with his father so the boy could have a better life, yet before she knows it, she's saying "I do" to a marriage of convenience. All Billie and Drew have in common is the heat that first brought them together, but can their sizzling passion lead to everlasting love?

At Avon Books, we know your passion for romance—once you finish one of our novels, you find yourself wanting more.

May we tempt you with . . .

- **Excerpts** from our upcoming releases.

- Entertaining **extras,** including authors' personal photo albums and book lists.

- Behind-the-scenes **scoop** on your favorite characters and series.

- **Sweepstakes** for the chance to win free books, romantic getaways, and other fun prizes.

- Writing **tips** from our authors and editors.

- **Blog** with our authors and find out why they love to write romance.

- **Exclusive content** that's not contained within the pages of our novels.

Join us at
www.avonbooks.com

AVON

An Imprint of HarperCollins*Publishers*
www.avonromance.com

*G*ive in to your Impulses!

These unforgettable stories only take a second to buy and give you hours of reading pleasure!

Go to *www.AvonImpulse.com* and see what we have to offer.

Available wherever e-books are sold.

AVONIMPULSE

IMP 081